THE LEGACY SERIES

SERIES TITLES

A Green Glow on the Horizon
Dawn Burns

Bodies in Bags
Jamey Gallagher

Apple & Palm
Patricia Henley

How We Do Things Here
Matt Cashion

Neon Steel
Jennifer Maritza McCauley

Release of Information
Kali White VanBaale

The Divide
Evan Morgan Williams

Yes, No, I Don't Know
Kathryn Gahl

The Price of Their Toys
John Loonam

The Caged Man
Calvin Mills

A Day Doesn't Go By When I Don't Have Regrets
J. Malcolm Garcia

These Are My People
Steve Fox

We Should Be Somewhere by Now
Stephen Tuttle

Burner and Other Stories
Katrina Denza

The Plan of Chicago
Barry Pearce

Trust Issues
K.P. Davis

Adult Children
Laurence Klavan

Guardians & Saints
Diane Josefowicz

Western Terminus: Stories and A Novella
Michael Keefe

Like Human
Janet Goldberg

The Hopefuls
Elizabeth Oness

Never Stop Exiting
Michael Hopkins

Broken Heart Syndrome
Anne Colwell

The Mexican Messiah: A Novella & Stories
Jay Kauffmann

Close to a Flame
Colleen Alles

American Animism
Jamey Gallagher

Keeping What's Best Left Kept Secret
David Ricchiute

Soaked
Toby LeBlanc

The Path of Totality
Marie Zhuikov

Shocker in Gloomtown
Dan Libman

The Continental Divide
Bob Johnson

The Three Devils and Other Stories
William Luvaas

The Correct Response
Manfred Gabriel

Welcome Back to the World: A Novella & Stories
Rob Davidson

Greyhound Cowboy and Other Stories
Ken Post

Close Call
Kim Suhr

The Waterman
Gary Schanbacher

Signs of the Imminent Apocalypse and Other Stories
Heidi Bell

What We Might Become
Sara Reish Desmond

The Silver State Stories
Michael Darcher

An Instinct for Movement
Michael Mattes

The Machine We Trust
Tim Conrad

Gridlock
Brett Biebel

Salt Folk
Ryan Habermeyer

The Commission of Inquiry
Patrick Nevins

Maximum Speed
Kevin Clouther

Reach Her in This Light
Jane Curtis

The Spirit in My Shoes
John Michael Cummings

The Effects of Urban Renewal on Mid-Century America and Other Crime Stories
Jeff Esterholm

What Makes You Think You're Supposed to Feel Better
Jody Hobbs Hesler

Fugitive Daydreams
Leah McCormack

Hoist House: A Novella & Stories
Jenny Robertson

Finding the Bones: Stories & A Novella
Nikki Kallio

Self-Defense
Corey Mertes

Where Are Your People From?
James B. De Monte

Sometimes Creek
Steve Fox

The Plagues
Joe Baumann

The Clayfields
Elise Gregory

Kind of Blue
Christopher Chambers

Evangelina Everyday
Dawn Burns

Township
Jamie Lyn Smith

Responsible Adults
Patricia Ann McNair

Great Escapes from Detroit
Joseph O'Malley

Nothing to Lose
Kim Suhr

The Appointed Hour
Susanne Davis

PRAISE FOR
A Green Glow on the Horizon

Dawn Burns' dream of America is a circus sideshow of small-town roadside attractions, and behind the scenes at these iconic museums and glorified gift shops, we find families profoundly devoted to whatever is on display. As Burns ostensibly explores tourist destinations, they are actually exposing the wider problem of spiritual abuse, engendered by blind faith and the plain old-fashioned refusal to see beyond one's own walls. Their tender and funny insights into the relationships between people and their beliefs reveal the way American religiosity so easily morphs into consumerism, cultural misappropriation, and absurdity. While some characters in these fabulist tales succumb to their worst impulses, the author never gives up on them, but instead, through masterful narrative, carries us all into the imaginative realm with humor and compassion that honors community and human complexity.

—BONNIE JO CAMPBELL
National Book Award Finalist
author of *The Waters*

With delicious humor and a masterful perception of the strangeness of the human condition, Dawn Burns writes characters you will never forget because they will haunt your dreams and follow you on road trips. They will persuade you to stop at their tourist attractions and help you look past the kitschy facades to see them in their weirdly fascinating lives. You will be pulled in by their unique voices and their very human desires and fears, and you will find yourself in places you never thought you'd be but that ultimately feel all too familiar. With Burns' latest, you will definitely laugh, probably cry, and wish this book would never end.

—CAIT WEST
author of *Rift*

Reader, to say you are about to embark on a spiritual journey would not begin to prepare you for the cross-country metaphysical trek Dawn Burns takes you on. These stories—testaments to joy and love, testimonies of insecurity and fear—ask you to bear witness to a great sewing together of threads into a perfectly unique, odd, unsettling-yet-comforting quilt of humanity. From emotionally lost mothers looking for love in the stars, to the double afterlives of a serial killer turned imaginary friend, from the traumas of religious isolationism to the many—contradicting—truths one tells themselves once they have healed, *A Green Glow on the Horizon* is "a celebration of who we are and what we do" as perfectly blemished beings looking for salvation. Nestled in these stories, Burns asks, "what kind of redemption can come without furious pain and suffering?" Reader, you're about to find out.

—RS DEEREN
author of *Enough to Lose*

A Green Glow is as daring as a high-wire act, and Dawn Burns walks that wire with no pauses and no missed steps. Somehow she holds the satirical and the affectionate in perfect balance. This is the rare book that manages to be wildly inventive, serenely wise, and delightfully zany.

—VALERIE SAYERS
author of *The Age of Infidelity*

Meet me at the crossroads of Sublime and Surreal, the Cartesian spring of genius that is cartographer Dawn Burns' *A Green Glow on the Horizon*. Here's the Bally: These tales are Double-took Dispatches for a Convention of Tricksters. This book is a Matryoshka of Defamiliarized Detours. Turns out there is a there there, and you can get there from here.

—MICHAEL MARTONE
author of *Plain Air: Dispatches from Winesburg, Indiana*

Dawn Burns understands just how weird the heart of this country can get. *A Green Glow on the Horizon* is for everyone who has traveled a lonely stretch of interstate and been unable—or unwilling—to tune out the sirenic pleading of the regional tourist trap. In the shadows of these dominant, billboard-friendly myths, Burns offers us characters we couldn't have imagined, stories we might not have noticed, and wonders we didn't know we needed.

—TIM CONRAD
author of *The Machine We Trust*
Midwest Book Award Winner

In turns wryly funny and heart-twisting, these compelling vignettes revel in their raw oddities. While each tale brings home its own unique souvenir, the common denominator among all the stories is an aim at understanding our deepest, truest selves. As Burns writes, "In the end we are all characters in each other's stories, aren't we?"

—COLLEEN ALLES
author of *Close to a Flame*

No writer I know of captures the essential surrealism of childhood and adolescence better than Dawn Burns. She gives voice to marginals: kids we grew up with and never really knew yet we see every time we look in the mirror. They wrestle with demons and angels in surprising places, finding horror, humor, and grace in a phantasmic landscape where nuance lies tucked under outrageous overstatement. *A Green Glow on the Horizon* is a compelling concoction of reality and compassionate, shimmering imagination, breathed into life on the page by a master storyteller. The world is our Tourist Attraction, and we are so much richer for sharing it with Burns and her unforgettable characters.

—JAN MAHER
author of *Heaven, Indiana*

Dawn Burns' dazzling range of storytelling—satiric caricature, social realism, mythmaking, and even stark horror story—serves the "sudden rush of sadness for all the stories people [are] unable to tell," as one of her conflicted characters puts it. *A Green Glow* will take your breath away by its too-too-real characters, its social candor, and above all else, its unashamed love of our ever-yearning ever-misfit humanity and the stories we attempt to make of ourselves.

—MARY CATHERINE HARPER
author of *The Found Object Imagines a Life*

A Green Glow on the Horizon is gently and lovingly curated—steeped with earnestness, hopefulness, copious amounts of humanity, and just the right infusion of whimsy. These characters would be fine company over a cup of Celestial Seasonings peppermint tea. I know that in a myriad of alternative universes—ones that Dawn must surely have visited—a version of me would be a card-carrying member of the National Association of Tourist Attraction Survivors. But until I find the portal, I am grateful for her sharing this travelogue.

—SCOTT HARRIS
Everybody Reads Books and Stuff, *Lansing, Michigan*

Dawn Burns' *A Green Glow on the Horizon* is a polyphonic ode to all those who dwell in the places that become the bizarro footnotes in other people's road trips. Burns takes us on a wild ride through small-town America, from places like Hell, Michigan, to The World's Only Corn Palace in South Dakota. *A Green Glow* is teeming with modern Midwestern fairytales and conspiracies alike that locate the fullness in the seemingly desolate, find the zaniness in the seemingly banal, and leave you basking in the afterglow.

—ELISE JAJUGA & CHRISTINE PEFFER
A Novel Concept Bookstore, *Lansing, Michigan*

A GREEN GLOW ON THE HORIZON

Tales from the National Association of Tourist Attraction Survivors

in which
Xavier breathes underwater for twenty-seven minutes,
Ezekiel stuffs squirrels for the Living Bible Museum,
Ruth wishes she hadn't lost her wishbone collection,
Rita rides to the top of Sombrero Tower,
Arabella devours herself in the Sonoran Desert,
Dawn sleeps in the Belle Gunness exhibit's garden cart,
Becky dismembers her mom's Cherished Twinklings figurine,
Layla loses herself in the Winchester Mystery House,
Bud steeps himself in a bath of peppermint tea,
Abigail becomes an otter,
Lauren embraces Jelly in a dream,
Valerie follows a green glow on the horizon,
and Hanna Susanna finds a home in Hell

DAWN BURNS

CORNERSTONE PRESS
UNIVERSITY OF WISCONSIN-STEVENS POINT

Cornerstone Press, Stevens Point, Wisconsin 54481
Copyright © 2026 Dawn Burns
www.uwsp.edu/cornerstone

Printed in the United States of America.

Library of Congress Control Number: 2026930238
ISBN: 978-1-968148-40-9

All rights reserved.

This is a work of fiction. Names, characters, businesses, places, events, and incidents are either the products of the author's imagination or used in a fictitious manner. Any resemblance to actual persons, living or dead, or actual events is purely coincidental.

Cornerstone Press titles are produced in courses and internships offered by the Department of English at the University of Wisconsin–Stevens Point.

DIRECTOR & PUBLISHER	EXECUTIVE EDITORS
Dr. Ross K. Tangedal	Jeff Snowbarger, Freesia McKee
EDITORIAL DIRECTOR	SENIOR EDITORS
Brett Hill	Paige Biever, Ellie Atkinson

PRESS STAFF
Brianna Loving, Lilly Kulbeck, Karlie Harpold, Samantha Bjork, Sophie McPherson, Andrew Bryant, Asher Schroeder, John Evans, Oliver McKnight

For SwampFire

ALSO BY DAWN BURNS:

Evangelina Everyday

I don't want to know which is you which is me this empty sky too much too much like the hole at the center of our deep space.

—Mary Catherine Harper, "Equinox Confession"

© Tammy Gordon

C O N T E N T S

Dedication — xviii
Editor's Preface — xxi

Storytelling Creed of the National Association of Tourist Attraction Survivors — 1

Letter from the Fort Wayne Children's Zoo — 3

The Roswell Diaries — 9

Born Beneath Pedro's Sombrero — 29

Raised in a Corn Palace — 47

Northern Belle — 63

The NATAS Editor Grapples with a Jelly Dream — 95

Cherished — 107

Taxidermy Tabernacle — 139

Under the Sign of Sleepytime — 177

The Thing Is — 207

"Writing in Clay: Discovering a New Language": A Case Study in the Therapeutic Benefits of Pottery with Tourist Attraction Trauma Survivors — 225

Go to Hell — 233

Epilogue — 253
Artists — 255
Acknowledgments — 259

Dedication

A Green Glow on the Horizon: Tales from the National Association of Tourist Attraction Survivors is dedicated to Xavier Buttons, the unsung mermaid of Weeki Wachee Springs State Park. Xavier, born with what is known to the medical community as sirenomelia—a rare congenital deformity marked by legs fused from ankles to abdomen—was as true a mermaid as has ever swum Earth's seas. Even so, Weeki Wachee never allowed Xavier to don a sparkly mermaid costume and perform in the mermaid shows which began their long tradition in 1947 when ex-Navy man Newton Perry trained young women wearing bathing suits and mermaid tails to perform ballet and eat bananas underwater.

Unlike Weeki Wachee's high school beauty queen mermaids with zip-up tails, Xavier was truly a mermaid both in body and in spirit, a being that swam on the boundary between human and fish. After dropping out of high school in 1979, Xavier sought employment at Weeki Wachee, the one place where Xavier (quite wrongly) believed uniqueness as a mermaid would be valued. An overlooked concession stand worker during the day, Xavier, who had been entrusted with keys to the tank room, became a mermaid for self and self alone at night. Entries from Xavier's journal reveal that not only was Xavier's "tail" perfect for swimming while being cumbersome on land, but also that Xavier was able to breathe underwater for up to twenty-seven minutes before surfacing.

On the morning of August 15, 1982, Xavier was found dead at the bottom of the tank, tail badly frayed and in the early stages of decay. Autopsy reports cite tail rot, a bacterial infection caused by stress and poor water conditions, as the primary cause of death.

This book is dedicated to Xavier Buttons, a true mermaid whose overlooked life of quiet contradictions challenges us to treat all those within our care with utmost dignity and sensitivity.

© Mary Catherine Harper

Do **you** have tourist attraction trauma?

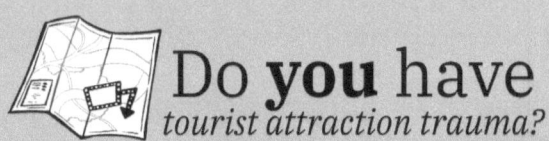

When **you say where you're from** do people say: "I stopped there once on my way to _____ ?"

When **people tell stories** of where they're from, do you stay silent and avoid sharing even though you have things you could say?

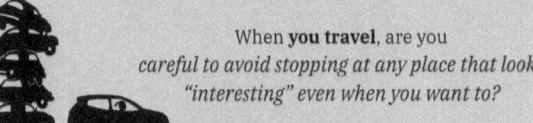

When **you travel**, are you careful to avoid stopping at any place that looks "interesting" even when you want to?

If you answered "**yes**" to **any** of these questions,

...you may be suffering from Tourist Attraction Trauma (TAT)

Call **1-800-555-TATS**

The call is free. The help is free.

Sponsored by the National Association of Tourist Attraction Survivors (NATAS), a non-profit research and recovery organization dedicated to helping Tourist Attraction Trauma survivors discover a healthy balance between their pasts and futures while living with confidence in the present.

Poster Design by Sofia Pagen

© Sofia Pagen

Editor's Preface

ON JUNE 15, 1996, MY FORMER CLASSMATE Dawn Tempers and I returned to Hanna, Indiana, our hometown. While Dawn came to Hanna intent on attending our five-year South Central High School reunion in nearby Union Mills, my arrival was most unexpected. I had no intention of attending the reunion—or, truth be told, of ever again setting foot in that small dot of a town on U.S. Highway 30—but on this day Dawn and I were drawn together by the toll-free helpline of the National Association of Tourist Attraction Survivors, NATAS for short. In Dawn's moment of personal crisis, she called seeking healing and restoration—a working through of her own deeply ingrained Tourist Attraction Trauma—as connected to the LaPorte County Historical Society Museum's Belle Gunness exhibit, which had been a shared childhood interest. I had already received the help of NATAS and was now employed to help facilitate awareness and change in others, even—and perhaps especially—my former classmate.

Still, as a NATAS senior counselor and the editor of this collection of survivors' tales, it is neither my experience nor my straightforward and unremarkable story that should take precedence here, and so I would like to share with you, in Dawn Tempers' own words, the events preceding her initiation into NATAS on that fateful June day:

Like so many who return home after a long absence, I stopped at familiar landmarks, mourned missing buildings and businesses, and tried (but failed) to incorporate into my mind and heart the new that I had never known. Given Hanna's size, my tour took ten minutes, at the end of which I found myself standing in front of the Hanna Branch Public Library. Shifting my weight from one foot to the other and back again, I felt uncertain, uncomfortable, and expectant in a way I did not like.

I cupped my hands to what had long ago been a bank's drive-up window and peered through a tangle of philodendron, past a Christmas cactus, and around a Venus fly trap until I glimpsed the open bank vault. Inside the vault stood a girl wearing a red nylon South Central Satellites jacket like I had once worn. I watched her pull picture books from the vault and stack them on the floor, and I said to myself children and innocence. Such a cliché! But then it wasn't really, not for me, and I wondered about the girl, what she had read and would read that would shape her on the inside, what she had done and what had been done to her that would color her soul.

I shook off my thoughts, walked the library's length of windows, brightly decorated with construction paper cutouts of flowers and smiling suns. Then I opened the door and stepped inside.

"Hello! How may I help you?" asked the librarian sitting behind the check-out counter. She was friendly. Too friendly. She was loud. Too loud for a library. Then her eyes widened and she exclaimed, "Why, you're Doris' daughter, aren't you?"

Doris. Yes, that was my mother's name—and, yes, I was her daughter, and that was all the librarian knew and needed to know about me. Daughter. That word always landed hard, even from the mouth of a librarian whose friendliness and familiarity had startled me. I forced a smiled I hoped would pass as casual.

"That's me," I said, gritting my teeth. "Doris' daughter. Is my mom still chain-reading Harlequins?"

The librarian busted out laughing and I looked away until she caught her breath again, wheezing out, "Oh, you bet! 'Chain-reading Harlequins.' You've got a way with words there, young lady! Your mom sure was right about you!"

"She sure was!" I choked out, feeling pressure building like I too might explode, only not with laughter. The librarian kept talking, sharing local gossip and tossing out surnames any Hanna person would recognize—Hunsley, Burns, Bechinski, Poe, Garner, Guse, Huhnke, Fritz, Cuff. I flipped through fliers on the community board. Hanna United Methodist Vacation Bible School. Lion's Club barbeque. South Central kindergarten registration. All the names and all the events were familiar, as though nothing ever changed in Hanna, and maybe nothing ever did, not even after living away from my hometown for five years. But then I saw it—something new, different, the bright blue corner of a flier pinned with a silver tack. My eyes were drawn to it, and so was my gut.

"Did your mom show you the latest about Oprah in the LaPorte Herald-Argus?" the librarian asked. As I feverishly worked to uncover the full flyer, she kept talking. Oprah Winfrey had been a common topic in LaPorte County ever since she'd bought a farm back in the late 1980s. "Seems Oprah's tired of her friends getting flat tires on the way out to her farm, thinks the county should fix them up with all the taxes she's forced to pay."

Farm.

When the librarian said "farm," my mind flipped back to 1908, nearly a century before, to that other farm in LaPorte County on McClure Road where Belle Gunness had done far worse than complain to county commissioners about rough roads. No one could have denied Belle was resourceful, taking matters into her own hands, thus forever becoming LaPorte's longest-lasting celebrity. But I couldn't think about Belle, and I couldn't think about my mother or my five-year high school reunion or the things I had or hadn't done, would or wouldn't do. I could only think about that blue paper because the more frenzied I felt on the inside, the more ordered I needed to appear to the librarian.

I pulled pushpins—red, orange, yellow, green, blue, white—from the other fliers and arranged the pushpins in a rainbow arc, then stacked the papers on the counter in a neat pile.

A slip of red and out the door. The girl in the red Satellites jacket was gone.

A voice. The librarian's. "Your mother..."

My mother? Which mother?

And then I saw fully the flier I had been seeking to uncover, bright blue and pinned in the corners with four yellow thumbtacks, flush against the board:

> **DO YOU HAVE TOURIST ATTRACTION TRAUMA?**
>
> When you say where you're from, do people say, "I stopped there once on my way to _____?"
>
> When people tell stories of where they're from, do you stay silent and avoid sharing even when you have things you could say?
>
> When you travel, are you careful to avoid stopping at any place that looks "interesting" even when you want to?
>
> If you answered "yes" to any of these questions, you may be suffering from Tourist Attraction Trauma (TAT).
>
>
>
> Call
> 1-800-555-TATS
> The call is free. The help is free.
>
>
>
> *Sponsored by the National Association of Tourist Attraction Survivors (NATAS), a non-profit research and recovery organization dedicated to helping Tourist Attraction Trauma survivors discover a healthy balance between their pasts and futures while living with confidence in the present.*

    I know that calling a seemingly coincidental but life-changing occurrence "fate" is out of fashion these days, but I can tell you three things: I never made it to my five-year high school reunion; I never became the serial killer Belle Gunness molded me from birth to become; I never regretted the phone call I made.

    A Green Glow on the Horizon: Tales from the National Association of Tourist Attraction Survivors is a personal labor of love, forged out of a deep need to share the stories of Dawn Tempers and others who have been profoundly impacted by tourist attractions. Dawn's story ("Northern Belle") and four others ("Born Beneath Pedro's Sombrero," "Under the Sign of Sleepytime," "Cherished," and "Taxidermy Tabernacle") first appeared in *Tourist Attraction Travesty: Tales from*

Tourist Attraction Trauma Survivors, an in-house publication of the National Association of Tourist Attraction Survivors' Hospital for Research and Recovery (NATASHRR). They are re-printed with kind permission from NATASHRR.

While I cannot begin to acknowledge every contributor by name, I would like to give special thanks to the doctors and counselors at the National Association of Tourist Attraction Survivors' Hospital for Research and Recovery in Florida, Ohio, most particularly to my dear friend and mentor Corey Shrilpa who taught me everything I needed to know about being a counselor myself.

To the rest who shall remain unnamed, lest I forget to mention even one, thank you for sharing your stories, letters, diaries, counseling session transcripts, even gift store receipts, all of which speak to the experiences of tourist attraction survivors.

These are your stories.

Thank you for letting me share them with the world.

—*Lauren Ambrite, 2009*

Storytelling Creed of the National Association of Tourist Attraction Survivors

This is the story I'm learning to tell.

This is the fear that threatens to choke the story I'm learning to tell.

This is the confusion underlying the fear that threatens to choke the story I'm learning to tell.

This is the sadness flowing through the confusion underlying the fear that threatens to choke the story I'm learning to tell.

This is the anger boiling up in the sadness flowing through the confusion underlying the fear that threatens to choke the story I'm learning to tell.

This is the story I'm learning to tell.

© Monica Friedman

Letter from the Fort Wayne Children's Zoo

Editor's note: While the Fort Wayne Children's Zoo is this letter's featured attraction, the exact location is of less importance than Abigail's (the letter writer's) perception of how a zoo context defines her relationship with Phillip (the recipient). The National Association of Tourist Attraction Survivors received this letter folded inside a map of the Fort Wayne Children's Zoo, with mentioned locations highlighted. An attached Post-it Note read, "Figured this was of more use to you folks than to me. Sincerely, Phillip." No return address was provided.

* * *

October 15, 2002

Dear Phillip,

Today, for the first time in months, I watch the otters alone. And I think about us.

I know your body too well to ever love you. I know the tan mole on your left shoulder and the black hair that curls upwards just below your navel. I know the rasping way you breathe after love-making and the plaintive wail of your stomach when you are hungry. But this is all I know.

Arranged marriages have something going for them. Blankness. The lack of memories, disappointments, even joys. In the absence of these, I could love you beyond minutes and hours. And maybe that love could overcome this place.

I remember when we first met. I stood sipping lemonade from a purple plastic ape outside the entrance to Orangutan Alley, debating whether to go in. You walked out and said, "It's not worth it. They haven't scooped the poop in days." Then you held your nose and made a sound as if you were about to be sick. I laughed, thanked you for the warning. "No problem," you said. "It is my pleasure to warn beautiful women of unpleasant things."

Nobody goes to the zoo alone. Families go so children can learn to imitate tigers and giraffes. Packs of teenagers go to taunt the monkeys, and maybe even sneak them candy. Young lovers go secretly hoping to glimpse mating kangaroos and tortoises. Old couples go to watch the families, the teenagers, the lovers, to sigh remember-whens. But alone? Nobody goes to the zoo alone.

Until the day I met you, I always had company. There had always been another—a friend, a sister, another secretary from the office—to accompany me. I suppose I could have found somebody that day, but just this once I did not want to be laughed at for making faces at the monkeys or hurried away from watching the otters play.

I believed you recognized all those things inside me, there outside Orangutan Alley. I may have blushed. I can't recall. You walked on alone and I watched as you began fading into a fourth-grade field trip. I hurried to catch up until, together, we were bucking the crowd of children and chaperones.

"I see you don't really want to be alone," you said. And so, I spent my day with you.

Somehow, we began meeting at the zoo twice a week. We always met on Sundays, then alternated Tuesdays and Thursdays. We always went to the otter pond but only sometimes to Orangutan Alley. I came to know your body in Australia After Dark, beneath the flickering EXIT sign atop the rocky cliff. No one ever disturbed us, and our cries were drowned out by the shrieks of bats.

I know we will marry like we have planned, that we will have a satisfactory life and add our quotient to the world's population, that we shall take our children to the zoo, even to Australia After Dark. You have talked about conceiving our children beneath the EXIT sign, but I fear such spawn would be flighty and dark. I want to conceive on a blanket of yellow in a field of green beneath a blazing red sun. I want any dark spot scorched from my children before birth.

Such a fantasy, this talk of marriage. I do not know you as I should. I have never known you outside the zoo. Remember when we hid inside Tiger Forest at closing time and spent the night at the zoo? We walked familiar paths, but everything seemed so strange. No laughing children. No popcorn vendors. No safari trucks making their rounds through the African Veldt. All was silent and when you spoke, I did not know your voice. That night was the longest of my life. We made love on the bank of the Indiana Family Farm pond, but Australia After Dark had never felt that down under. We had the zoo to ourselves, and we were strangers.

Can we even know each other apart from the zoo? In my mind I draw your body—eyes, nose, limbs, feet, even the tan mole on your left shoulder—to exact proportion, create your fragrance with chemicals, flowers, and dung. I even taste your mind, biscuit-dry with certitude. But all of you is mingled with the fluttering of bat wings, the odor of popcorn, the vendor selling alfalfa pellets in ice cream cones for the petting zoo goats.

Today I watch three red-bellied woodpeckers—two females, one male—on the tallest tree behind the otters. The male jackhammers the thickest part of the trunk, each beak-strike determined and exact. The females flit from branch to branch, then fly away. I think they would like to leave the zoo behind.

I wonder if I am flighty and you, determined and exact. You never look to either side but press on, as if in one hour you could penetrate a tree ten times as dense as your head. How is it you keep your grip, vertical against the trunk? I would think you would fall. I would wish you to fall.

No. We are not these woodpeckers. Woodpeckers don't belong to the zoo. They can, should they choose, fly away at any time. Life does not work like that for us. If we flew away, I fear we would be devoured by all that is different between us.

I think if we were truly meant to marry, my soul should have changed by now, should have mingled with yours, that our two souls would have fused into something new and wholly unique. Some say souls meet through the eyes, and I remember when you first caught sight of mine. I had been doing nothing more than watching the otters when I turned to you, you who were always ready to move on to Australia After Dark, and said without hesitation the one thing that was in my heart, said that otters were God's playful angels. But my words were not what made you gasp. In that instant, I saw you seeing through my eyes to my deeper soul, and while I could not tell whether you were pleased or frightened, I felt relieved that my soul was no longer hidden.

Only once have I glimpsed your soul, that time I chanced to see you outside the zoo, at the intersection of Coldwater and Coliseum. I caught your eyes and glimpsed a rainbow trapped beneath an iron grid. I tried to peer deeper, but you removed your sunglasses from your jacket pocket and placed them over your eyes, as a drunken pirate would replace his patch which had fallen off during a brawl. As if he could cover his shame. You said the sun was too bright, that you had an appointment to get to, that you would see me at the zoo as usual on Sunday. And then you hurried on. I did not cry, but my soul wept. That was the only time we met on the outside.

I tried to love you after that day on the street, to go on as if our universe were the zoo. Once in Australia After Dark I asked if you had a soul.

"A soul? What's that?" you asked.

You laughed. "I am Batman," you said, taking our blanket and turning it into your cape. "Do you not know Batman has no soul? I am just a figment of a cartoonist's imagination." You flapped your imaginary wings. Another time I would have laughed.

God's playful angels splash about. Liquid eyes and white whiskers, water cats that exist somewhere between fish and mammal, water and land. They watch me watching them, inviting me as they always do to strip down, get wet, plunge beneath, play as if there is no zoo.

By the time you read this, I will be an otter.

—Abigail

© Heidi Reichenbach Finley

The Roswell Diaries

Editor's note: In July of 2001, Salvation Army thrift store staff in Las Cruces, New Mexico, discovered a battered green spiral notebook with tire tracks on its back cover behind a bookcase full of Harlequin romance novels.

Matthew, the store manager who mailed the notebook to the National Association of Tourist Attraction Survivors, was baffled as to how such a personal item had made it to his store, let alone onto the sales floor. He knew nothing of the notebook's origins beyond the obvious fact that it had been run over by a vehicle. "I don't have a clue how it got down to Las Cruces from Roswell," Matthew wrote in the letter accompanying the notebook, "but I sure would be interested to learn whatever happened to the kid who wrote this."

Except for the diarist's first name (Valerie) and age at the time of her writing (thirteen), her identity remains unknown. NATAS welcomes any leads regarding the writer of "the Roswell diaries" which has become a vital resource in Tourist Attraction Trauma studies.

* * *

August 1, 1998

We're moving. Again. Mom tells me, "It's for the best," but that's what she said when we ended up in Tacoma a year ago. This time Mom says she wants an alien baby and the only way to get one is if she moves us all to Roswell. Van and Velma don't seem to mind, but I don't want to go. Van's only three and too young to care where Mom takes him. Velma's going to be in first grade, but she's too weird to have any friends so she doesn't care either. I'm not too young, I have friends, and I care. A lot.

August 2, 1998

Today I asked Mom why she wants an alien baby and all she said was, "I need a new challenge, Valerie." A new challenge? I told her she should take up knitting or bowling or maybe even give marriage another try. "I plan to," she said. Then she got all dreamy and asked, "Wouldn't you like to have an alien daddy?" YUCK!! Who wants an alien dad? I sure don't.

August 3, 1998

We're in the car. The 2 Little Vs are asleep in the backseat. Mom said she needed a map-reader so I'm up front. We've been on the road since 4:00 this morning and now it's nearly noon. I begged Mom to let me bring Bruce and he's asleep between us now, stretched out on his back, showing off his white belly patch. Bruce didn't like being in the car at first and howled a lot and sweated from his paws, which seems weird to me, but most of all he just shed. There's gray cat hair all over the seat from the first hour of the trip but he's fine now. I've been feeding Bruce Cosmic Catnip treats and letting him drink out of my water bottle when he's thirsty.

"We'll get you an alien cat in Roswell," Mom said.

She says I roll my eyes too much. I don't think I do. Who wants an alien cat? I sure don't. I wonder, though, do alien cats have antennae?

I'm back. I'm tired of listening to Mom so I told her I had to write in my diary. She's still talking but I'm not even pretending to listen. Here's what she sounds like when she talks nonstop: "Oh, alien men are great. Alien dads are great. Alien cats are really great. Just think, you'll be going to school with aliens, and we'll live in an alien house with alien TV and eat alien TV dinners blah blah blah alien, blah blah blah alien, blah alien, blah blah blah blah." She makes me sick.

I had a hard time explaining all this to Brandi. Even though Brandi's supposed to be my best friend and should understand me immediately like we've got some kind of psychic connection, she's kind of flaky sometimes.

"Mom's moving us again," I told her.

"Where to?" Brandi asked.

"Roswell," I said.

"Where?" Brandi asked again.

"Roswell," I repeated, "like in *The X-Files*."

"Like in what?" Brandi asked.

So I tried to tell Brandi about Mom wanting to marry an alien man so she could have an alien baby. And how the only way Mom thought she could do so was to go all the way to Roswell, halfway across the country. I tried to make it sound like it really could happen too, or at least I didn't try to make it sound like it couldn't. I talked like this was just what Mom was doing and it was just the way things were and so that made it OK, because, really, girls my age should still believe in their moms, shouldn't they? I mean, believe in their moms at least a little bit because if I couldn't believe in Mom then the whole world and all its bigness and uncertainty would just be too terrifying to even consider, right? Because I'm thirteen, and I can't really take care of myself or Van or Velma, even though I already mostly do. But I'm THIRTEEN and I shouldn't have to, and I don't even want to think about that right now because the truth is that it could happen, that this move could turn out really badly and I could have to take care of myself and the 2 Little Vs.

I don't even know how to think about that yet and I really don't want to have to think about that, but I especially couldn't even begin to explain all that to Brandi who has lived in the same house in Tacoma all her life with her mother who's the church organist and her father who's an undertaker at Scanlin's and her older brother Mick who just graduated from high school and still isn't going to leave town to go to college, just live in the basement and learn how to undertake from his dad.

"Oh!" Brandi said, looking like she finally had it all figured out. "You mean like *Star Trek*! Maybe you could beam me up for a weekend sometime!"

But she doesn't get it. Even though Brandi's supposedly my best friend and we have this psychic connection thing going, even she doesn't get it at all. She doesn't even get that *The X-Files* and *Star Trek* are not even close to the same show, so how could she ever understand that my mom is moving us clear across the country so she can have an alien baby?

So I just told Brandi I didn't think it worked like that, but then she acted all mad like I didn't like her anymore. Brandi started saying I probably had other people in mind I wanted to beam up first instead of her, that I was just going to forget all about her once I moved. She can be soooo annoying sometimes! But I'm still going to miss her.

We stopped at a McDonald's just outside of Salt Lake City and ate supper, which really was just lunch at night. Honestly, I'm not sure what to call our meal. When I tried to get Mom to take the Boise exit at noon since we were all so hungry, Mom just wanted to keep on the road, so instead we ate stale pretzels and Cheerios straight from the box until they ran out. Then we just chewed Juicy Fruit and Big Red to keep us from thinking about being hungry. But when we reached Salt Lake City five hours later, even Mom was hungry, so she got herself a Quarter Pounder with Cheese and I ordered for the rest of us—Happy Meals and cookies for the 2LVs, a Big Mac, large fries, large Coke, large chocolate shake, and cherry pie for me. Filet O' Fish without the bun or sauce for Bruce. I'll say one thing good about Mom, when she's excited about something, you can get her to buy you anything so long as you're willing to take advantage of her mood. I feel pukey now, but I don't know when I'll get a meal that good again. Mom's gone kind of quiet now and isn't chattering away as much as she was earlier. Looks like she's getting mopey which isn't good for any of us. Uh, oh. She just asked, "Do you think an alien man will really love me?" So I said, "Uh huh. Sure, Mom," and tried to smile up at her because the last thing any of us needs right now is Mom losing faith in herself halfway to Roswell.

August 4, 1998

Finally, the sun is up enough for me to see, and I might as well write since there's nothing to look at except sand and saguaro and yellow billboards that read, "The Thing? Mystery of the Desert! Exit 322," but now I don't even see those. I asked Mom if we could stop and find out what The Thing? is, but she said we don't have time, which isn't at all true but since she's driving, we drove by Exit 322 without stopping. Mom's been driving all night, pushing through Utah and on into Arizona, one state away from New Mexico and her beloved Roswell. I slept off and on, waking up when the car veered into the left lane and another car honked at us, which made Mom start singing "When You Wish Upon a Star" really loud to keep awake.

Ok. I'm going to write some things I didn't think I was going to have to write, things I don't want to write but I have to. I just hope Mom doesn't open my diary.

See, the thing is, I'm sure there aren't aliens in Roswell. I know we're going to get there and Mom's going to be so disappointed she's going to crash, really crash bad this time, and I'm going to have to take care of the 2LVs by myself and that scares me. I hope for all our sakes that she finds an alien man she can marry and live with happily ever after, because that would mean the rest of us wouldn't live half bad. But I'm convinced that's not going to happen. Here's why:

1) Mom has never found even a human man who can live with her for more than a year.

2) The only evidence she has of alien men living in Roswell comes from a story in *Weekly World News*.

It's not that I don't think *Weekly World News* isn't credible about a lot of things like the Bat Boy and the face on Mars, but when Mom called the Roswell Chamber of Commerce to request more information about Roswell's Humalien compound, I heard a deep booming laugh followed by silence and knew that the man on the other end had hung up on her.

"It's ok," Mom told me casually, too casually to be comfortable, as she tossed the cordless phone onto the ever-growing mountain of bills and junk mail on the coffee table. "That's what the *Weekly World News* said would happen. They just don't want their town overrun by outsiders."[1]

I was angry then. Not angry at Mom and all her hopes and dreams of finding an alien man who could give her an alien baby, but angry at the man at the Roswell Chamber of Commerce who could have said something different. Could have done something other than laugh. Could have maybe

---

[1] What follows is the portion of the *Weekly World News* article from the July 1998 issue believed to have spurred Valerie's mother to make her cross-country move to Roswell:

"Roswell, New Mexico, home to the 1947 alien spaceship crash is now home to bi-speciel families! Tucked away in a quiet corner of Mac Brazel's ranch is a thriving community of Humaliens (human-alien) living life as nature never intended! As many as fifty alien men from the planet ZugZug have made their home here with red-blooded American women! The alien men, averaging in height from three-feet, five inches to four-foot, express a preference for dwarfish women who are often overlooked by the American male."

cared enough about the crazy woman on the other end of the line to ask if she had any children and get her address and phone number and say he would send her brochures and a calendar of events and make like she was welcome in his city. Not because Mom really was welcome but because he was just a little worried about her—and even more, about her children—so that he could contact the Tacoma police and have us looked in on so that maybe this stupid road trip that is going to end terribly wouldn't even have had to happen. Or at least if it did happen, somebody else on this whole huge planet called Earth would know about us and worry about us and look after us, even just a little. Even just enough so that if we all turned up dead somewhere along the way, somebody would know our names and would know even a small piece of our story.

Maybe it wouldn't have made a bit of difference if the Roswell Chamber of Commerce man hadn't laughed, but just knowing that he knew our names (that he knew we were out there), and just believing somebody else cared even if nobody really did would have helped me feel a little less responsible, a little more ok with being the normal child of a crazy mother. No. Not even a crazy mother, just a lonely mother. A very, very, lonely mother. A mother who would wander the earth and the stars trying to find the one man who could love her, never realizing she could start loving her kids at any time.

But now I do sound angry at Mom. Angry and bitter. And what good does that do me in the middle of this desert? Keep it together. Keep it together. Valerie, you've just got to keep it together for your sake and your whole family's sake, because if you don't, then where will you be? Keep it together, Valerie, just keep it together.

I'm back. We're an hour from Roswell and the 2LVs have finally stopped puking. Van was first. He puked without warning, straight onto the back of my seat. After that, Velma started in, and Mom didn't have anywhere to pull off or anything for them to throw up in, so the puke just went all over. By the time Mom pulled over at a run-down Sunoco, the car felt like this puke sauna. Since Mom can't handle being around sick people, she got me a bucket of water and an armload of scratchy brown paper towels from the bathroom. Mom set me to work cleaning the car and the 2LVs while she scurried back into the air-conditioned gas station like she'd melt if she didn't.

As I was stripping off the 2LVs puke-soaked clothing, this shiny silver Ford Astro with a California license plate pulled up and I watched as these perfectly tanned parents and their two perfectly tanned children—one about Van's age and one about Velma's—got out to stretch their legs and load up on Pringles and Dr. Pepper. Since there was nobody else around but them and us, we couldn't ignore each other, even though I willed myself to be invisible, staring straight through them and smiling, expecting their faces to drop, waiting to catch them glancing at us from the corners of their eyes the way people usually look at us. The way that makes me uncomfortable. The way people can say so much without a single word, can say without even looking, "Yes, we know you're there, but forgive us for not really looking because if we did, you'd only be ashamed because of who you are and then we'd be embarrassed about your being so different from us, and really, we have nothing to say to each other and we don't want to be embarrassed about your existence in this world but still, we are embarrassed, and there's nothing that can be done about it. If we were to enter your world, then we would have to examine our own and your memory would haunt us. We wouldn't know what to do with that so it's better, really, just to look away, and I'm sorry, but that's just the way life works."

The dad and kids dropped their eyes to the pavement and hurried past us to reach the bathroom. But then the mom walked over to me. I was kneeling in front of the 2LVs wiping Van's bare chest with wet brown paper towels which weren't holding up too well with the water and the scrubbing, leaving little brown balls sticking to Van's skin like tiny leeches. "Looks like someone's not feeling too well," the woman said gently, and she was actually really nice, not fake nice, but nice nice.

"Hold on just a minute," she said, then went back to her Astro. When she returned, she had a plastic tub of Huggies baby wipes and crouched down beside me and started wiping off Van's chest, which made him blush. "These will work better, I think," she said and smiled, looking up into my eyes but also wondering, I could tell, where my mother was and what I was doing taking care of these kids when I was only a kid myself. And just when I could tell she was thinking this, Mom came out of the Sunoco with ten alien head air fresheners to hang in our car.

Since Mom's my mom and I've known her all my life, she sometimes seems almost normal to me, but then there she stood before me, all twitchy in her excitement with her bullfrog eyes bulging out of her squinty weasel face, her silver hoop earrings clinkety-clanking back and forth, her hands waving around these alien head air fresheners that were the same bright green as her fingernail polish. And even though I'm used to how Mom looks and acts, not everybody is, and this tanned woman from California clearly wasn't. Her lips got all tight as Mom, holding her nose, handed me the alien heads. Then Mom gave a little wave to the woman who was cleaning her son, *her* son, not the son from California who had this woman as a mother. This woman who smelled like oranges and cocoa butter. I was embarrassed and ashamed.

For myself? For my mother? For this stranger who didn't know anything about us and so must assume everything, and was probably making half-right assumptions? *It's not like she doesn't love us*, I thought but did not say. And my mom, who has no self-consciousness and is excited about getting to Roswell today, told this woman, "We're meeting their new father today." And though it might have been almost ok if Mom had stopped there, she didn't stop there but added, "He's an alien."

"Do you mean he's from Mexico?" the woman from California asked, trying harder than most to be kind, to give Mom the benefit of the doubt.

"Oh no," my mother said. "He's from the planet ZugZug."

I could have died.

The woman looked from my mom to me, and she must have known it wasn't a joke when she looked at my face, burning with shame. As Mom was hanging up the alien head air fresheners in the car and the 2LVs were putting on clean clothes in the backseat, the California mom took one more wipe from the Huggies tub. I thought maybe she was going to clean her hands, but instead she removed my glasses, cupped my chin in her palm, and wiped all the sweat and grime from my face.

When she finished, the woman who was not my mother but whom I wished could be, handed me the Huggies and whispered in my ear, "You can keep these." And then she and her husband and their two small children who were the same ages as Van and Velma but were probably named Mike and Maggie climbed back into their silver Ford Astro and drove away. Forever.

Back in the car, Mom yelled at me for throwing away the 2LVs pukey clothes and dressing them in clean clothes—the only extra set Mom had packed which she said were their dress clothes for meeting their new alien dad. "Sure, Mom," I said. "Whatever you want to believe."

The ten air fresheners hang all along the windows of the car. They smell like pine, but they look like shrunken alien heads.

August 5, 1998

Like the spaceship that probably never even was, my mother crashed in Roswell last night.

At first, she was excited, as were the 2LVs who perked up as we were driving into Roswell at sunset. Van had been sleeping, and the first thing he saw when he looked out the window was this huge green alien. Van thought it was real and in his sleepy voice said, "Daddy?" But the alien was tied to the ground with long ropes and held a sign that read "Roswell Honda."

I could tell Mom was nervous because she wasn't jabbering on about alien dads and cats and schools. I pulled Bruce onto my lap and he curled up and started purring and nudging my hand with his nose, which he somehow knows to do when I need him most.

Mom stopped at a McDonald's and bought one cheeseburger which she split five ways "for a snack," she said since we'd feast when we arrived at the Humalien community. I used the wipes from the California mom and cleaned all our faces and hands when we were through, starting with my own and the 2 LVs, then moving on to Mom's. Beneath the slick strong fabric of these pure white wipes, my fingers smoothed the creases under Mom's eyes, filled the pock marks in her cheeks, caressed the angry scar on her chin that she had always called a Christmas gift from her father.

In the bathroom, Mom brushed her hair and gave me a comb to take care of myself and the 2LVs while she began applying make-up in front of the mirror: first blush and powder, then lipstick. She finished and turned to look at me as I combed out Velma's tangles.

"Do I look beautiful?" Mom asked, and I swallowed hard and said, "Yes," even though her lips were bright green and her cheeks were pale blue with glitter stars, and I wanted to say she looked like a freak. I wanted to ask what was going to happen when we got out to where the Humaliens supposedly lived and found nothing there, but in that moment I had no choice but to believe that she would find a wonderful four-foot eight-inch alien man who would love her unconditionally, who would be her husband, and who would be our dad. I had no choice but to hope that even though Mom and her alien husband wouldn't be like the California couple at the gas station, they would be our parents, stable and settled, not moving from place to place. But that's not how it happened.

The drive out to the old Mac Brazel ranch was quiet. The 2LVs sat up straight and tall in the back seat like Mom told them to, and they didn't say a word. Mom gripped the steering wheel and drove straight ahead: a woman with a purpose. Bruce sat on my lap and looked at me and I looked at him, his green eyes glowing in the darkness. He didn't purr and I could scarcely breathe.

When we arrived, there was nothing besides some sleeping cows beneath a starless sky. Still, Mom got us all out of the car and told us to stand in a straight line, to smile and reach out our arms, as if the Humaliens were hiding in some parallel dimension and we had to show our good intentions before they would show themselves to us. But when they didn't come out of hiding and all we could hear were rumbling cow snores, my mother said, "Maybe they've moved on. Maybe they're nomadic." So Mom piled us back into the car and drove on through the night, out in the New Mexico countryside, looking for a green glow that would lead us to where we belonged. But there was nothing. And when the sun began to rise, I looked over at Mom, still gripping the steering wheel, still determined, but now with blood-shot eyes, tear furrows down her painted cheeks, and lips still green except where her natural color showed through from nervous biting.

"Do I still look beautiful?" she asked with a crooked half-smile. The alien air fresheners around the windows blew in the breeze and clacked together.

"Oh, Mom," I said, and began to cry.

What are we doing here? Where will we go? There are no aliens, and there is no Humalien compound, but with no money, we have to stay. And I guess here is as good as Tacoma, as good as anywhere, or at least it's no worse.

August 6, 1998

Somehow we found our way into town last night, and then Mom saw the thing she thought she was looking for, a spaceship lodged into the side of a building that had a big marquee with black letters spelling out "International U.F.O. Museum." By that time, Mom was really out-of-touch with reality, and when I pointed out that it was a museum and not the Humalien compound she believed it was, she put a finger to her lips, shushed me, and said, "You'll see." But I didn't see, and what was worse was that she thought she did.

From the moment we stepped inside, it was clear that we were in a museum. Statues of aliens greeted us. To our right was a stand where visitors could pay for a set of headphones and a tape recorder to listen to the story of the 1947 crash as they walked through and looked at the exhibits. The 2LVs stuck close to me as Mom collapsed in front of a four-foot tall silver alien and began to weep and kiss his feet. From all corners of the museum, people came and encircled Mom. They whispered about her, but these weren't the whispers I was used to, the ones about her being weird, a bad parent, a drain on society's resources. A man with long red hair tied back in a ponytail whispered, "Abductee," and then one by one, strangers approached and wrapped their arms around Mom and the statue.

Mom had broken down completely by then and couldn't say a word. With her smeared make-up and green lips, I could see how she might have looked like an abductee to them. At first, I spoke up. I tried to say the problem wasn't that she was an abductee, but that she couldn't find any aliens to abduct her. But then these people picked up the 2LVs and the man with the ponytail reached for my hand. When I saw we were walking towards vending machines and everyone was digging in their pockets for quarters, I jammed my hands deep in my jeans pockets, shut my mouth, and followed.

I had forgotten where we were when I woke up this morning and opened my eyes to see doctors with white masks covering everything below their eyes. But then I blinked, saw them again, and realized they weren't real doctors, just dummy doctors in the *Roswell* movie exhibit I had seen the night before. I still didn't remember how I had come to be there exactly, but I reasoned that some time after eating snack bags of Cheetos and Chips Ahoy I must have fallen asleep on the table, or fallen asleep somewhere else in the museum and then been brought here, but it was weird because, even though I knew I had slept in an exhibit of a movie set, everything was so real—the stainless steel operating table, the blinding bright examining lights, the glass window on the other side of which I could see the faces of museum staffers and tourists looking in at me. So I scooted off the table and held up both my hands in Spock's "live long and prosper" sign (one of the few things I'd learned from Brandi) and tried to waddle like E.T., feet turned outward. I must have looked convincing since the tourists started snapping pictures and the staffers started writing notes.

Even though Mom hadn't come to her senses, at least we had a place to stay, food to eat, and people to take care of us, all of whom were willing to believe we were Humaliens. Outside of the alien autopsy exhibit where I had slept, I found the 2LVs playing tag in front of a huge, crashed spaceship and some not-so-real aliens. I couldn't find Mom, but since I didn't figure she was much good to us right now, I didn't look all that hard. So instead, I started going around the museum looking at the exhibits and reading all the newspaper articles and the museum's commentary on the 1947 crash. They left no room for me to doubt that aliens had crashed, no room to believe instead that maybe, just maybe, what crashed was a weather balloon and not a spaceship.

A spaceship crashed. The government covered it up. End of story.

Even though I cannot look straight on at their evidence and not believe, the weird thing is that deep down I still don't want to believe because that could make Mom right instead of just some crazy wannabe abductee, and if she really is right, then why do I feel so messed up inside?

Why do I feel like I should be on guard against even these good things that seem to be happening to all of us here in Roswell?

The man with the ponytail who calls himself Scottie fed us bologna sandwiches and brownies for lunch. He watched us as we ate, but except for my funny E.T. walk and my "live long and prosper" hand signals, there was nothing out of the ordinary about us. Scottie thought that we were "out of this world" and kept saying so, over and over again. The 2LVs acted perfectly normal except for telling Scottie they were from ZugZug when he asked. I explained matter-of-factly that the reason I had alien traits and they didn't was because I had grown up learning ZugZuggian mannerisms before we left our home planet, but that the 2LVs were too young to retain any of them and adapted more easily to Earth ways. This seemed to satisfy him. When he asked if we had bologna on ZugZug, I explained that we did, only instead of being made from pork byproducts, bologna on ZugZug was made out of animals called zigs (like pigs, only they're green with antennae and radioactive tails). Scottie wrote down everything I said.

I admit, though, I felt bad about lying to Scottie because he was nice to me and the 2LVs and seemed understanding about Mom. "She's had a rough time, hasn't she?" he asked, and I said, "Yes," because it was the truth. There was no doubt that Mom had had a rough time, even if she brought it on herself. "She told me your father was going to meet you all here in Roswell, is that right?" Again, I said, "Yes." Van stopped chewing his bologna sandwich and shouted, "Alien daddy!"

I told Scottie our dad was scheduled to arrive last night, and that the reason Mom was so messed up was that she was worried about him. "They've had a tough relationship," I said, hoping I sounded mature and wise. "He did abduct her, after all, but she's grown to love him, even if they don't see each other often. He travels a lot and doesn't like Earth much. That's why last night was going to be so special. Dad was finally going to live with us."

"The amazing thing," Scottie continued, "is that you all look so much like your mother, so human." Then I had to go into this long explanation about how alien genes are recessive and sometimes, in mixed breeds like us, can go almost unnoticed, especially when not influenced by the surrounding culture. It got to be exhausting making all this up and trying not to contradict myself. But I answered all his questions, from my favorite ZugZuggian food "azzip," which I hoped he wouldn't recognize as "pizza" spelled backwards, to my favorite ZugZuggian game "Zogonopoly," to where I would travel to if I could go anywhere on ZugZug—Zisneyland. I was glad that was Scottie's last question because I was running out of lies!

Then Scottie took us to the library to see Mom. All along the left wall stood tall bookshelves filled with books about aliens and spaceships and government conspiracies, but I hardly even noticed those before I saw Mom at the far end in front of a mural of a crashed spaceship with alien bodies sprawled all around. The mural didn't surprise me, but what did was that she was acting like it was real! She'd found a miniature alien, a one-foot high green rubber alien with big black eyes, a pot belly, four fingers on each hand and four toes on each foot, and a face all crimped up like a little old man's or a dwarf's. Mom had wrapped the alien in a pastel green baby blanket and stood cradling it like the alien baby she'd wanted so badly. She cooed to it in a strange alien-sounding voice and sang it a lullaby with lots of Zs and seemed to have forgotten all about her 3LVs: Velma, Van, and me, Valerie. Scottie seemed to realize Mom's behavior was problematic, not normal, but he just repeated something he'd said earlier—"She's been through a lot, hasn't she?" Then Scottie shook his head and looked very sad.

"She thought he would be here," I said, with less enthusiasm than before. "She thought her true love would be here."

"Maybe," Scottie said, putting his arm around my shoulders, "maybe he'll show up yet."

I shrugged off his arm, walked right up to Mom and looked her straight in the eyes but she didn't recognize me at all, so I started to scream, "What about us? What about your Three Little Vs?" Mom was just silent and smiling.

"I think it's best we let her have some space," Scottie said, leaning over and whispering into my ear. "She's not the first woman who's come here in this condition, and they need time to heal, time to be separate from the world."

I was tired of all my lies, so I told Scottie the truth. I told him we weren't really Humaliens and that Mom was nuts, but he didn't believe me. I even stopped with the E.T. waddle I'd been doing all day. Scottie was still kind, but he shushed me, said he'd seen all this before with women like her. I thought then of the man from the Roswell Chamber of Commerce who laughed as though he'd heard women like my mother before, a man who did not share Scottie's sympathy but did share his lack of understanding.

In my mind I saw my mother broken down into tiny square boxes, looking like the robots I liked to draw on graphing paper in art class. I saw Mom being made to fit these patterns of "women like her" so that men like Mr. Roswell Chamber of Commerce and Scottie of the Stars could know how to respond in ways that made sense and that made Mom more manageable. Gone were her round bull-frog eyes and hoop earrings and ever moving, ever twitching body. In this version, my mother lost her texture of eye wrinkles and acne pits and Christmas scars. She was flat, the feel of crisp squared paper beneath my fingers, and I wanted to cry when Scottie said again that he'd seen it all before with women like her because I knew he had never seen my Mom at all.

August 7, 1998

We left the museum early this morning and are riding with Scottie in a grey Toyota hatchback with a "Beam me up" sticker on the back bumper. I don't know what will happen to us tomorrow or the day after or the day after that. We have Scottie who feeds and clothes us, who cares for us, who says he loves us. I do not know if Mom's ever going to get better. She sees what she wants to see, needs to see. Mom's sitting in the front seat beside Scottie, still cradling her alien baby, and Scottie is dressed in an alien costume, grey-green in color. When I started this diary, this would have bothered me, but now I guess I'm just glad to have a place where I am no longer the only alien. Van, Velma, and me are squeezed together in the back seat and Bruce is behind us in the back window, panting and sweating from his paws. We're heading out toward the same place where the aliens weren't two nights ago, and Scottie's not telling us what we're going to do once we get there. He talks softly to Mom and reaches over to stroke her hand now and then with his rubbery alien fingers.

"It won't be ZugZug," he says gently, "but it will be close." Mom looks up at him—her alien man—and smiles.

We're pulling off the main road now, and in the distance I see a green glow on the horizon. Maybe, just maybe, we're almost home.

© Mary Catherine Harper

Born Beneath Pedro's Sombrero

Editor's note: Rita's story epitomizes Tourist Attraction Trauma (TAT) and is a foundational case upon which doctors based Tourist Attraction Trauma theory. Paradoxically, Rita's story also complicates initial TAT theories proving that the trauma that so often results from tourist attractions is not absolute or unchangeable but can sometimes be transformed into Tourist Attraction Triumph.

* * *

I was born beneath Pedro's sombrero during a thunderstorm in early March. Mom labored seventeen hours, long enough for management to tack up "SEE WOMAN GIVE BIRTH BENEATH PEDRO'S SOMBRERO!" on billboards fifty miles to the north and south along I-95. Even in the rain, hundreds came to watch my birth. We received no royalties, though Mom got a free t-shirt with a cartoon drawing of her in labor with me, wearing a sombrero just like Pedro's, coming out from between her splayed legs. "Pequeña Pedrita," they called me after that. But even then I preferred just plain Rita.

South of the Border. Stuttering neon, greasy food, tacky T-shirts, and sweatshop snow globes to last a thousand lifetimes.

Hell. Home.

Doesn't matter which word I use.

Now I can't say whether growing up north of here would have been heaven, purgatory, or maybe just another kind of hell. That's not for me to know. Still, having seen road-worn tourists by the thousands, all sharing a glazed yet guarded look, I cannot confidently claim South of the Border to be the only hell on Earth.

As a kid I spent whole afternoons drinking Pepsi and eating Pop-Tarts straight from their silver foil package, observing the gas-pumping tourists watching me over the tops of their cars and minivans. And when we looked at each other, an unsettling awareness passed between us, both knowing about each other the things we could not see about ourselves. So we looked away, the tourists to the pumps in their hands, me to the Pepsi in mine. Sometimes we closed our eyes against the brightness of the sun and sky, at ease only in the shadows of our own minds.

Kudzu. That's what I knew tourists to be. Kudzu multiplying madly, vines and leaves grasping to hold onto something, going everywhere all at once yet nowhere at all. Beautiful from a distance out there on I-95 when they were still travelers. From the top of Sombrero Tower I watched lines of cars moving forward in both directions, going all the places roads can go, unstoppable and also beautiful in their motion. Mysterious and exotic and powerful, going to places I could not see, to destinations beyond my vision.

Travelers pull off on Exit 1, become tourists, invade. Kudzu tumbles out through sliding minivan doors, clamors for cheap hot dogs and flashy bumper stickers, and crawls over all the Pedros. Kudzu sneaks inside the Dirty Old Man shop, putts balls at the Golf of Mexico, sometimes even swims and sleeps at the Pleasure Dome. Which is good, I guess, because without kudzu's grip, this sad and desperate place just might blow away.

Maybe it's good that South of the Border is here to give an invasive species a place of welcome, even if only for an hour or two, before they twist back out on I-95 with empty bladders, full bellies and gas tanks, and photographic proof of life at the top of Sombrero Tower, having paid their own ransom before heading on their way to consume someplace else, some dreamscape too far away for me to see.

I wondered sometimes what exactly it was that kudzu believed about me.

First memory: I lick Pedro's toes, flake off scratchy brown bits that scrape my throat when I swallow. I cough but they don't come back up. I swallow again, but they don't go back down. They stick where I cannot see, paint me brown on the inside.

From the very beginning, I felt like something less. But mostly I think I just felt scared all the time. My first four years, I swear I never looked up, never realized there was more than Pedro's sandaled feet, big enough to crush one so small as me.

Maybe life wouldn't have been so bad if Mom hadn't had to work the toilets. Maybe life somehow would have been better if Mom hadn't had to clean up pee from all the kudzu brat boys, unclog toilets stuffed with bloody pads, and bleach down diarrhea-splattered stalls. Mom used to try and smile, be friendly, show the "true spirit of Pedro." I remember. But after a while she just sat by the door in her orange plastic chair, smoking her Slims, staring through them all. By then I had started to truly see South of the Border, and when I started to see, I became angry. On my sixth birthday, I took the keys to my mother's broken-down brown Chevette and chiseled my name—Rita—in the big toes on both feet of the Pedro by the main entrance.

The address on our junk mail read 3346 Highway 301 North, Dillon, SC 29547. That confused me. We never lived in Dillon but at South of the Border. I never understood why our mail wasn't sent to:

Dolores and Rita Epiphyte
Bright Orange Trailer with Broken Screen Door
and "No Trespassing" Sign
Behind Pedro's Pantry West
South of the Border, SC 29547

The summer after I turned eight, I met a kid named Louie who was waiting for his dad to come out from the Dirty Old Man's Shop. Louie was hungry and Pop-Tarts come in packs of two, so I gave him one of mine. Between bites, crumbs falling from his mouth, Louie told me that he lived in a town called Wanatah.

"Wanatah," Louie said, "means 'knee deep in mud' in Potawatomi." Louie must never have left Wanatah before because he couldn't shut up about how he loved Pedro-land and the Golf of Mexico and most of all the Sombrero Tower—how he loved our rusted out, shit-smeared Sombrero Tower, only he didn't say it was shit-smeared and rusted out. "Oh Rita," he said, "I'd love to live here. I wish I were you."

I gave him a drink of my Pepsi which stopped his mouth long enough for me to think but not long enough to say that I would trade lives with him in an instant, that I would rather live in Wanatah, wherever that was, than live at South of the Border.

See, nobody living at South of the Border likes it. Some are pretty good at self-deception for the sheer sake of survival, sure, but like it? Nobody really likes living here. I knew just enough from reading the hundreds of brochures in the Pleasure Dome lobby to understand that South of the Border is not like some national park. If I had lived in a national park I wouldn't have been so dissatisfied because, really, it's not the tourists that bother me most and I would get to be out in nature where things are beautiful all the time. Or, if not beautiful all the time, then at least always real. If I had grown up in Yellowstone and Louie had come along and told me how lucky I was, I'd have said, "Yeah," because it would have been true. And if there were a giant concrete Mexican named Pedro at Yellowstone, let alone seven of them like at South of the Border, nobody would even notice because they'd be too busy watching the geysers and looking for bison. Nobody would take Pedro's picture. If anything, there'd be a big "FREE ADMISSION TO ANYBODY WHO DYNAMITES THE BIG GUY WITH THE HAT" sign at the gate.

Living at South of the Border I saw thousands of kudzu tourists, none of them happy when they arrived, and all of them sick when they left with five-dollar Pedro T-shirts stretched over their bloated bellies. Still, I envied the visitors because they got to leave, got to go home to somewhere better than South of the Border where the neon doesn't ruin the sunsets. Somewhere better or at least somewhere real, even if it was knee deep in mud. I wondered if they even realized how lucky they were. Lucky like my dad.

Maybe it was lucky that I never knew my dad—a balding gap-toothed trucker with silhouettes of naked women on the mud flaps of his sixteen-wheeler—and lucky for mom that she only knew him for twenty-seven minutes. Mom met him in the Dirty Old Man's Shop when she was delivering a case of chocolate undies after her shift at the toilets.

"Hola, Señortita!" That's what Mom says he called her, "Señortita," when he called her over, and from what I've been told, that's pretty much all he said before hauling her off to the cab of his truck. The least he could have done would have been to treat her to one of the Pleasure Dome's "Honeymoon Suites: Heir-Conditioned at South of the Border."

I have no illusions about Mom loving him. I have no illusions about him someday coming back for me. Better that way. Who needs some shriveled up kudzu clinging to us with gnarled woody roots?

I knew plenty of other kids like me—fatherless kids whose moms cleaned toilets, sold T-shirts, or worked the Sombrero Tower. Some spent their days watching trucks roll in and through, hoping their fathers would recognize them. Those were the kids whose mothers told them their fathers loved them. Those were the mothers who believed the fathers would one day return and want to be their husbands. My mother knew the truth and said nothing about my father, or if she said anything at all, she spoke of how my father was once alive but now was dead, or must've been as she'd seen and heard nothing for years. I pitied the kids who waited and hoped. I pitied them, but still wondered what hope would feel like.

It's hard to live at South of the Border and not have at least six days of the week be down days. On down days, it's hard to move, to do anything at all. But on down and dissatisfied days my skin seems an uncomfortable fit that I itch to get out of. I was having one of those days when it happened.

I had spent the morning riding the glass elevator up to the top of Sombrero Tower, then back down again. There wasn't much to see from the elevator, just smeared pigeon poop and feathers clinging to the glass, but I liked the motion of moving up and down, up and down, and I liked the rush that came when I stepped from the elevator, walked to the lookout railing, leaned down, and felt both awe and fear as my gut bottomed out, like I was free falling even with my feet still firmly planted on Sombrero Tower's metal grating. I had run out of quarters after my fifth trip, but Beulah was having a down day and didn't care whether I paid, so I kept riding. When the elevator opened at the top of what would be my last ride of the day, I stepped out and walked to the railing, gazed out over this not-so-vast, not-so-perfect place, wishing but not expecting to see something grand. All I saw were the same old roofs of the same old buildings —Rocket City, Pedro's Hot Tamale, El Drug Store, Mexico Shop East, and Mexico Shop West. South of the Border was as flat, gray, boring, and desperately sad as it had ever been. I counted the Pedro statues. I watched the traffic on I-95. Smart travelers passed by. Kudzu took the exit.

Then I saw her. Out of the corner of my eye, I saw her, bright and gleaming against the rusted railing, this woman I had not seen on any of my forty trips up the tower that day. I knew right away she wasn't kudzu, but I couldn't quite tell what exactly she was. She is so vivid in my mind, yet I can't quite conjure her up. Sometimes I picture her in a butter-yellow sundress, and sometimes I think she wore a wispy green shift. I know her hair moved in waves, that she rippled like a mirage in the South Carolina summer heat. Kudzu stepped off the elevator, vined around her to look over the railing, but I could see through kudzu as if they were no more than ghostly vegetation.

She turned to see me seeing her, so I stared down at my feet, flip-flopped and filthy. I moved to the opposite side of Sombrero Tower.

"Why don't you jump?" she asked, her words like warm honey, her breath a blazing chill on the back of my neck. I felt the rush of free fall, but this time without the fear.

I knew that I could plummet all the way to the ground and stand back up. She hadn't asked, "Why don't you kill yourself," or "Why don't you rid the world of your presence?" She had asked, simply, "Why don't you jump?"

I surveyed South of the Border below—Pedro's Diner, Autobahn Club, Golf of Mexico, Ice Cream Fiesta.

"You won't die," she said. "You won't even stub your toe."

I closed my eyes, saw my mother leave work unpaid to come and rescue me, saw me jumping up and saying I was just fine, saw another line added to my title, another billboard, a new job.

PEQUEÑA PEDRITA!

SEE THE CHILD BORN BENEATH PEDRO'S SOMBRERO

JUMP FROM SOMBRERO TOWER

EVERY HOUR ON THE HOUR!

I would have made a good Old Faithful geyser. But I shook my head. No.

Aside from the packet of oyster crackers Beulah had given me that morning, I had eaten nothing since the day-old chocolate doughnut Mom had brought home from Pedro's Diner the night before. I had hallucinated all kinds of things at the top of Sombrero Tower on days like this, mostly tourists walking around with hamburgers for heads and French fries for legs. I tried to test whether this woman who stood behind me might be a hallucination, but she didn't morph into some other creature when I turned to face her and did my rapid blink test. She didn't change, only flickered the way that neon lights flicker against the black of night, a staccato pulse of colors.

"My dear," she said, locking eyes with me between blinks, "how hungry you must be!" She cupped my face in her hands, smoothed back my straggly hair, and pointed to the bird poop and feathers that peppered the cement under our feet. "Tell those bird droppings to turn into burgers and they will." But this I refused to even imagine, so disturbing was the idea of food coming from pigeon poop, even if I would have been well fed. So my stomach continued to rumble. My ever-present hunger remained.

And then she did one final thing. She stretched out her arm, motioning over all of South of the Border and said, "See all this?"

Now, I had watched scenes like this in movies, and whenever some mysterious person stood at a high point and said, "See all this?" the next line was invariably, "All this could be yours."

But this woman said, "I can rescue you from all this."

And I was hers, all hers.

It's hard to recall the order of events that followed. I know I came down from Sombrero Tower, though I do not remember taking the elevator. I know the woman said her name was Aurora, that when we walked she was just a little behind and to the side of me, that I moved within a cocoon of honey mist. I know she told me I was "meant for something greater." I know she always called me "Rita," never "Pequeña Pedrita." I know I never asked questions. I know I never went hungry.

I suppose I should have asked, "Where will you take me?" And I certainly should have asked what she meant by "something greater." But I didn't.

We walked and Aurora talked, my mind buzzing with possibilities. She fed me small yellow cakes that both satisfied and made me ever hungry for more. She told me all I had never known about a place beyond the Borderland.

"I chose you," she said, looking me full in the face, "to be my sister."

How stupid I was! I did not know what "sister" meant. Oh, sure, I knew the basic biological meaning, but beyond that? Not a clue. We walked past Pedro's Pantry West, past the Autobahn Club, all the way to the Golf of Mexico. "I'm going to bring this place down," she said quietly, even mercifully as I think about it now. "Bring it down and clean it out."

I guess when she said, "bring it down and clean it out," I expected something dramatic, something earth shattering, like she'd bring in tanks and heavy artillery, dynamite all the Pedros and short circuit the neon, leave South of the Border in rubble. I expected she would set up her own system to replace the old one, set the two of us up in charge, and we'd be fair and just and righteous, exalting those who did right and condemning those who did wrong. The toilet attendants would become bosses, the bosses would become toilet attendants, and the truckers who stopped at the Dirty Old Man shop would be castrated. She would make things right because she could, and I would help her.

I saw our first opportunity to make things right that first night when we went to meet Mom as she was getting off work. It was Friday, payday, and like all other paydays, her boss had lowered himself to visiting the toilet attendants as they exited. My mom, who had the least seniority even after years as a faithful worker, had to stand in the back of the line. Aurora and I watched from a distance as one by one the attendants got their cash-filled envelopes, and as opening the envelopes they were forced to frown rather than smile—sad, resigned frowns as if nothing would ever change for them. Ever. I thought I could help Mom by getting her all the money so she'd at last have more of something, be better and bigger than all the rest.

I didn't know how we could grab the cash and get away, but I felt somehow Aurora had power and believed that people with power took what they wanted. If I made the first move, I reasoned, Aurora would follow, convinced that what I wanted would be what she wanted. So I ran forward, grabbed the envelopes out of the boss's fat hand, and started running.

"Come on, Mom!" I yelled.

"Pedrita, you fucking cunt!" the boss yelled. "Get your ass back here."

I thought Mom would follow, but she didn't, and neither did her boss. When I turned around to see what had gone wrong with my plan, I saw Mom's boss, puffed up and red like a giant hot tamale, grab the front of her shirt and pull her up so close I could almost feel the hot blast of his breath, smell its sour, smoky tang. I'd messed up. Mom had to give him his money back or be fired or worse. I was old enough to know that Mom's boss had jobs worse than cleaning toilets, and as I watched his fat sausage fingers squirm over Mom's breasts, I knew he knew this too.

But then Aurora, who hadn't followed me, slid almost invisibly alongside my mom, eased her hand between the boss's hand and my mother's breast. The boss didn't seem to notice the change, but my mom did. Her eyes softened and her jaw unclenched. My mom smiled for the first time I could remember, even as the boss screamed and cursed and moved his hands over her. Standing there with a stack of envelopes in my hand, I felt stupid.

So I got it in my head that the Pedros were the problem.

That night, after everyone was asleep, I armed myself with a spray can of red paint and wrote "Rita" on every Pedro, telling myself as I did so that when I had marked them all with my name I, not they, would have the power. But seeing my name spelled across the knees of all the Pedros still standing tall, still grinning down at me, only made me look down at my feet, which gave me another idea. So I snuck into a trucker's cab, stole a screwdriver from his toolbox, and started chipping away the big toes of all the Pedros, filling my pockets with concrete. But my attacks only made what was already ugly and distasteful even uglier and more distasteful, and now I had not only signed my name to them, I had made them less whole. With heavy pockets, I went home and waited for what I knew must happen next, and then it did.

BAM! BAM! BAM!

I was asleep in my bed when South of the Border's so-called border patrol busted down our broken screen door, armed with a search warrant. My mother cried, but I just stood watching. When they found the toes I felt numb, almost relieved. I had thought I was doing something important, something great and covert and defiant, but all that grandness, all my striving towards something greater washed out of me when I was turned over to the Dillon police. I had messed up. Again.

Standing before the court, that unsettling, ungrounded feeling came once more—like I was sliding outside my own body into somewhere else. I watched from above as the judge extended his arm through his black robes to point at Pedrita, stone-faced and ashamed. And I wondered where her bravado had gone, what had happened to her sense of rightness as I rested invisibly on unseen branches, with Pedrita not looking up. I listened as the judge sentenced Pedrita to forty hours of litter control in the town. I watched her head drop and wished she could raise it. I saw my mother weep and beg and promise a full month's wages to spare her daughter such a fate. I saw that Aurora stood not behind Pedrita but behind my mother, hand on her shoulder, squeezing it slightly. And then just as suddenly as I had felt myself separate, I slipped back inside myself, constrained by the tightness and heaviness of ill-fitting skin, full to bursting with mixed-up feelings. Grateful to my mother, ashamed and confused at myself, and angry with Aurora for not stopping me. As we walked back to South of the Border, I tried to give my mom a hug but she didn't hug me back, as if all that mattered was being late for her shift at the toilets. So I hung back and Aurora linked her arm in mine.

"Why didn't you tell me?" I demanded. "The least you could have done is told me."

"You didn't ask," Aurora replied, her voice so soft. "You needed to find this out for yourself."

At that moment, I remembered what it felt like to hang loose from those branches.

My brain is numb, my fingers paralyzed. I want to write, get right the words to explain this radical thing that has happened. My hands hover but won't write, not even in spasms. My brain refuses to conjure the words that should come, words to make sense of impossible events. *Aurora.* Her name like waves crashing, pulling back into itself and out again to sea. *Aurora. Aurora.* Endless ebb and flow. *Aurora.* Tongue tumbling in my mouth. *Aurora.* A footfall on sand. *Aurora.* Swept back and churned up in undertow. Let it out, take it in. Begin somewhere, anywhere. Begin with Aurora saying, "I'm going to bring this place down, bring it down and clean it out."

Frightful liberation. That's what I felt. Like for the first time I was aware that I was separate from South of the Border, aware that what had sustained my whole life hadn't been Beulah's oyster crackers or Mom's stale donuts, but had come from the air around me and from the rain when it fell. I was Spanish moss hanging from live oak, looking like a part of that twisted tree but with no roots except toward the sky. I may have been born beneath Pedro's sombrero, but I had never understood that it was the thunderstorm that mattered.

Trust does not come easy to me, and I cannot hold hope in my hands. But I know that Spanish moss can blow into the sky and soar as a bird in flight, or dive into the sea and surface as a dolphin. Holding tight to nothing, I could become anything, could become everything, could even become nothing at all.

Strange how I could have been pregnant for nine months without knowing. I should have suspected when I first felt the stretching inside, the early cramps of growth that tugged in mostly small ways but occasionally in sharp and sudden ways as well. I thought, naively, these cramps were just more of the same, waves of menstrual cramps that could feel like change but never got me anywhere except back to where I had begun. Those pains were never more than temporary, part of my body's way of saying, "You may have potential, but you will never fully realize it."

I should have known when, in quiet times, alone and away from Aurora, I felt a rhythmic thudding, a hard pressing from the inside, somebody wanting to get out. But I shrugged it off, even when I could see with my own eyes that something inside was moving. Knees, elbows, fists striking out, stretching my skin. I don't know why I didn't know, but I am glad I didn't. Because had I known, had I any idea how I was to end and begin all over again, I would surely have aborted my half-formed self.

For nine months I traveled with Aurora on the outside, away from South of the Border. Away from the Sombrero Tower, the Golf of Mexico, and the Pedro statues, I could see and breathe and hear and taste and touch better. Everything was better and life felt more alive. Aurora, though, wasn't always kind. I can't say she was cruel, exactly, though she sometimes seemed so in the way of a midwife who must one day sever the umbilical cord.

Oh, I know how confusing this all must sound. And if I could write down in concrete details and facts all that had happened, I would. Really, I would, but I lack the language. Gestation and birth—particularly one's own—are such confounding experiences that language and logic fail, facts do not exist, and the only truth that remains is the proof of one's birth and the sweet-small swell of afterbirth that quickly disintegrates, leaving no trace.

All I recall, all I can share, are fragments.

Aurora takes me to the Fort Wayne Children's Zoo, shows me brave tigers pacing back and forth, back and forth behind glass at Tiger Forest. I think they are beautiful and strong. I am glad they are here behind glass so that I can see them.

Aurora cries for them in this place. I do not understand her tears, cannot possibly understand why she would want them to be anywhere but in this zoo.

Swimming. I have never before gone swimming so Aurora takes me to Lake Wawasee. I don't know how to float or swim or breathe underwater so I flail and go under, flail and go under. Water rushes into my nose and mouth. I gag and spit, gag and spit. Aurora laughs, floats on her back, dives under, surfaces ten feet from where she'd started. She swims like an otter, fluid and beautiful. Aurora takes my hands and when she pulls us both under I am ok, as if she is a mermaid who breathes for us both.

I stand at the edge of the Grand Canyon, frightened by how huge it is and how small I am. I want to go back and sit in the car but Aurora has locked the doors and pocketed the keys. We have crossed the do-not-cross rope and she skips along the edge. I am so scared that she will tumble over and be gone from me forever. Aurora seems not to care.

At Disney World, Mickey Mouse squeaks a muffled and mousy, "Welcome to the Magic Kingdom," and I say hello. But then Aurora calls him Amanda, and from somewhere deep inside the rubber suit sings a steady sweet voice. "Oh, Aurora! How are you, my sister?"

The Sonoran Desert, domain of the dry and the dead. I have hurt Aurora, or is it me I have hurt? I did not mean to, but I have. Something about a knife, about cutting. Accident? I can't recall.
"I know you want to be born," she says, "but not yet and not this way. It is not time." I am angry that I don't know what she's talking about and can't understand why she must always talk in metaphors. I don't remember even holding

a knife. Her tears fall as she stitches together a slit in my abdomen. I feel nothing, only lay there silent and scorched between sand and sun, waiting for night to fall and the saguaro to bloom.

The edge of the sky is a cold white place, and I blaze and burn inside. Between contractions, Aurora soothes my scalded lips and starved tongue with tender morsels of cool sweet cake. Inside, a wall breaks and I am pulled under the surface. I am drowning, but still can't let go of whoever is inside fighting to get out, even as the contractions quicken. Aurora cries, "Push! Push or you will die!" and presses a cold cloth against my forehead.

Contraction.
Thunder inside me.
Contraction.
Aurora.
Contraction.
But I can't!
Contraction.
Can't let myself push.
Contraction.
Can't let myself swim.
"No!"

Aurora throws herself into the North Wind and the bitter cold of night, dives into the sky, fluid with waves of brilliant green. I hear a roaring laugh, too big for any one body.

I push.
I scream.
I turn inside out.

I begin to swim. I just swim and swim and swim, not sure what I am swimming toward or away from, only knowing I love my body in motion, love the water's push and pull on me, love the taste of salt in my mouth, the motion of water around me and through me. Just water, everywhere water, and me seeing all the way to the pulsing red horizon on the edge of forever. Drunk on salt water, somersaulting with joy, feeling within myself the first shimmer of becoming. Taking in my mouth small new fingers that wiggle and twist until I find my thumb, just hold it inside, sucking. Again, I swim and swim and swim until my swim stretches the red horizon, clings to me, takes on my shape. Tasting like iron, feeling like a balloon, smelling like blood, sounding like Rita, Rita, Rita footfalling in my head. Red and veined, moving and alive, me and also me. I push my face into the translucent horizon. I somersault back and find only more horizon rounded up and around me. I curve over, encircle myself into myself as tightly as I can.

The pounding of the surf. The beating of two hearts. The pause in my swim. Punching out. Kicking through. Saltwater spilling out and me sliding through to find where my sea has gone, to reclaim it.

I open new eyes and see my deliverer for the first and last time, glowing green on the horizon.

And then, as a newborn, I journey back from the edge of the world to the place where I was first born.

I rest above the kudzu now, Rita Epiphyte. When Mom comes home from her ten-hour shift at the toilets, I slip off her stained canvas shoes and place her feet in a soothing bath of Epsom salts. I feed her toasty loaves of buttermilk bread and steaming bowls of chicken soup with rice, and I tell her that I love her.

© Jan Bechtel

Raised in a Corn Palace

"Like a time capsule with the lid off."
—*Description of South Dakota in a Corn Palace video*

Editor's note: In her letter protesting the National Association of Tourist Attraction Survivors' "slanted perspective," Ruth Michelle Mitchell wrote:

> I don't understand you NATAS folk. How can you feel so afflicted by your homes? How could you all want to flee? I think you're looking for something to blame, so you choose to blame the places you're from, choose to turn your backs on your heritage. Well, I have no bizarre story to tell, no "Tourist Attraction Trauma" to brag about or suffer through, and while travelers may see the Corn Palace as one of only two places worth stopping on their drive across South Dakota, that's not what the Corn Palace has been to me.

Surely, if there is any testament to the possibility of positive tourist attraction experiences (what Ruth steadfastly terms "Tourist Attraction Triumph"), Ruth's story is it.

* * *

As I pack up my life, I wish I hadn't lost my wishbone collection. I've had my collection since I was a girl no older than six, and have added to it every wishbone I've since had the pleasure to break. When I was a child and my mother would prepare the chicken for Sunday dinner, my brother Mike and I would always pull the wishbone.

"You pick," Mike would say, holding between his thumb and forefinger the center knob of bone, and so I would choose which end would be mine, which end I would stake my wish on. Then I would grab hold, the bone warm and slippery as the bird from whose body it had come, close my eyes, make a fervent wish, and pull. A splintery crack. The looseness of a bone broken free. A prayer that I might have the better end, that my wish might be the one destined to come true.

"What'd you wish for?" Mike would always ask, no matter who had won or lost. "C'mon, tell me what you wished for." Though I never asked, Mike would always tell me what he had wished for, from a new baseball glove when he was eight to Dad not seeing the dent in the Bel Air's back fender when he was sixteen—but I never shared my wish. Not even once.

Instead, after dinner I would hurry upstairs, close my bedroom door behind me, and pull a black scrapbook bigger than the family Bible from beneath my bed. My wishbone collection. With a dab of rubber cement, I would glue my half of the wishbone to the heavy yellow paper, and I would write the date and my wish underneath in pencil. Then, if I had the losing end, I would take a red pencil and draw a straight line through the abandoned wish. But if I had the winning end, I would take a gold crayon and draw stars all around. Sometimes, wish recorded, I would close my scrapbook and slide it back under my bed. Sometimes I would read over past wishes, marking down whether they had come true or were at least closer to coming true than when first wished. Silly, I know, but even now, sixty years since I began collecting, I keep my wishbones, and record every wish and its date. Sometimes I even bake a chicken not because I'm hungry, but because I need to make a wish.

So when I started packing to move from my Mitchell, South Dakota, home to Chicago ("so great that nobody even needs to say it's in Illinois," my daughter Emma brags), and I found wishbone fragments strewn across the attic and heaps of scrapbook shreddings used for rat bedding, I broke down and cried. But even after a good cry, I couldn't walk away from my life of wishes—some with dates, some without; some answered long ago, some never to be. Inside an award-winning model of the Corn Palace Emma had made in eighth grade, I found a black hat box full of postcards from other people in other places, and before Emma could catch me, I dumped the postcards in the black trash bag she had brought up for clearing away my wishbone collection. Instead, I began to box up all the pieces that remained. And I wished I had a wishbone to wish upon again, to wish that all the mess were cleared up, that I could put all those years back together again, that I didn't have to leave any of it behind.

Emma, she doesn't understand. She gets impatient with me.

"It's just stuff, Mom," she tells me. "Just stuff you don't need, stuff you can't hold onto."

This she tells me as she and her son, my grandson, Evan help me clear out my place, reducing my belongings by eighty percent since I can't take everything I own to Chicago. I know I can't take everything, but how can I keep from wanting to? I want to believe Emma means to be kind and helpful, but sometimes the words that leave her mouth sound cruel, callous.

"Why save wishbones in the first place?" she asked as I handed her the trash bag full of postcards believed to be my wishbone collection. "That's just weird. And you had to have known rats would find them someday—they're just bones, after all."

But I hadn't known rats would find them someday, hadn't even thought of them as bones. I tried to explain that they weren't "just bones," that they were instead a lifetime's worth of wishes, my hopes and dreams made visible, the ebb and flow of my desires, my worries, my life.

"Mom," Emma said, stopping my speech. "They are chicken bones. That's all they are."

But if chicken bones are all my wishbone collection is, then what is the Corn Palace?

"Just corn," Emma says when describing the Corn Palace to her Chicago friends. "Sure, it makes for a pretty photograph, but really, when it comes down to it, the Corn Palace is just corn and grain and straw."

There was a time when Emma wouldn't have said that. A time when Emma was different. She never would have described the Corn Palace as "just corn." Why would she when it had always been so much more? Every August as a child, Emma eagerly awaited the Corn Palace Festival, hoping to win Longfellow Elementary's Corn Palace mural contest, and even though she'd lose every year, she still kept trying.

Then in eighth grade the mural contest went away, and in its place came the Davison County model competition. That was the year Emma won grand prize with the Corn Palace she made out of wooden shingles and painted PVC pipe for turrets. I knew it was neither the shingles nor the PVC pipe that won Emma the prize; it was the way Emma so cleverly constructed the central onion dome by supergluing the disassembled slivers of my copper wind chimes—patinated like Lady Liberty's gown, shimmering green at sunset in New York's harbor—to my decorative fruit bowl's plastic pear. When Emma stood smiling on the Corn Palace Festival's main stage to say a few words, Emma declared, "Of all the wonders America has to offer, the Corn Palace of Mitchell, South Dakota, is the most wonderful wonder of them all."

I was so proud.

I wish that time could be again, at least for a little while.

For Emma, leaving the Corn Palace at eighteen years of age may have come easy, but for me, leaving will be anything but. I know that. No, I didn't grow up inside the Corn Palace, not literally. Not in the sense of being born in that building and never leaving its four walls like some of the sad folks I've heard about at the National Association of Tourist Attraction Survivors. But if you also had been born and raised in Mitchell, South Dakota, you would know what I mean when I say the Corn Palace is my home because it would have been your home too.

Every small town has a gathering place. A place to cheer on high school basketball teams, to eat popcorn and hotdogs, to drink Pepsi. A place to watch local theater productions of *Oklahoma* and *South Pacific*, and to see the occasional entertainer who comes in from outside. For Mitchell, that place is the Corn Palace. Aside from the murals made of corn, grains, and grasses, aside from the tourists wearing fanny packs and sunglasses who take pictures outside and wander aimlessly inside, aside from the keychains and mugs for sale, the Corn Palace is just a place to gather and to grow up and to be with other Mitchellites. The Corn Palace is a place to belong. As the video that only tourists really watch proclaims, the Corn Palace is "a celebration of who we are and what we do." What exactly this means, though, is harder to pin down. Who are we? What do we do? Even in the beginning, way back in 1892, there was disagreement. The Native Americans called this area—called South Dakota—"the land of visions." The settlers termed it "the wild west." For me, the Corn Palace and Mitchell, South Dakota, have always been and always will be "the place of belonging."

Who I am: Ruth Michelle Mitchell. But that is only a name.

What I do: I live. As best as I am able, I live alongside people I love, hate, am indifferent towards—people I know because they are part of Mitchell and the Corn Palace is part of them. It's only now that I am about to be pried out of my place like some too-old split cob of corn that I can feel the sticky tar paper holding me in place, wanting me to remain in the great mural I have been a part of since the day I was born.

I was born Ruth Michelle Helgelien, belonging in every way to this place, and I loved the feeling. I belonged to my family, to the Corn Palace, to Mitchell, to South Dakota. Extended outwards, you could say I also belonged to America, to Earth, to the universe. But, really, I've never thought much beyond Mitchell. My parents were good people. Hard workers. Lovers of family and of place. They weren't so much thinkers as doers, and what they did, they did well. My dad, Tru Helgelien, established and ran Tru's Value, the local hardware store. My mom, Eleanor, transformed the basement of our house into Eye of the Beholder, a beauty parlor where I'd find her faithfully cutting hair every afternoon I returned from school. And if ever I needed to talk to Mom or Dad, I was welcome wherever they were, whatever they were doing, even if they were working. Dad would ask a customer to step aside so he could wait on me first; Mom would set aside her shears to give me a welcome home hug.

Out of two children, I was the younger. My brother Mike, three years older, was always protective, showing his love by worrying about how the guys I went out with would treat me. And because the guys I went out with knew my brother, they never disrespected me. I was safe. I was happy. I was loved. But most of all, I belonged, fitting into my family, into the Corn Palace, into Mitchell like a perfectly sawed ear of corn. And when I married Bo Mitchell at seventeen, I fit even better, belonging even in name to the great Mitchell mural.

My life has been marked by the changing designs on the Corn Palace. Each year a new mural replaces the old one, having lived out its life and purpose as art for humanity and as The World's Largest Birdfeeder. Strange how making a home in a place can slowly, beautifully, naturally wear it out, lead to its end. Birds and mice, even rats I suppose, need food and shelter, and year after year after year the Corn Palace provides just that. I suspect the animals don't notice the murals, the sweeping portraits of Abraham Lincoln, Elvis, Crazy Horse, a man walking on the moon, and rodeo riders. I suspect birds don't ever suspend their flight within sight of the Palace to admire, just admire, the artistry, the pictures, the words, the shaping of thousands of bushels of corn and wheat and wild oats and so many other beautiful gifts of the earth into pictures that mean more than what they are made of. But for the birds it must all mean something, mustn't it? For the birds, the Corn Palace means they don't have to scrounge for food or seek out small backyard feeders. For the birds, the Corn Palace is a smorgasbord of the grandest scale where they can feed day after day after day and never go hungry.

Strange how the Corn Palace can be a place of both permanence and constant change. The big changes everybody notices—the stripping of the old mural, the tar papering in preparation for the new, the placing of cob after cob of thirteen different colors of corn to create images never before seen in grains and grasses. We who live in Mitchell, we watch these big changes as they take place from early spring through late summer, but can we see the daily disappearance of grain that happens even as the mural is being created? From one day to the next, can we tell how many birds' bellies have been filled? We would prefer to stand at a distance and admire the largeness of it. We glory in the fact that we can't say precisely how many kernels of corn remain and how many have fallen. But then one day, all at once, it seems, we look at the Corn Palace and see that it has become old, worn, full of gaps where grain once was, showing off the tarpaper beneath. We see that life has taken its toll, and we both mourn and yearn to start all over again.

I can look at the Corn Palace any time of day or night and it looks different each time because of where the sun is in the sky, or the moon, or seemingly neither when armies of clouds roll through. If I want, I can drive out in the country and see fields of corn and wheat and rye that stretch out for miles and miles. Just seeing forever like that, seeing visions sometimes like the Indians did and feeling the wildness of the land like the settlers did, this part of South Dakota's a special place. I worry that in Chicago I won't be able to see the land or the sky or the sun or the moon, though I'm pretty sure I'll feel the wind. I don't know what it will be like to trade in my Corn Palace that changes every day, that feeds and houses the smallest of God's creatures, for buildings that do no such thing, that just stand there tall and gray and steely, like hundreds of silos that hold no grain, but hold only people and papers and money and things. Some days I think it will kill me, this change, this place called Chicago. Some days I think I shall be unable to breathe Chicago air, that every breath will slowly poison me until one day I can breathe no more. But then I consider Emma and Evan, my heart shifts, and I know that I will go because I must. I will go because I love.

Emma and Evan, they need me, and for love of them, I would move anywhere, even to Chicago—a city that is always expanding, forever moving, a city worlds away from The World's Only Corn Palace. I have tried to persuade Emma to come home to Mitchell, to return to the place of her childhood. But she tells me Mitchell is "too small," "too stagnant," "too stifling."

"No offense, Mom," Emma tells me, "but I outgrew Mitchell the day I left for college." I do not understand how she could have "outgrown" Mitchell when all I have done every day of my life is grow into this town, deepening my roots only to find that they keep going deeper still. But I'm trying to respect her, to let her be who she needs to be, even if I don't understand exactly why.

What I do understand is that Emma is alone in a big and busy place with an eight-year-old son, that she needs to belong somehow to someone—even if that someone is just her mother from Mitchell, a town her Chicago friends don't recognize until she says, "You know, the Corn Palace." But even then some of them still don't recognize it. I imagine Emma shrugging off Mitchell, saying that it's "just a small place," a "good place to raise kids maybe if you want to keep them ignorant of other cultures, but not a place to live if you want to get anywhere in life."

Is it important to say why she wants me with her? Why she needs me? My daughter knows something about the loss of a husband just as I do. No, not just as I do. Different. I know about the loss of a husband after forty-five years of marriage and the raising of a child to adulthood. I know about the loss of a husband as someone who has lived through good and bad times with a husband, times of exuberance and joy, and times of indifference and hostility. Emma, she knows about the loss of a husband she hardly had time to know, a man who was a lover and a father for just under nine years, hardly long enough for the marathon of married life to settle in and stick, which likely explains why he left. Not that it's ever easy to lose a husband—I have missed Bo every day for the six years since a heart attack stopped him as he was walking home from the post office—but losing someone you've just begun to really grow into, who seems suddenly to have grown tired of loving you, seems harder somehow. And to have a young child to care for and raise all alone? There is no question Emma needs me.

Emma tells me she's glad I will be coming to live with them, that she's excited to have me in Chicago. "We'll go to Chinatown on Sundays," Emma tells me. "I'll treat you to real Chinese food, not the dumbed down sweet and sour and General Tso's you get in Mitchell. And Evan, he'll introduce you to bubble tea, this great milk tea with black tapioca balls you suck up through a big fat straw."

    I will not be returning to live again in Mitchell. Emma and I don't speak about this, but we both know it is true. We are getting rid of too many things for me to come home later. Once in Chicago, settled and living day to day, my house will be put up for sale. Somebody will buy it and I will not even return to see it sold, to say goodbye. My daughter jokingly refers to my "senior moments" when memory fails me, when names I've always known are lost, keys are misplaced, groceries-to-be-bought are forgotten. I laugh about these moments too, but I know that we both know more will come of them, not less. We both fear that one day I will slip headlong through the fog that teases at my head even now, will slip headlong and drown in forgetfulness. Only it won't be the past that I forget. It won't be Mitchell or the Corn Palace or any of the wishes I have made that fade from memory, but Chicago and Emma and Evan. By then, I'll be no help to Emma, no help to Evan. Instead, I'll become a burden, an inconvenience, a useless, placeless, empty cob of corn. Maybe I'll even forget to wish on wishbones when they come my way. This is a matter I try to think about as little as possible.

    What do I wish for now? For things to be the same? No. Not really. Life changes, people change and move and die. I can't wish for Bo, dear husband that he was, to be back because he had to go when he had to go. I know that. I could wish for Emma to return to Mitchell, but I know she won't, that she can't, that once you leave a small town it always seems smaller than when you were in it. Guess that's why I'm glad I never left. Guess that's also what worries me about Chicago. I think I'm past the age where leaving my home will be an exciting adventure. Mitchell, South Dakota, is my world, the Corn Palace my compass.

    "You can go online," Emma tells me. "Every day, twenty times a day, you can go online and see the Corn Palace web cam." But even she knows that is not the same. Not the same as feeling the mid-July sunshine beat down on me from all angles. Not the same as feeling the bitter January wind whip my hands and face. Not the same as seeing the Corn Palace always standing in sunshine and snow through all my own struggles, whatever they may be. A constant companion to change with, to face every glorious or miserable day of life. That's the Corn Palace for me.

"I am sixty-six years old and I am moving." How many times a day I say that to myself! Before my morning shower, I stand naked in front of my bathroom mirror and watch my lips move to say those words. "Good luck," I sometimes say next, or "you're crazy," or "Emma and Evan, they need you." Sometimes I say nothing. Still, I look at myself in the mirror, my saggy sixty-six year old body from which all the fight for firmness has gone out, and I wonder what Chicago will do to a body like mine, a body meant to relax on the front porch with a good book and little else to do but eat chicken and noodles with mashed potatoes and a few green peas for color. A body like mine is made to play cards and bingo with Alwilda and Mildred and Phoebe, all friends with names and bodies equally saggy and resigned to aging gracefully. A body like mine is not meant to go to Chicago, not meant to take the subway, not meant to try new things like sushi and Chinese food like "real Chinese people" eat, not meant for any type of tea but iced Lipton.

Last night over dinner, my arm stretched halfway across the table to grasp the end of the wishbone that Evan had not chosen. I wished just once that Emma and Evan could need me here in Mitchell. Here where cars don't bunch up on expressways like rats inside some slow digesting snake. Here where skyscrapers twice the height but not nearly so majestic as the Corn Palace do not restrict and channel the howling wind. Here in the land where the sky—no matter its mood—is a constant companion, where visions can still be seen, where there is still some wildness to be had, where belonging is every bit as important as being. I closed my eyes and let Evan pull, knowing in my own bones that I held the shorter end before I heard the snap.

"Guess what I wished for, Grandma," Evan gasped, waving his winning end. "I wished..."

"Hush!" I commanded, more strongly than I'd meant, my eyes rising to meet his. "You hold onto your wish and keep it close. Don't ever share it."

"But I want," Evan stammered, "I want you to know. Please!" he pleaded. "It's about you, Grandma, and it's important."

"All the more reason not to share," I said, half-wondering, half-wanting to know. "You just keep that wish safe inside, keep it to yourself."

Evan's eyes dropped then to look at his wishbone, still pinched between his thumb and forefinger. I could tell he had to have something to rest his eyes on so as to keep from looking sad and disappointed and I said, more gently now, "You just hold onto that wishbone and your wish, and after we've had a slice of cherry pie, I'll show you what you can do with it, what I have done with all my wishbones."

Emma sighed but didn't interrupt.

"But Grandma," Evan said, lifting his eyes to mine, "what if I never get to pull another wishbone?" He lowered his eyes again and began to turn between his fingers this wish of his. I watched its turning, watched the smooth gray surface of bone give way to the brown-red marrow where the bone had splintered, then go gray again. Evan's fingers stopped and I watched as his closed fist turned into an open palm to catch the wishbone, then closed again. Evan didn't look up but mumbled, as if embarrassed, "I don't think they have wishbones in Chicago—I've only had them here."

"But you eat chicken, don't you?" I asked, holding back both laughter and astonishment.

"Sort of," Evan said, "only I don't think Chicago chickens have skin or bones like Mitchell chickens. Chicago chickens are thin and flat and covered in ice. Mom buys them by the bag."

I glanced over at Emma who shrugged her shoulders and said, "I just buy the frozen breasts—less mess, all meat."

Now, I'm not so backwards that I hadn't heard of such a thing, hadn't seen the bags of breasts in the freezer section of Coburn's, but I've never wanted anything less than the whole chicken, never wanted anything less than all of it—breasts and thighs and drumsticks and wings and wishbone.

"Don't you get tired of eating only white meat?" I asked Emma, imagining bland baked breasts staring up at me from a plate in Emma's Chicago apartment. "The same old thing over and over?"

"It's not always the same, Mom," Emma said, picking up her knife to cut chicken free of a leg bone. "I cook them in so many ways—stir fried with vegetables, tossed with fettuccine, glazed with honey and lemon. Believe it or not, Mom, I'm a good cook. And versatile."

Emma didn't add "unlike you," but I wondered if she thought it sitting there at my kitchen table, my usual summer Sunday dinner of roast chicken, mashed potatoes and pepper gravy, buttermilk bread, sweet corn, and sliced tomatoes spread out on the table before us. I wondered if she thought I wasn't versatile, if she thought I was just typical and maybe a little boring.

"Mom is a good cook, Grandma," Evan said then, looking up at his mother who seemed relieved to have her son's support, "but she never makes anything like this. When you come to Chicago, can you find real chickens like this one? Real chickens with wishbones too?"

"Oh, I think I can find chickens with wishbones in Chicago just as well as in Mitchell. Well, maybe not just as well," I said, wondering where on earth Emma bought groceries in such a big city, "but if they've got them there, we'll find them."

"And if they don't?" Evan asked.

"If they don't have chickens like this in all of Chicago, well, then," I said, thinking what next to say even as I was speaking, "well, then, I guess you and me will just have to drive all the way back to Mitchell to buy some, won't we?"

"Oh, wow! Can I, Mom?" Evan asked, jumping out of his seat. "And can we stop in at the Corn Palace when we come for the chickens?"

Before Emma could give her permission, I had already said "Sure. Why not? You know why the chickens in Mitchell are so tasty, don't you Evan?" I asked.

"Because of the wishbones?" Evan asked.

"Well, maybe in part, but even those flat iced chicken parts your mom cooks once had wishbones," I answered. "Let me give you a little hint," I said. "You know all that corn on the Corn Palace?"

"Yeah…" Evan said.

"Well, the chickens around here, they eat the same corn as what gets put up on the Corn Palace to make all those pictures you see."

Evan's eyes widened.

"From the time I was born, every chicken I've ever eaten in Mitchell has been a Corn Palace chicken. Every chicken has been…"

"Royalty," Evan whispered, gazing at the winning wishbone he held out before him.

"Absolutely right," I said, recognizing only then that every wish I'd ever wished in all those years, every wishbone I'd ever pulled and saved, every wishbone destroyed by some attic rat had been in its own way a royal petition. "Chances are," I added, thinking then of the whole chickens that must surely exist somewhere in Chicago, "chances are even some of those chickens in Chicago have a little of the Corn Palace inside them, and we'll find them, wherever they are."

"Promise?" Evan said, raising his right eyebrow in its own question.

"Promise," I said.

And then, as if Evan's wishbone had found its way to some long-forgotten treasure chest, I felt a small click deep inside and remembered how, as a girl, I had believed that Mitchell was a kingdom ruled by the kindly King Maize and Queen Rye. And as the bone turned in the lock, the impulse to bow low flooded through me. I remembered how, whatever event had brought me to the Corn Palace—whether it was one of my brother Mike's Kernels games or a Jimmy Durante show—I would slip away to go and stand in the entranceway, to silently and without words bring my wish before King Maize and Queen Rye. Never was I scared that my wish might be refused or, worse, that I might be sent to the executioner. Instead, I was just hopeful that I would be heard, even if my wish wasn't granted.

In that moment, I was glad the wish I had made would not come true, and I knew then what my wish would be a week later when I sat eating chicken at my daughter's kitchen table in her Chicago apartment. For some time, I have felt like God was holding the top knob of a celestial wishbone, urging me to wish for either Mitchell or Chicago and pull. But since I cannot wish for either, I will wish for both. I will wish for love and understanding towards Evan and Emma. I will wish that resentment not creep in upon me when I am far away in Chicago and think about Mitchell. I will wish for appreciation of new things like bubble tea, for a more sensitive palate to love that which I don't know. I will wish for peace to reside within me, for the Corn Palace to be always present deep within so that I need not long for home, staying connected instead to the home inside of me. And I will even wish for Evan to continue his own wishbone collection away from my eyes after I have shown him how to start.

© Kelcey Ervick

Northern Belle

Editor's note: Dawn Tempers' testimony was first presented in the "Surviving the Dead and (In)Famous" session of the fourteenth annual conference of the National Association of Tourist Attraction Survivors (NATAS) in 1997. "Northern Belle" was subsequently included in *Tourist Attraction Travesty: Tales from Tourist Attraction Survivors*, an in-house publication of the NATAS' Hospital for Research and Recovery.

* * *

On the outskirts of Hanna, Indiana, where U.S. Highway 30 and County Road 450 West meet, stands an old farmhouse with peeling white paint, a sagging roof, and broken windows. This was my childhood home. Even so, I did not sleep here. Instead, from infancy to age twelve, I slept in the Belle Gunness exhibit of the LaPorte County Historical Society Museum.

Both my parents worked nights. We had no extended family in the area to take me in, so while my father drove to Bethlehem Steel in Burns Harbor, my mother drove twenty miles to LaPorte to work as a cleaning lady at the museum, taking me with her each night.

The closest thing the museum had to a house was the Belle Gunness "Lady Bluebeard of LaPorte" exhibit. No, this isn't quite true. The museum did have a Victorian living room, but my mother thought the Belle Gunness shed was more like the house we lived in than the plush velvety Victorian couches. And, in truth, it was. Constructed out of wood siding from a shed on Belle's original property, my nightly home had an antique meat grinder, a window to look out of, and a plump Belle standing guard, waiting for Norwegian suitors and watching over me. My mother tells me that when I was a baby she—while cleaning distant corners of the museum—would hear me cry, but that by the time she reached me with a bottle of formula, I would have quieted down, my eyes fixed on Belle's solid, unmoving figure. My mother knew only what she could see: that Belle was a stiff, lifeless, inhuman thing, and that I never took the bottle. I knew only what I had experienced: my belly filled at Belle's breast.

Psychologists say that first memories are important, and to honor that theory, my first memory is this: a gnawing in my belly, a groping of hands and mouth in the dark, a latching onto flesh like rocks, a filling of mouth and belly with a milk so bitter and so sweet that I cannot stop suckling, a softening of that flesh in my hands, a gripping ever tighter so that even when Belle's milk has stopped flowing, she will stay with me.

As I began to crawl and later to walk, I climbed out of my crib during the night and wandered around Belle's cramped quarters. A sliced finger taught me not to touch the red-tinted ax leaning against the wall. A splinter in my heel reminded me to step around the sharp bone fragments that littered the floor. But nothing stopped me from crawling inside the garden cart, and when I did, I awoke the following morning with a gunnysack draped over me and with a memory of Belle's rough lips having brushed my cheek, her warm breath smelling like boiled cabbage and tapioca pudding, smelling like the taste of her milk.

Six days after my fifth birthday, I began kindergarten at South Central Community School Corporation, a rural school for the children of Hanna, Union Mills, and Wanatah. The night before my first day, my mother gave me a bath at our house on the corner of U.S. 30 and 450 West and the next morning when her shift ended, my mother dressed me at the museum. As I was leaving, Belle hugged me and whispered in my ear, "Be nice to the boys, and they'll give you their milk money." I buried my face in Belle's skirts and cried as my mother pulled me away and out to the car for the drive to school.

I remember my first day of kindergarten well. The teacher asked us what our bedrooms were like, and I listened as my classmates described walls papered with balloons or dragons or race cars or Barbies. When I said my bedroom was made of old shed siding and that a woman with hips like armchairs and breath that smelled like cabbage and tapioca whispered to me in the night, my teacher ended sharing time and sent me home with a note which I gave to Belle, not my mother. At recess, the Barbie girls and the race car boys clustered at the base of the curly slide to whisper and point at me. Only one boy, Duane, wanted to play, but all he could talk about was his bedroom wallpaper—baby blue with giant earthworms dressed like cowboys and Indians. Still, I was nice to Duane, just like Belle had instructed, and he gave me his milk money with which I bought a second chocolate milk. Even then, the teacher saw that Duane had none and made me share.

We talked at night, Belle and I, and sometimes I stayed awake all night, nestled down in the garden cart, listening. Often Belle told me about growing up in Selbu, Norway, gathering spruce twigs for the family fire which burned quickly and gave little warmth. Townspeople teased her, called her "Snurkvistpåla," meaning "Paul's daughter spruce twigs," and she hated them for it.

Belle told me about one little girl in particular, Brynhild, a pretty girl with yellow curls and rosy cheeks loved by everyone who knew her. Everyone except Belle. Belle told me Brynhild was cruel, and that she used to invite Belle over to play with her dollies but would never let her touch them without wearing gloves, and even then would only let her play with Mollie, the one-eyed doll with a splintered face. Belle told me how Brynhild would hand her a pair of gardening gloves and say, "You can play with Mollie, only you have to wear these over your hands, and you can't ever never kiss her." Belle told me how mad Brynhild made her, how one day when Brynhild had left the room, she yanked off the gloves, tore off Mollie's clothes, ran her hands up and down Mollie's body, and kissed her all over.

"And then," Belle said, a thin smile cracking her face, "I ran into the kitchen and found her mother's meat cleaver. *Whack!* Off went Mollie's head. *Whack! Whack!* Off went Mollie's arms. *Whack! Whack!* Off went Mollie's legs. And then I put Mollie all in pieces in a gunnysack and tossed her in the corner."

I was enthralled. I thought about the Barbies the girls brought to school each day and wondered where I could get a cleaver and whether it could hack through their plastic bodies as well as through Mollie's wood and stuffing, for even though I never had a desire to play with Barbies, I liked the idea of chopping them into pieces.

"What did you do when Brynhild found out?" I asked.

"Found out?" Belle laughed. "She never found out. Why, when Brynhild returned, I was wearing the gloves and told her, 'Mollie just got up and walked away.' Brynhild believed me, of course, because I 'would never lie to the best friend I had in the whole world.' Oh, but how she screamed when she opened the gunnysack to get potatoes for her mother and there was Mollie, all in pieces! And I screamed and cried and carried on even more than her. 'The troll!' I cried. 'The troll that lives under the bridge! That nasty old troll! He's to blame!' I sobbed. And Brynhild believed me because she had no reason not to."

Making close friends at school was hard, perhaps because I loved Belle too much—needed her too much. Sometimes I told Belle about my day, about how the other kids teased me for sleeping at the museum and not at home. And how they made fun of me because my parents worked nights instead of days, unlike all their parents who were mostly farmers and housewives. They even made up a little singsong taunt:

*Dawn's a stupid night girl with a stupid na-ame
And her Mama's stupid too or she would have named her Du-usk.
Stupid, stupid Da-awn doesn't sleep at ho-ome.
Stupid stinky Da-awn smells like poop and cabbage.*

There wasn't even any sense to their song, and that last line was just so not true. But when you're five, the dumbest and most untrue things other kids say hurt the most.

When I tried to tell them about Belle who talked to me during the night, they called me a liar. And when our teacher made us draw pictures of our families, I drew Belle holding my hand with my parents standing behind us.

Dawn is a weirdo, thinks she lives with Be-elle.

While my classmates teased, the teacher gave my picture a "Messy Duck" stamp for the bold blacks and browns that broke through my own carefully drawn lines.

Then one Monday morning in second grade, as I stood alone during recess on the blacktop where I always stood alone watching everybody, I saw Alan move away from the boys playing football in the grass—felt as much as watched him walk towards me. His mouth puckered and his brown eyes widened like maybe even talking to me was a dare, so I looked back to the boys who had been playing football;

they had been standing there watching Alan but now, in one quick motion, they turned back to look at the grassy field and one of them threw the football high in the air and caught it again. All the boys piled on top of him so now it was just Alan, alone, moving towards me, and then the tips of his red canvas Converse shoes were touching the tips of my black ones as his lips parted and his too-determined, too-controlled voice spilled over me like barrels of nervous vomit.

"I went to that museum, Dawn," Alan said, "I went there with my mom on Saturday because she's writing a paper for her English class at Purdue North Central, and so I had to go there because I couldn't be home by myself and so I saw her, I actually saw that Belle Gunness woman you're always talking about and you know, don't you, Dawn? You know, don't you, that Belle's just this big fatso doll and her face is all cracked and she stinks and she wrote letters to lonely men and then she killed them and she probably wasn't even a woman anyway—just a man dressed like a woman who could lift a hog off a cart all by herself and could kill that hog all by herself. Her kids were really stolen from other women she killed and fed to her hogs like lots of those poor men except for the ones she buried in her back lot, and she never died in that house fire. In fact, she's probably still alive. Why do you love her so much anyway, huh? Why? Cause she's not even for real in that museum, but she's out there somewhere, she's out there, that Bluebeard in Skirts, that Hell's Belle, that Gunness Monster, that Butchering Widow, that Mistress of Murder Hill, 'cause those are the names she earned, those are who she really was, who she really is even if she's so old she's got to be dead by now if evil like that can ever really die, but it's not like Belle could be there with you anyway so why?" he stopped.

Alan stared at me then like he was afraid of me even though he'd known me since kindergarten and always just teased me before but this was different because he was both teasing and not teasing and I didn't know what that meant when somebody did that except that inside it didn't feel at all good to me but strange and a little scary. "Why do you say Belle loves you when she's just a big fat stuffed doll and her face is all cracked and she stinks anyway?"

I couldn't answer. I had no idea what Alan was talking about. I looked down at my feet and saw Alan move two steps back. I had slept in the Belle Gunness exhibit of the LaPorte County Historical Society Museum all my life, but never once had I visited it, never once had I seen any of the things Alan spoke of—if they even existed and he seemed so certain that they did, so certain, having been to the museum with his mother. I had always entered Belle's shed from the side, and she had made me comfortable there. Never once had I wandered around the front, seen what else might be on display.

"Liar!" I yelled, hoping my volume would drown out my sudden fear. "Belle's my best friend! Belle loves me! Belle has always loved me, and Belle is real and she tells me the best stories, true stories, like the one about Brynhild and Mollie and how she took that cleaver and . . ."

Alan took off running the second "cleaver" slipped through my lips. His red South Central Satellites jacket grew smaller in the distance as he ran away from me and away from his football playing friends and towards the woods. As I watched him run, I thought about the axe and the bone fragments where I slept. I knew I did not know how to explain those away, though until Alan had made Belle sound so cruel, so "evil" (had he really used that word?) I had never once questioned why they were in Belle's shed, and knew I could not risk questioning them now. I could run after Alan, tell him all about Belle's good qualities, but none of that would make any difference in how he thought about her, and he could never really understand. Nobody could, I knew that.

So I stopped. Stopped telling my "stories" about Belle. And then I started. Started denying any connection to Belle for the sake of having friends. Within weeks, classmates gradually stopped avoiding me, and some of them even let me play hide-and-seek, though I was always "it," Like I was a thing and not a person. During all this, Belle never gave up on me, never lost faith. When, guilt-stricken, I told Belle one night what I had done, how I had denied her to my classmates, Belle stroked my hair and said, "You are very clever, Dawn, for the only way to get what you want from people is to pretend that you aren't who you really are, that you don't know what you really know, that you don't do what you really do."

I'd been holding inside all the things Alan had said about Belle, but that night I told her all of it, and I asked if they were true. She wrapped her arms around me, kissed my forehead, and replied, "Not all of it, my darling Dawn. And not the way they tell it. Sleep well tonight, and tomorrow night I shall tell you more."

Now, for as long as I can remember, I have had dreams I could not explain—dreams which may have been dark but were never frightening beyond what I could handle. Before I could verbalize it, I always felt that I was invincible in my dreams, regardless of how vulnerable I might have felt in waking life. Perhaps it had something to do with Belle's breast milk, some immunity to fear that she had transmitted. Regardless of what horrid things happened in the dreams, even when I was being chased or hacked to pieces, I was always in control. The night after Alan said all those horrible things about Belle, I had the following dream.

I was on the green hills of Norway, leading a lamb home to my family who lived in the valley. The lamb looked healthy and plump with its woolly and well-combed coat, but when I reached down to pet it, brittle bones crumpled under the weight of my hand. I looked down to where the lamb had been, but instead of the lamb, I saw only a pile of gray bones and a few tufts of wool that clung tightly to the bones so the wind could not blow them away.

Panic. Sheer panic. For the first time in a dream, I felt panic. The air grew cold and the wind picked up, scattering the bones across grass that was no longer green but red, the most brilliant shade of red. I looked down into the valley, saw smoke billowing from the chimney of my house, and remembered I had been sent to bring home a lamb to roast in celebration of my father's finding oak to burn rather than spindly spruce. But now, there was no lamb.

What could I do? I had promised to buy the lamb and bring it home for Dad to butcher, but what would happen if I came home without it? I didn't want to consider that. What if, instead of a live lamb, I brought home a dead one? Chopped into pieces and wrapped in paper? What if that thing I brought home wasn't even a lamb? Would they know? How could they? I thought of Brynhild, then headed toward her house in the valley.

In the next instant, I was sitting at the long wooden table, eating dinner with my family. Dad was telling me how thoughtful I had been to prepare the lamb myself, to save him from the messy job of slaughter. "What a fine butcher you are," he said, carving up Brynhild's leg, then putting some on Mom's plate and on his own. When he offered me a slice, I declined, saying I wanted only boiled cabbage for dinner. My pockets bulged with Brynhild's gold and silver coins, and I thought that, tomorrow, I would buy a proper lamb.

The night following my dream, Belle—as she had promised—began to share the truth of her story with me. I had no need to ask questions, no need to prompt her, for she controlled both her telling and my understanding.

"Nothing," Belle began as she tucked me into bed, "hurt my heart more than the suffering of my fellow Norwegian countrymen. To see them arrive in America alone, only to be tempted by American women and American ways. I met and married Mads in Chicago when I was twenty-five—more than three times your age," she said, brushing my cheek with her fingertips. "Not because I loved him but because he needed me, a strong Norwegian woman of reputable character. I was his link back to Norway. How he longed for the old country, for the green grass and shimmering blue lakes! He spoke endlessly of Norway, all the while making all the American money he could to ease the ache inside of him. But it didn't," she sighed, bending low to kiss my forehead, the odor of tapioca sweet and creamy on her breath. "He even gave me four babes, four plump, blonde, Norwegian babes we named Caroline, Axel, Myrtle, and Lucy. Not even his children could ease his ache, and when Caroline and Axel died, well," she paused, "that made his ache all the worse.

"All the time Mads used to talk about Norway, and for seventeen years I did my best to make him feel at home, to make him feel he was back in his home country, but my efforts did no good. 'Belle,' Mads would say to me, 'if only I could be back on those green hills of Norway. I would give anything.' Well," Belle went on, smoothing her skirts over her knees, "not even I could give him that, and all the Norwegian puddings and marzipan I fed him could not return him to those green hills. So one night I said to him, 'Mads, you will never be happy here, here in America. I will take you back to Norway the only way I know how.' He was such a gentle man, and in such anguish that he said, 'Belle, do what you must. I am a brave man, and I cannot stand this life any longer.' And so it was that I told Lucy and Myrtle to kiss Papa goodbye, told them that he was going to take a trip back to Norway. And then I brought Mads a mug of warm eggnog with a little something extra and wished him well on his journey home.

"That Mads was well-insured was of no concern to me, for I had no desire for my own gain. Yet, why should I not keep the money? He would have wanted me to live well, for though I never truly loved him, he had certainly loved and needed me, wanted the best for me. He wouldn't have minded. He would have wanted as much."

Belle went on to tell me about buying the farm on McClure road in LaPorte with the insurance money Mads left behind, and about marrying Peter Gunness. And she told me how Peter was not so much a lonely Norwegian as an angry one, a man with a violent temper that flared up when he drank.

"One night," she said, "I was dusting a shelf while Peter, in a sober moment, sat reading in his favorite chair. On this shelf sat a sausage grinder, and as Peter sat and read, it became clear to me that, like Mads, Peter also missed Norway, though he didn't speak of his longing as such but drowned it with drink. And as I was thinking this, my hand brushed up against the meat grinder. Now, I'll confess I made no move to stop the grinder as it fell, but I also did not directly hit him with it. And anyway, it was all for the best. The children and I were better off without him, and he had such a wealth of insurance that we were able to live well for quite some time."

As for the other men, Belle blushed when she spoke of them. I told her about a letter Alan had mentioned, one she had written to Andrew Helgelien, and she recited several lines from memory:

> *I went to the post office this morning and had the great pleasure of receiving one of your very welcome letters. Many thousand thanks for them all—I keep them all as I would a great treasure. You truly do not know how highly I prize them as I have not found anything so genuine Norwegian and real in all the*

> *twenty years I have been in America. I do not think a queen could be good enough for you and in my thoughts you stand highest above all high and I will not let anything stand in the way of my doing anything for you or so that we can meet each other.*

Then she paused and shrugged. "Well," she said, "what else did he have in his life? His brother Asle?" Belle laughed. "Fool!" But I didn't know whether it was Andrew or Asle of whom she spoke.

"Those letters I wrote, to Andrew and to the others, brought them fond memories of Norway, gave them something to look forward to when they finally made the trip, most from the Dakotas, to Indiana. Why," she said, grinning, "even you know how much fun it is to keep secrets from people, or to believe something or someone better is waiting for you. But then when you finally see that thing, get that thing, all the joy goes out of you, for what you expect is never as good as what you end up getting."

As Belle talked, I curled up on my side and burrowed all but my head under my blanket of burlap, warming to the truth of her. I thought back to all I had desired and been disappointed by—my first bicycle with busted tires that Dad brought home from the dump, the birthday party only Duane attended—and I understood. Belle was right. What's more, Belle was everything I had always known her to be, everything Alan had said she wasn't. Belle, keeper of my nights, was good, true, and wise. As much as I knew the warmth and comfort of burlap in the night, I knew I had made no mistake in letting Belle love me.

"Yes, Dawn," Belle went on, "I gave these men hope, loved them through words. I made each one of them believe that what awaited them at my farm, what awaited them in my arms, was a better life. And then I preserved them from bitter disappointment by releasing them from life at the height of their joy. And you should have seen them, too. Especially Andrew.

"When Andrew arrived, I had a feast prepared of all those things he most loved and best remembered from Norway, ending the meal with Andrew's favorite, cream pudding. Afterwards, we went together to the bank where he added his money to mine, as true a marriage as any ordained by church and state. And then we had one night of passion, true bliss for Andrew—of course, you're too young to understand all of that, but someday you will—and I closed our night by kissing him on the forehead and giving him a mug of warm eggnog with nutmeg and," she paused, "a little something extra. He passed over happily, a smile on his face, all his earthly needs met in me. I fell asleep beside him and awoke only when his body grew cold."

"Then what did you do?" I asked.

"Well," Belle said, patting my leg, "that's a private matter, and not all that important, but I did have to hide him, to preserve the sanctity of his memory. For though our time together was brief, I gave Andrew something special, something he needed. His money was but a token of what he owed."

Over the course of Belle's telling, the museum clock tolled the ten o'clock hour, then eleven, then twelve, then one, and then two. I did not understand everything Belle had told me, and I don't think she expected that I would, but I understood enough. Certainly, what I did not understand, could not yet and could maybe never understand, I simply trusted. Somewhere in the space between the tolling of two and three o'clock, I fell asleep in the lap of my true mother, my hair fanned out across Belle's broad skirts. I slept well that night and for many nights after.

Two uneventful years followed Belle's night of disclosure. At school I did not mention Belle, nor did my classmates.

Until fourth grade. Until *Gnista*, the high school play that all us elementary kids were taken to see.

I remember only bits of *Gnista* now, and I confess I did not pay it much attention at the time, knowing the truth as Belle had told it. I do remember a high school girl with smoother skin and a much slimmer build than Belle's, dressed in turn-of-the-century garb. My classmates thought she looked convincing, but she only made me laugh. I remember the fake Belle holding a sausage grinder above her unsuspecting fake husband Peter's head, bringing it down with great force, and the fake Peter falling dead to the floor, so very different from the truth as Belle had told it to me.

Perhaps *Gnista* could have faded into the background. Certainly, it should have. But after the play, our fourth-grade teacher Mr. Johnson spent the rest of the afternoon sharing the "facts" of the Belle Gunness story, showing slides of black and white photographs—the scarred and bloated head of Ole Budsberg; the twisted and decaying body of Andrew Helgelien in the garden cart; men with shovels and pickaxes looking for the bodies of Belle and her three children in the burned basement remains while curious onlookers peered down at them. Not only did Mr. Johnson not tell the truth as Belle had told it, he also spiced up her stories with rumors nobody has ever confirmed, including the one which had everybody talking at lunch.

"Little did the townspeople of LaPorte know," Mr. Johnson whispered, "in their morning sausage, they were eating the bodies of Belle's victims, for Belle's sausage was famous in LaPorte." Lauren Ambrite, a student new to my class that very day, called the hamburgers we had for lunch Gunness Burgers and the name stuck, not only for that week, but for all our school years.

If I had an ally at school, it was Lauren. After *Gnista*, she began hanging around, asking me questions about Belle. At recess, we hung upside-down from the spider bars—which she called "cages in a medieval dungeon"—and watched as wind whipped the sand below ("a cauldron of boiling oil," she called it). When we walked the low balance beam at the boundary between the playground and the soybean field, she commanded that each time one of us lost her balance and fell, a crocodile chomped off a limb ("arms first, then legs"). And when I talked about Belle, Lauren didn't want to know Belle's noble motives, only wanted to hear gory details. Peculiar. Even so, Lauren was the closest thing to a friend that I had, and we spent all our time at school together.

"I want to meet her," Lauren demanded one recess in sixth grade as we played Klutzy Derby, the goal of which was to kick the legs out from beneath the other person. She had just succeeded in making me the klutz for the fourth time in ten minutes, and I was more concerned with wiping the gravel off my skinned leg.

"Come on, Dawn, I want to meet her," Lauren said. I watched as tiny dots of blood rose to my skin's surface. "I know," she went on, my pain not her problem, "why don't you see if I can stay over at your place." We had a peculiar understanding, Lauren and I. When Lauren said, "your place," she meant the museum, Belle's place, which was more my place than that house on the corner of U.S, 30 and 450 West. Lauren, of all the people at school, was the only one who ever got it right.

I was pleased by Lauren's interest, the only interest that had ever truly been shown in me and in Belle whom I held so dear. Pleased but also frightened about sharing Belle, frightened that Belle might somehow love Lauren more. And that wasn't such a weird idea because by sixth grade, Belle and I were beginning to have some differences.

"You can fuck boys now," Belle had said, standing over me the morning of my first period. Belle, not me, had been the first to notice; she had smelled the blood even while I slept. I had grabbed at the warm wetness that seeped through my underwear and smeared my thighs, then lifted my hand to my face and felt panic burn my throat at the sight of my own blood. "You can fuck boys now," Belle said again in a monotone that sounded like the iron I smelled in my blood, "and if you get in trouble, I know what to do. I've helped many girls in trouble in my time." And she told me of the "many girls in trouble" who had come to her to rid themselves of boys' unwanted seed. "The two kinds of people I helped the most in my time were lonely bachelor farmers and desperate girls in times of trouble."

The central piece of furniture in Belle's house, as she told me on my first morning of being a woman, had been her long oak kitchen table upon which she performed her most important services. As I wiped the blood from my thighs with the burlap bag and did my best to dress for school without spreading the mess, Belle told me of one poor soul who had come to her on a night in January 1908. "I was taking care of Andrew that night there on the kitchen table and had forgotten this girl had made an appointment. What could I do?" she asked, shrugging her shoulders, "I used my kitchen table for both tasks.

"This girl, Annie I believe her name was, must have come first to my front door and knocked, but I couldn't hear her knocking with all the wind that night, so she came in the back door and saw me with Andrew before I knew she was even there. I heard the backdoor slam, heard Annie shout to whomever had driven her to the house, 'She's got a man in there on the table! And she's hacking him to pieces with an ax!' I chased after her, of course, not to hurt her but to explain, but she was gone with the driver whose horses kicked up dirt in the moon's half-light. Had I thought to put down the axe, perhaps she would have stopped running and returned." Belle sighed, threw up her hands, continued. "When I returned through the back door, I nearly tripped over the bag of money Annie had brought to pay for the removal of the unwanted seed—$27.53, all coins. All the money she must have had in the world."

Because I didn't plan to get into "trouble," Belle's story about Annie didn't have much effect, nor did her promise to "help me." Even though Belle gave me permission to "fuck boys" at the age of eleven, this wasn't something that particularly appealed to me. I suppose this was when the distance between Belle and me began to grow. She wanted me to follow in her footsteps and help the sad lonely men of the world while making a living for myself, but I wasn't yet ready for that and wasn't sure I ever would be.

At first, I tried doing what she wanted, and I fucked boys. Or perhaps I should say, I was fucked by boys. Or perhaps I should say, fucked by one boy. Or perhaps I should say, and this is the most accurate, was kissed and mildly fondled by one boy, Duane, who even in sixth grade had earthworms dressed in baseball uniforms on his bedroom walls. Even so, I told Belle that I fucked boys, but when she asked for proof in the form of money and bodies, I had nothing to show. So she got angry and yelled, "You'll never amount to anything! I'm ashamed to call you my daughter!"

At that, we both paused, and at first my eyes started to well up with tears. But then, overcome with rage, I thoughtlessly yelled back, "I'm not your daughter. I only sleep here."

"Only sleep here." What simple words. But acknowledging this fact for the first time was the most difficult thing I had ever done; admitting I was not Belle's daughter was only the beginning. After those words slipped from my mouth, I desired all the more desperately to be Belle's daughter, though I knew I didn't have what it took to do what Belle required.

Because I knew that Lauren, not me, had what it took, I was hesitant to invite her to spend the night. I worried that Belle might claim a new daughter, that I wouldn't be the one. Even so, I couldn't help but give Belle what she wanted, believing somehow that if Lauren could do what Belle most wanted, then Belle would thank me for bringing her Lauren. So desperately did I need to remain Belle's daughter that I believed I could secure my own place with Belle alongside Lauren. I was right about Lauren becoming Belle's new daughter; I was wrong about securing my own place.

How well I remember the first time Lauren spent the night with Belle and me! Lauren and I walked out of school that late October day into a new world, everything having changed since morning. Air which had been warm and sweet was now cold and bitter; leaves which had pulsed green with life were now the brick red color of dried blood. As I slipped my arms into my red Satellites jacket and hunched over against the wind, Lauren pulled off her sweatshirt and raised her face to the sky. The wind shrieked, in a voice I knew but did not know, "Not my daughter, not my daughter, not my daughter."

Lauren and Belle hit it off from the start, and I could tell Belle loved and needed Lauren, but in a different way than she had ever loved or needed me.

"I hear you killed a lot of people," Lauren said straight out when she met Belle.

"That I did," Belle replied, nodding.

"I hear you stole men's money," Lauren said.

"That I did," Belle replied, grinning.

"I hear you even killed your own children, some for insurance money, some just to make people think you'd died in that fire," Lauren said.

"That, too, I did." Belle replied and extended her hand to Lauren.

"Cool." Lauren said, taking Belle's hand and giving it a firm shake.

I was deflated.

There was no talk of helping lonely Norwegian men, no explanation or justification. Lauren didn't require the soft sell, and I could tell Belle was no longer interested in what I would or would not do for her. That night, Lauren stole a carom board set from one museum display and a leather belt from another. In the confines of Belle's shed (which was just the right size for two but too small for three), we played Punishment Pool—a game of Lauren's invention which resulted in ten blows from the leather strap for every shot missed. Between Belle and Lauren, I ended the evening with burning red welts across my legs, butt, and back. In one night, I had fallen out of Belle's favor, and when I awoke the next morning, I saw Belle not as my living, breathing mother, but as a stiff stuffed doll with a cracked smile across her paper-mache face. And then I saw Lauren, completely entranced, talking to Belle as I had the previous night and for all my nights before, pausing to listen and laughing every so often at Belle's stories. I did not doubt that Belle was speaking, though I could no longer hear her.

Within a week of Lauren's first night at the museum, she came to school reporting that her parents had died in a house fire, and I was surprised nobody but me noticed how coincidental this was given the fire that had destroyed Belle's farmhouse. As I was Lauren's only friend, my parents felt they had no choice but to accept Lauren's decision to come and live with us. At night, Lauren slept under Belle's watchful gaze and I, no longer welcome, began sleeping in the Victorian living room. The red velvet couches were so plush, so comfortable compared to my cot in Belle's shed, but I could not sleep. The sound of Lauren's voice and the memory of Belle's kept me ever awake. I could not help but miss them both. Sometimes I thought I even heard Belle's voice, but when I went to the shed and looked inside, hoping to be welcomed back with open arms, Lauren turned her back to me and Belle refused to be anything more than a stuffed and lifeless doll.

One night I did sleep, but my head was full of nightmares. I had become Brynhild's doll Mollie, and I knew my fate before I saw a figure—Belle's figure—appear, looking down at me, shaking her head, a butcher knife in one hand and a gunnysack in the other. When I awoke, Belle was standing over me, the ax from her shed at her feet, but she was looking straight ahead as she could only do—stuffed thing that she was. My mother, coming to get me at the end of her shift, asked how Belle had gotten all the way over to the Victorian exhibit, but I could not explain.

"Well, she's got to go back," my mother said, and I couldn't agree more. My mother left me with Belle while she went to find a moving dolly. Belle's silence was more hateful than her anger.

Months went by, and on the morning of August 15, 1985—my twelfth birthday—my mother woke me from the Victorian living room couch and stated that I was old enough to sleep on my own at home while she and my father went to work at night. Lauren stayed. And I didn't know how to feel about that so I didn't feel anything at all.

"Whatever Lauren wants to do, she can do," my mother said firmly when I told her where Lauren was, "but you, my daughter, seem at last to have outgrown Belle." Then she laughed as she said, "Why, until a few months ago, I thought the curator would have to build a separate exhibit just for you."

And then I laughed too. I hugged my mother, my flesh and blood mother who smelled of bleach and nicotine, and for the first time, felt strangely loved.

I no longer slept in the Belle Gunness exhibit, and I never went to the museum, even requesting exemptions from school field trips to the museum. I wallpapered my bedroom with bright yellow daisies and daffodils, making up for that day in kindergarten when everybody but me could talk about their beautiful bedrooms with their beautiful wallpaper. Only problem was, nobody had cause to ask me about my wallpaper, and I didn't feel easy within such beautiful walls. Neither did Belle become a thing of the past so quickly. At school, sitting beside me at our shared desk, Lauren talked about Belle so incessantly that I couldn't help but envy their closeness, even as the boys in our class began disappearing one by one—first Alan and the blonde Norwegian-looking ones, then all the rest. Of course, this alarmed the teachers, and police were alerted, but Lauren could pass so easily for normal that no one ever suspected.

Ben Folkert's disappearance had been sloppy. Anybody would tell you that. Usually the boys went missing in the nighttime along with their coin banks shaped like He-Man and Gizmo the Gremlin, stolen from their bed stands or bookcase headboards. Nobody could say whether the boys had been stolen away or left on their own; they were just gone. But not Ben. Not Ben who had come to school with twelve crumpled dollar bills in his pocket, birthday money from his snowbird grandmother living the high life in some Florida trailer park outside of Weeki Wachee Springs. Not Ben who went outside with the rest of us for morning recess during that first week of March but did not come back.

Laredo, still wearing her goofy Care Bears moon boots and rainbow scarf when the rest of us had shed our winter gear, had gone looking for Ben who had just that morning checked the "YES" box on her "Will you be my boyfriend?" note, then forgot to wait for her at recess. That day I played our crocodile game alone as Lauren said she had to stay inside to practice fractions. So when Miss Lesion blew her recess whistle, I lined up along the boundary between sidewalk and mud with my classmates, all of us orderly and contained. All of us but Ben who did not return and Laredo who ran screaming from the far woods, Ben's beloved Chicago Cubs cap dripping blood onto her moon boots. Our orderly line fell apart as my class ran to the security of our room, shrieking about murder. As if waiting for us all, Lauren sat hunched over our desk, chopping whole numbers into fractions. I eased in beside her and rested my head on the desk's fake wood surface, liking its coolness against my flushed cheeks. Lauren looked over at me but said nothing, as if she had done nothing more than chop up boring old numbers all recess. I didn't say a word to her about Ben.

She knew.

We both knew.

And besides, her boots were caked with mud.

My stomach in knots, I sat at my desk, hands in my lap and picked at my already stubby fingernails until my fingertips were raw. Miss Lesion and the principal stood quietly behind two brown-uniformed LaPorte County police officers who asked questions about Ben's family, whether we had seen any strangers lurking around the playground at recess or any other time and whether anybody on the playground saw anything at all. Nothing. Nobody said a word. Then one officer rifled through Ben's desk for clues, so I tidied the contents of my half of our desk, stacking textbooks neatly in one pile, papers in another, loose crayons and pencils in my blue crayon box. Anything to be busy. But I could do nothing about Lauren's tangled half of our desk, and so I worried about what might be found if they searched our desk after Ben's. Lauren's bloodied pocketknife? Twelve crumpled dollar bills? I both wished for Lauren to be found out so I could be done with her, be done with Belle, but even more I knew that I could not afford to lose Lauren, to lose them both. I didn't need to worry. Lauren passed so easily for normal that no one ever suspected her and the police only asked us questions about creepy strangers, not classmates.

Soon enough the police left the room, the principal dismissed school, and we walked outside, Lauren linking her arm in mine.

Junior high came and went, then high school, and increasingly I found myself alone. When Lauren wasn't busy mauling some guy up against his locker, she still talked to me, but I grew tired of hearing about her boyfriends and about how dumb and old-fashioned Belle was; how Belle stunk like cabbage and how she preached at Lauren what she should do with her life when Belle hadn't a "fucking clue about the world since 1908," how after graduation Lauren was "getting the hell out of that museum" to do her own thing, something bigger and better than even Belle had done. I listened but did not listen, and when I opened my mouth and spoke, Lauren did not hear me. But then, nobody did.

On an early day in June 1991, dressed in robes as red as blood that tastes its first air, Lauren and I stood facing each other, pressed close amidst a crowd of jumping, shouting classmates. Lauren had done her share of jumping and shouting, mixing in as only she could do, me awkwardly standing and shifting in her shadow. We knew this was it, the time to say goodbye and to walk our separate ways, the time to move out into the world and on to better things than South Central, bigger places than Hanna, Union Mills, Wanatah, and even LaPorte. Lauren and I had never been ones to embrace, but we had no choice, here on graduation day when the only thing for anyone to do was to clutch each other so tightly that only letting go would bring relief. Her body in my arms felt like I always imagined mine to feel to Belle—sharp and bony, delicate in the way of bones too old for one's flesh. I smelled in her the cabbage she hated, the tapioca she thought so old-fashioned, and I smelled too her cheap perfume and the cologne of many boys. In me, I feared she smelled blood and so I shrank into myself, remembering Belle's long-forsaken command: "You can fuck boys now."

Lauren and I pulled away then, our robes separating like velvet curtains until we stood separate and alone, a dark and empty stage between us. Lauren told me something as she turned back into the crowd, but I could no longer hear her.

On my drive to Hanna for my five year South Central High School reunion on June 15, 1996, my first return in five long years, I felt what I had not in the least expected—the old pull and call of Belle, present from the moment I crossed over the threshold of LaPorte. Disconcerted but determined to drive straight—to decide my own path—I gripped the steering wheel of my red Ford Astro so tightly I thought for sure my knuckles would slice through my skin. At the crest of the highway bridge overlooking the museum—Belle's home, my home for so many years—I refused to look in Belle's direction though I heard her voice, heard her calling to me in a way I had not heard since before Lauren had entered our lives.

"Come home," Belle pleaded gently. "I need you, Dawn. I need you to come home to me," she crooned, sounding so loving, so alone.

I refused to listen, couldn't afford to listen, so I turned the radio to Sunny 101.5 and cranked up "Let's Get Physical," a song I'd hated since sixth grade aerobics. Had Belle's voice, Belle's words, come from outside, maybe I could have overcome her, but she spoke from deep within, from a part of me I had long believed dead. I tried to drown out her voice with my own conscious, careful voice telling myself what a good life I had had since leaving Belle, how free, how independent, how in control. I considered my husband Lloyd and our infant son Andrew who bore the same name as one of Belle's victims, "a way of letting him live again," I had thought when I—not Lloyd—chose the name. I told myself how much I loved my husband and son; how much I knew that they, not Belle, were the ones I needed, were the best thing for me; how I knew their love was real and good and honest. *But do I need them?* I wondered in spite of myself, and then *Do they need me?* And I heard Belle's voice answer from deep within, "They may love you, my darling Dawn, but they don't need you. They don't need you like I need you. And I need you more than ever, just as you need and have always needed me."

Somehow I kept driving, on past the museum, on past Dairy Queen, on past Five Star Supermarket and Maple Lane Mall. Five years gone and my body still knew how to autopilot: left on IN-39, stop at the flashing 4-way at U.S. 6, straight until U.S. 30, then right. Pass the sign to Hanna, cross the railroad tracks, slow down and ease left to make the turn onto 450 West, cross over U.S. 30 then turn right into the first driveway. Home. Only I didn't make that final turn but drove past home, then on by the cemetery, then left towards the center of town until I found myself on Thompson Street at the Hanna Branch of the LaPorte County Public Library. And then, not quite in command but not quite under Belle's either, I found myself inside the library, staring at my salvation tacked up on a bulletin board, a bright blue flyer for the National Association of Tourist Attraction Survivors asking "Do You Have Tourist Attraction Trauma?"

I can say now what I knew then: Had it not been for NATAS, I would have returned to Belle. And I would have returned not simply because she controlled me but also because I wanted to be under her control. I would have returned with bowed head and open hands, willing to submit to the plans Belle had had for me since I suckled at her breast, eager to receive whatever she cared to give in return. For in those twenty-six minutes it took to drive from LaPorte to Hanna, I had begun to savor Belle's voice within me, hearing her even through the radio as Elton John pleaded with his absent lover in "I Guess That's Why They Call it the Blues." All my old demons had returned.

But something in me, something in the muddle of this murderous middle ground, had the sense to know I needed help even when I wasn't sure I wanted it, had the sense to call the toll free number on the NATAS flyer. And within an hour a white NATAS van pulled up outside the Independent Order of Odd Fellows on Moore Street where I sat on the curb, sobbing. Except to say that he was round and dressed in green, I hardly remember the man who helped me inside, offering me a seat next to a silent passenger. Maybe I should have been surprised when, after my sobbing had subsided, I opened my eyes to see that it was Lauren who sat beside me looking every bit as controlled and calm as I was not. Truth is, I wasn't surprised. Instead, I simply asked, "So why aren't you at the reunion?"

"I had better things to do," she said and grinned. "I just figured it was time for me to get this Belle Gunness business behind me once and for all. You know, move on and have a normal life and all." Then Lauren punched me hard below the shoulder, the pain bringing me back to our shared childhood. "God, how I've missed you!"

The NATAS van sped us down the highway to Florida, Ohio, to the NATAS Hospital for Research and Recovery. Lauren and I did not talk but knew somehow it was right that we should be together. I spent the next six weeks in recovery—sometimes alone, sometimes with Lauren. When together with a therapist, Lauren did most of the talking, speaking first of Belle's cruel brilliance and later of her outdated finesse with her letters and her Norwegian spiel. I just listened then, but when apart from Lauren I found myself talking about Belle's warmth, love for me, and then of that cruel moment when Lauren first appeared and began to take Belle away from me.

I spent many therapy sessions worrying aloud about what Lauren said about me in private, how she must have seen me as so needy and helpless and cowardly. I felt so inferior to Lauren and so desiring of Belle, jealous yet fascinated by the one who had stolen Belle away from me because she was what I was not. Lauren and Belle were always cold to each other. And they were so honest.

"You know, Dawn," remarked my therapist one day, "you talk nearly as much about Lauren as about Belle." This surprised me, but perhaps it shouldn't have, Lauren having become the one who was everything Belle had wanted in a daughter—no, not daughter, accomplice—who had become all those things I could not be.

Belle Gunness told me long ago, "the only way to get what you want from people is to pretend that you aren't who you really are, that you don't know what you really know, that you don't do what you really do." I think about that now and then, about who Belle was and who she pretended to be—about who I still expect myself to pretend to be. Looking at Belle's life and all the people she killed and all the money she made, I think that she may have been right, for surely she could not have gotten all she ever wanted had she not all those years pretended to be someone else. Belle just never got anything she needed.

I think of my husband Lloyd and our son Andrew, think of our home which we have filled haphazardly with scratched and strained furniture from other people's lives, cheap reproductions of Margaret Keane's big-eyed children, and a special bedroom shed for Andrew made from corn crib siding from my childhood home at U.S. 30 and 450 W. There are no pictures of Belle in Andrew's shed, but neither are there soft brown teddy bears or baby blue quilts. Andrew has his "Gunny" instead, made from a burlap gunnysack with black button eyes, a red-stitched mouth that cannot open, and dried apricot ears. When Andrew asks me to play with Gunny she never talks for herself, but it is Andrew who talks for her, telling her what she says and making her dance insanely exhausting dances.

When Andrew begs me to speak for Gunny, these are her only words: "I cannot control you. I can't even love you. Look at how silly I am, all limp and stuffed and harmless! Look at how you can do with me anything you choose!" And so Andrew does. Dragging Gunny through mud. Throwing her down the stairs. Biting off her apricot ears.

And this so reminds me of Ole Budsberg's scarred and bloated head which, if I am to tell the truth, I am drawn to even now. I find I can't mourn for Ole's lost life or the lives of any of Belle's victims, can't feel the sadness their surviving family members must have felt. I know that I should, that any decent human being would, but in truth, a part of me still admires Belle, still imagines the version she told only to me—only to me and nobody else, not even Lauren—to be the whole truth.

I guess I'm also thankful to Lauren for doing what I could not, for becoming the daughter Belle desired and arriving just in time to fuck boys and kill boys and take whatever money she could get. Even so, Lauren wasn't the slut I had mistaken her for, just a businesswoman of a new generation, carrying on Belle's trade 100 years later with no one the wiser except for me.

Stitching on Gunny's new apricot ears in the predawn dark of a sleepless night, I sniffled and shivered from chills that come from deep within during times of illness. I could no more control my thinking than I could control my needle that stabbed at Gunny's rough hide. At times like this, Belle would rise up from the dusty corner I had allotted her in my soul, longing to stretch her limbs and try her voice. She still had her place just as I had mine, so I invited her out for awhile, just to see the rising sun. Blanket clutched around me, I waited for warmth, waited for dawn to embrace us. For only then would she cease her movement, cease her speaking. Only then would she become both substantial and transparent, both body and ghost. Growing up I saw Belle as flesh and blood, never transparent like a ghost. Except for those moments between her and Lauren when I saw her cruelty for what it was, I never saw through her.

Morning arrives and dawn burns away the shadows of night, tempers Belle so that I see her as she is, scattered particles of dust, of ash, caught for one brief moment in the swirl of air around me. I dare not catch my breath lest she stay, lest she take up residence. Even so, Belle is and always will be, must be, a part of me. In the early light of dawn, I sip warm eggnog with nutmeg, and I dream of that little something extra.

Afterword by the Editor

There have been three developments of significance since Dawn Tempers initially wrote her account.

First, the Belle Gunness exhibit, along with the rest of the LaPorte County Historical Society Museum, took up new residence at 2405 Indiana Ave. in LaPorte, an improvement from the cramped county complex location next to the county courthouse. Belle's shed and imposing figure remain a popular attraction on the new museum's basement level, though the museum as a whole seems too spacious and well-lit for Belle.

Second, April 28, 2008 marked the 100th anniversary of the fire that destroyed Belle's house and led to the discovery of the bodies on her property. Bruce Johnson, long-time elementary school teacher at South Central, chaired the Belle Gunness 100th Anniversary Committee. Among other noteworthy events leading up to the anniversary of the fire, Bruce Johnson organized presentations by folklorist Janet Langlois (author of *Belle Gunness: The Lady Bluebeard*) and University of Indianapolis graduate student Andrea Simmons who is leading a forensic investigation to solve the mystery of whether the headless body in the Gunness farmhouse basement belonged to Belle Gunness. Bruce Johnson also placed a wreath on the grave of Andrew Helgelien, a moment of historical significance captured by no less than *USA Today*.

Third, the childhood home of Dawn Tempers which once stood "On the outskirts of Hanna, Indiana, where U.S. Highway 30 and County Road 450 West meet" no longer stands. Having been condemned for many months, the house was destroyed, first by heavy machinery, then burned by the Hanna Township Volunteer Fire Department during a practice exercise in February 2008. Stopping by to see the final flickering flames on February 14, while on a visit to her parents, Dawn had the following to say:

> Pulling into the driveway, I saw a part of what I had always seen: the front steps, the leaning juniper tree my cats once climbed, the lane leading away from the house and down to the woods. What I did not see was my home. Only a basement remained, a basement that looked, I suppose, like the basements of other burned down houses, that looked to me like pictures of the basement of Belle's burned down house. Only there were no bodies here. No bodies in the basement of this house or in the garden, or near the corncrib, or even back the lane to the woods.

As a final but necessary NATAS clarification, albeit an unfortunate one, it must be noted that while Dawn Tempers and this editor, Lauren Ambrite, were classmates at South Central High School, no part of Tempers' story about Lauren is true. Yes, there was a series of mysterious disappearances as Dawn's account so vividly relates, but Lauren and Dawn did not have a close connection to each other, and no evidence has been found linking Lauren Ambrite to the alleged crimes. Phyllis Tempers (Dawn's mother) who has worked as a night janitor at the museum—both the county complex and Indiana Avenue locations—since before Dawn's birth corroborates this account, stating that she knows of "nobody who has ever slept in the Belle Gunness exhibit besides my daughter."

My perusal of Tempers' case as a senior counselor with NATAS coupled with my own personal recollections leads me to conclude that Tempers was suffering from false memory at the time of her writing. All the same, her account does offer insight into certain long-term delusional tendencies that may exist even after treatment for Tourist Attraction Trauma.

© z the goblin

The NATAS Editor Grapples with a Jelly Dream

"When they start making fun at me, I say, 'I can see you for nothing right here, but you had to pay to see me.'"
—Percilla Bejano, aka Percilla the Monkey Girl

For all my years working for the National Association of Tourist Attraction Survivors, both as a senior counselor at the NATAS Hospital for Research and Recovery (NATASHRR) in Florida, Ohio, and as this book's editor, I find myself in a moment of crisis, my life's work called suddenly and sharply into question. I am not who I was when I began, I am uncertain about who I have become, and I don't know who I am now supposed to be.

When I sit down to write editor's notes and add researched footnotes, I adopt my most objective and rational voice, while in my head I hear a litany of questions in a voice that is my own.

Who am I to bring these stories into the world?

Should these stories even be brought into the world, and once in the world, who will listen? Who will care?

Does it matter if anybody cares? Anybody…or nobody?

Does any of this—any of anything—matter?

Do I matter? And if I matter, to whom?

To all these questions, I have one unsatisfying answer: "I don't know."

And because I don't know—because there is no absolute knowing to be found, no certainty—I am afraid.

What am I afraid of? Well, I fear I've been going about *A Green Glow on the Horizon* all wrong.

I fear there's no right way to go about this (and no wrong way either).

I fear I will never finish, and I fear I will finish, and I fear that if I finish, I will be finished.

My fears have been stopping me cold.

Then last night—an ordinary Saturday night where I fell asleep on my futon with my pug dog Pongo during the last half hour of *Saturday Night Live*—I had a dream that, on waking, brought the kind of relief that comes only with letting go, letting be.

You see, dear reader, I have worked so hard for so long to enforce critical distance and objectivity that this has begun to do more harm than good, both to me and to the survivors whose stories the whole world needs to hear. Yet I know that those stories are only a small sliver of who these people are. I know that even if I were able to endlessly spill out stories, I could only begin to approximate these ever-evolving lives. As Oscar Wilde writes in *The Picture of Dorian Gray*, a book I read in senior English at South Central High School with Mrs. Corey Shrilpa, "'Who are you?' To define is to limit."

That overriding awareness left me paralyzed, the granular details of people's lives overwhelming to me. Until I had my Jelly dream.

On waking from my Jelly dream, I felt relieved, for the dream revealed that I had not, as I had feared, taken on the role of the ringmaster like that ringmaster wearing a black top hat with a red satin bow who lured me to see Percilla the Monkey Girl at the 1982 LaPorte County Fair with the promise that I would see her whole hairy body.

What I expected to see at the tender age of nine was an ape-girl in a cage, shaking the bars and howling. Instead, I saw a bearded grandma in a short-sleeved cheetah-print dress, rocking in a wooden chair like my own grandmother's. As her hands knitted a bright orange scarf, she said, still looking at her yarn, "Welcome, everybody. Please come closer so everybody can see, and don't worry, I won't bite."

A mass of bodies pressed me forward until I was standing on tiptoes looking over the plexiglass frame that circled Percilla's stage which was covered in the same indoor-outdoor carpet as at Wright's Barnyard mini-golf in Valparaiso where I had once gone because I'd earned two free tickets for Bible verse memorization at Vacation Bible School. At the front of the crowd, trapped between Percilla and the people, my stomach clenched from the smells of powder fresh deodorant, Polo cologne, and the B.O. tang of bodies in August's humid stew.

I looked at Percilla, and Percilla raised her eyes from her knitting and peered straight into mine, our brown eyes locked as though we were the only two people in the tent. *Help me,* I thought as she began her story, but she was there to tell her story and I was there to listen, whether I now wanted to or not.

"My name is Percilla Bejano, and when I was born in Puerto Rico on April 26, 1911, my body was covered in thick black hair like you see me today." Percilla set down her knitting on her lap and raised her arms, her fingers pointing to the top of the canvas tent as stage lights made her forearm fur sparkle. I gasped. Percilla lowered her hands to her lap, picked up her silver needles, continued knitting her scarf and her story.

"People stared," Percilla said, "and the priest at our home parish in Bayamón suggested an exorcism might cure me, but instead of an exorcism, my father, desperate to find a cure about why I was so different, left behind my smooth-skinned mother and six siblings and brought me to America where doctors told him I had hypertrichosis which means the same thing all of you are thinking as you look at me: I had and always would have too much hair!" At this, Percilla stretched her arms wide like Jesus on the cross. "So my father who called me 'a hairy little girl' did what he thought best for me and for the rest of our poor family. With freak show promoter Carl Lauther, they began exhibiting me as The Monkey Girl, and when I was six and my father died, Carl Lauther adopted me and became my legal father. I'm a trained singer and dancer and have been performing my entire life. In 1938 I met Emmit Bejano, The Alligator Man. We fell in love and eloped, then returned to the stage as The World's Strangest Married Couple on our own terms."

Still looking at me, Percilla smiled.

"I'd like to sing a song for you now," she said, setting down her knitting again and walking over to a wooden stand that held a suitcase record player, the kind on which my teacher liked to play "Great Green Gobs of Greasy, Grimy Gopher Guts" with its line "mutilated monkey meat" which made me wince and laugh at the same time.

"This song is my beloved Emmit's favorite," she said as she placed the arm of the record player down, and the record began to spin as the needle awakened "It's a Long Way to Tipperary" while Percilla the monkey grandmother began to sing and sway from side to side, all the while looking only at me as I ran my tongue over my extra set of bottom teeth, wondering if I, and not this lady with a beard, was the freak. Percilla looked so odd but seemed so normal to me, and here I was looking so normal and feeling like the hyperdontic freak I was. In that tent I stood frozen on my tiptoes while Percilla danced on stage, industrial fans blowing at high speed to keep Percilla cool in the August heat while

I felt like I was being pulled down into a swampy bog, with no will-o'-the-wisp to illuminate my way.

While my Percilla memory may seem to be a sidetrack, it really matters to my Jelly dream, for I no longer carry the discomfort I once felt over having to face that I am an animal: Percilla is a grower of hair and I am a grower of teeth. Underneath everything, we animals are just people, and I never have been a ringmaster. I gather these stories for you, dear reader, not to show off people's weirdnesses but to validate their individual selves.

And so right now it matters that I tell the Jelly dream which I felt compelled to write as a letter to one of the characters in the dream who happens to be Oscar Wilde.

September 20, 2008, 7:58 a.m.

Dear Oscar,
   In my dream you have a friend named Jelly you want me to meet. We are in Des Moines, Iowa, location of 1972's *A Thief in the Night*, the Christian horror film I watched in the Redemption Hall basement that made me terrified of the Rapture and worried I would be left behind. I am following you to where you live and we must walk through an alley to get there, an alley that stretches up a steep hill—steep by Midwestern standards—between bland backsides of storefronts. The building on my left is a crumbling yellow stucco. The building on my right is brick the dull color of dried blood. As I follow a short distance behind, heavy things weigh on my mind. I have not had a good week.
   I carry your book *The Picture of Dorian Gray*. You open a wood-framed screen door, and I want to enter but then I drop your book and turn around to see it slide down a steep slope. I run back down the hill after it, rage building inside of me. This dropping of your book is one more little thing I do not need. As I run, I scream, "THIS HAS BEEN

ONE FUCKED UP WEEK!" I am unable to stop myself even as I feel Des Moines citizens would not take kindly to such language. By the time I reach your book, Percilla the Middle-Aged Monkey Woman holds it in her hairy hands. Percilla says, "I understand."

Now Percilla and I are standing together on the sidewalk, both of us now looking up at a mural of a wrinkled old woman on the alley wall. The mural is as large as the screen at Plymouth's Tri-Way Drive-In where I watched both *Gandhi* and *E.T. The Extra Terrestrial* with my family in 1982. The old woman's deep brown eyes are open wide, overwhelmed by some awful thing appearing in the sky, and that's when I see her teeth—so many extra teeth, just like mine—in the black hole of her mouth. Percilla takes my hand, turns to look at me, and smiles. Percilla, like me and like the woman in the mural, has an extra row of teeth. We are a sisterhood of hyperdontia.

I like Percilla but cannot stay because I must find you again, Oscar, find you and this Jelly you have said I must meet. I drop Percilla's hand and pick up *Dorian Gray*, now twice the width it was before the fall, its spine cracked. I feel sad about this, but take comfort knowing a broken book is better than a book that isn't read.

I thank Percilla, then hurry up the alley. I know she stands watching me from the bottom of the hill, know that if I turned around and asked her to join me, she would. But I do not turn back, worried that if I turn around and look at the artist I want to be, God will turn me into a pillar of salt.

I find the door you have entered, Oscar, but I can't figure out how to walk through it because it opens between two floors, like the elevator in *Being John Malkovich*. The top part is a small screen door, maybe a foot and a half high, and I can see the floor of this place, and I can tell that the room is a kitchen with black and white chessboard tile floor. Ceramic bowls on the floor by the hulking white 1940s refrigerator hold crunchy cat food and water. I crawl into the upper room, thinking I'll see you, but you are not there, and I still don't know who Jelly is, whether Jelly is your roommate, or a lover, or a bunch of grape goo in a jelly jar. I call out your name, "Oscar!" You do not respond.

The living room does not seem like the type of place where you would live, Oscar, nor is this a place I can rest. The marmalade orange walls are dingy, not bright like you, and the mint jelly drapes cover the windows so completely that what light gets through casts a puke green glow. Even worse, the room is furnished with my Aunt Carole's matching set of velour furniture—couch, loveseat, and La-Z-Boy—patterned with rustic grain mills and sheaves of bound wheat. Do people still buy these, Oscar? Not like Aunt Carole once bought hers from a furniture showroom in the 1980s but from thrift stores? Did you choose these? Did Jelly?

I open a door at the far end of the furniture-cluttered living room and find stairs leading to an attic. I hear voices and follow, climbing stairs carpeted with frayed red shag, stepping over crumpled clothes as I steady myself against the fake wood paneling that makes up the walls. The only light in the attic comes from a small greasy window at its far end. The ceiling is angled downward so the only place I can comfortably stand is in the center.

Here is where I find you, Oscar, and, I presume, Jelly hunched low in your shadow at the bottom of the angled ceiling.

And now, to try to describe Jelly, the most difficult thing to do.

Jelly is small, a child I think, maybe as young as a toddler. Must be very young because I know at one point you mention a diaper change. Jelly is a genius of some sort, and draws pictures, creates worlds out of them. Jelly is a creature of the past, the present, and the future, and at different points in the dream I see Jelly and his work in these various stages.

In appearance, Jelly is the color of burnt sugar. Jelly looks more androgynous than markedly male, though I identify Jelly as "he" from the beginning. Jelly is not unattractive, but the overall effect of his appearance on me lies at the nexus of attraction and revulsion.

I realize now that I am outside of my dream that in Jelly I see you, dear Oscar, and Gandhi and E.T. and Percilla and Xavier and Abigail and Valerie and Rita and Ruth and Dawn and also the me I avoided becoming through all my therapy with NATAS but have to feel and embrace now.

Jelly unsettles me because Jelly seems to know me. I can't hide from Jelly. And so I avoid looking directly into Jelly's every-color eyes, afraid I will be undone. Jelly doesn't seem to have the same effect on you, Oscar. I watch you talk with Jelly, hear the rise and fall of your natural conversation.

Suddenly I notice a retrospective of Jelly's artwork is playing on a big screen TV, narrated by a man with a British accent who may or may not be David Attenborough but sounds like him. I suspect the program is BBC produced. The retrospective reveals strange patterns and worlds, a unique vision. The sketches are disturbingly beautiful, even though the foundation is, and could be said to be a child's sketches. Both you and I are drawn to Jelly's art. Jelly seems not to realize the power of Jelly's work. Certainly, Jelly does not boast about it. What Jelly has done—and the BBC retrospective shows this nicely—is fill in the sketches with color and shading and depth. In so doing, Jelly's art has changed and matured. These sketches begun in Jelly's child state have been layered and transformed into all the Jellies that they have ever been.

The retrospective shows this process by overlaying the initial drawings with the more developed ones. Some of these have even been animated. The effect of all these things is reminiscent of the Beatles' *Yellow Submarine* movie and of Terry Gilliam's *Monty Python and the Holy Grail* animated sequences. I remember one image especially well, a sketch of a tree that starts small and grows and flowers and produces strange fruits with sharp geometric angles, unlike any natural fruit which is always rounded on the edges, no matter what its overall shape. Jelly's work is beyond mere nature, is visionary.

I am glad you wanted me to meet Jelly. I am also unsettled because I so understand Jelly's work even though I am at a loss for words to match my understanding. But isn't that true about all of us, as you yourself have said?

In the retrospective, an art professor with a Midwestern accent uses words to explain what he thinks Jelly's work means. From the way he looks beyond the eye of the camera into the far off horizon, I can see that his words make him feel important and even superior to Jelly and the art he'll never be able to feel.

All I can do is feel all the Jellies altogether without limit—young, old and feeble, and in their prime. Jelly's art doesn't progress chronologically, but rather is all of these simultaneously.

My attention is pulled from the BBC retrospective to Jelly themself. Jelly is older and working on "coloring in" a picture Jelly is drawing on a twisted mobius of stark white paper. Jelly draws my attention to what Jelly is doing, and I watch, amazed. "Coloring in" is more than simply coloring between the lines. The coloring adds a certain wisdom and sorrow and longing to the child Jelly's stark lines. The picture is both the same and not the same. The picture is everything Jelly.

I still don't really know who Jelly is in relation to you, my dear Oscar. I don't even know if you live in this place with Jelly. It seems to me that you must, but the clutter in the attic room, especially the scattered clothes that trip me up when I walk, seem so uncharacteristic of you, so unrefined, so broken. Maybe the clothes are Jelly's. Maybe they are yours. Maybe both. That you seem to belong in this place, that you don't move to leave or to ask permission to do one thing or another makes me think you must belong here, as uncharacteristic as it first seemed.

At some point you and Jelly and I are all tired. We lie down to sleep together on an unmade mattress on the floor with twisted sheets that none of us bother to un-twist. I lie beside Jelly who curls into me like the child Jelly is, wrapping their arms around my neck. I smell Jelly's fruity-soft hair, but I don't feel myself to be offering comfort and protection to Jelly as Jelly's pose would imply. Rather, Jelly's embrace of me communicates how deeply Jelly knows me, how ok I am. Then you, dear Oscar, spoon me.

I am in the embrace of the holy and profane.

With warmest affection,

Lauren Ambrite

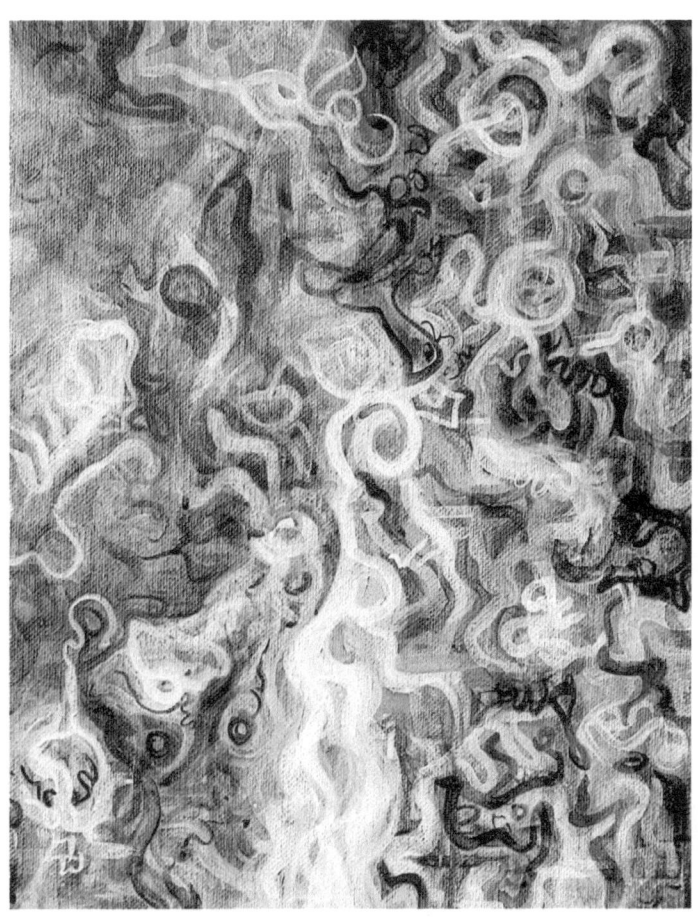

© z the goblin

© Lux Burns

Cherished

> "*Cherished Twinklings are all about what it means to laugh, live, and give, and that's no phony baloney.*"
>
> — *Tina Slaughter, 1992*
> *on receiving the Niceness of Art in Society Award*

I left home the morning after I broke Mom's "Home Run" figurine. Any other of her 114 Cherished Twinklings and I could have remained, but Tina Slaughter made this one especially for Mom after Joey got struck down by lightning at his first tee ball game. I left home not to run away but to reclaim sanity, both Mom's and mine. Dad was the eternal unspeaking presence I never had to worry about—he never voiced his thoughts or opinions, and if he was not exactly sane, he at least kept all his insanity inside. So when I heard, "You know, Becky, I'd feel better if I knew where you were," and turned to see Dad standing in my doorway, I dropped the socks and underwear I'd been trying unsuccessfully to stuff along the edges of my mostly packed suitcase.

"Shit, Dad! You could knock first, you know?" I said, dropping to sit on the edge of my bed.

Dad smiled and moved beside me, picking up scattered socks and tucking them inside my suitcase with his long pale fingers, leaving my underwear where they lay. Then from his back pocket he pulled a sheet of paper folded neatly in quarters, unfolded it, and smoothed out the creases. Dad seemed unsure about handing it to me, so I leaned over and saw a picture of what looked like an old brick church with the words, "National Association of Tourist Attraction Survivors Hospital for Research and Recovery, Youth Resources Center. Florida, Ohio," bolded underneath.

"They're good people, Becky," Dad said, his eyes glued to the paper. "I called and talked to Roy, a caseworker. They have a bed ready. I will cover all costs."

I said nothing.

"Of course, I can't make you go," Dad said softly, "and I won't, but," his voice faltered, "well, I just think this would be a good step towards"—his shoulders lifted, then fell again—"towards whatever happens next. They are"—he said again—"good people over there. NATAS is a good place, good people. I would tell you if they weren't. Heck. If they weren't, I wouldn't be telling you anything."

Dad handed me the paper and I just sat beside him, breathing in the faint paraffin scent of the Ivory he used to wash his body and his thinning brown hair, listening to the steady motor of his breathing. "God!" Had it been this long since Dad and I had been so close? Had it really been three fucking years?

I wanted to find a way to close the gap between our bodies, to physically touch him, but then I felt embarrassed and dropped my eyes to the NATAS paper, burying my feelings between the printed words. I thought about Dad, all those hours he spent on our boxy old Hewlett Packard with the dial-up connection, him searching with a purpose I had not known until now. I wondered how long he had looked, what else he had found, what thoughts he had had all those weeks and months and years—three of them now—since Joey. What thoughts had he had about me? I chewed my bottom lip, focused my mind on the date at the bottom of the print-out. Five months had passed since then. Five months of Dad holding on to this page until this exact moment when I would need it most. Me and Mom and Dad all needed this somehow in all our differing ways. I looked up. Fuck. Dad's soft blue eyes had gone to water and just seeing that made mine spill over.

"I'll go," I said, letting my tears fall as though I could not feel them. "Thanks." We just sat there trying to be strong, holding ourselves back from the broken state that would make my leaving impossible.

"She doesn't know about NATAS," Dad said, looking down. "I thought that was best. Best for now."

I nodded. Dad wasn't hiding the truth from Mom, only choosing when she should find out, as she someday would. Dad placed his work-worn hand on mine and let it rest there, gentle but certain. I closed my eyes and leaned my head against Dad's shoulder, wanting this impossible moment to remain, both dreading the morning and itching to get the hell out of this place where I never had and never would fit. At least NATAS was a place to go to maybe sort out this mess. Better than running away to God knows where.

As the sun refused to rise, I clutched my orange shag pillow and curled up in the back row of a half-empty Greyhound headed to Ohio. Dad's idea. The Greyhound, the hospital, and the pillow. I should have thought of the pillow myself, but I hadn't, and Dad knew what I needed. With me gone, Mom and Dad sure didn't need the pillow at home. Mom had been trying to throw it out for years, but I had loved it since Dad gave it to me for my fourth birthday. With its fraying edges and wild color, my pillow was everything that made my mother recoil, everything her beautiful Cherished Twinklings world was not. Everything I was, and even more so with its strained stitching and lumpy stuffing.

Let's face it. I've always known Cherished Twinklings was bullshit, or if not bullshit, just "off." Either Cherished Twinklings was off or I was off, and I wasn't always sure which was the truth. But I knew—I fucking knew—Mom's collection of big-eyed children was creepy. I knew nobody could laugh and live and give all the time, and I knew the beauty and pain of living were too vivid and too strong to be contained in pastels.

I knew all this long before Mom moved us into Bumbly Bunny RV Park. I knew it because I had lived it, lived it long before my brother died, long before my mom packed up our possessions—Dad and me among them—and moved us as close to the Cherished Twinklings Encouragement Retreat as she could get. Problem was, I knew it, but nobody else did, so maybe they were right and I was wrong. But I couldn't make myself see things differently, and I couldn't tell anybody what I knew to be true because then everybody would brand me as "wrong" or "crazy." I never met anybody from the outside that I could tell, not even the tourists, because they were insiders too. Nobody who wasn't already a believer journeyed to the Encouragement Retreat.

I grew up in New Paris, Pennsylvania, a far cry from the real Paris where people know what it really means to laugh and live, even if giving is bullshit everywhere. But in New Paris, everything was anaesthetized, sanitized. No lifeblood pulsing here, no devouring carnality to either avoid or indulge, nothing alive in this town that was hardly even a town, and even less at Cherished Twinklings Encouragement Retreat. Absent of danger, lust, and hunger, even just staying awake was hard to do. You could sleep your whole goddamn life away, and everybody did. Everybody but me. I was born wide awake and screaming bloody murder. I embarrassed my mother from the start—bright red, splotchy, downright ugly, a "complicated" birth that ripped my mother from hole to hole.

Talk about being born into a nightmare! I would have preferred zombies plodding after me to eat my brains. I would have preferred gore, dismemberment, ice picks through my eyes. But what I got was a nightmare where everybody's always too fucking pleasant, too shit-eatingly courteous, too goddamned programmed to say cute things like, "May your seconds be super sweet," and "Laugh, live, and give every minute of every day." Just too fucking nice.

And then when something happened, when something bad happened, when I was five and ran through a plate glass patio door and got sliced up something awful, Mom grabbed up the figurine of two pastel children patching each other up with flowery handkerchiefs and wrapped pink bath towels around my arms and legs. Even so, I bled all over the living room carpet and through the towels, fascinated and frightened by the sticky sweet blood that streamed through my skin. And maybe Mom was scared, but all I remember her saying as she looked at me in her rear-view mirror was, "You're going to be fine, honey. Love and laughter heal all wounds," and all I remember her doing in the ER after the doctors had stitched up the gashes and bandaged the scrapes was press these cold, hard Cherished Twinklings children to my chest even as she turned her face from me, her flesh and blood daughter. But my pain didn't go away and my blood didn't go away. Just stayed hidden to everybody but me, under the bandages and under my skin, me afraid my skin would burst open again and not knowing how Cherished Twinklings could ever help take that fear away from me when not even my mother could look at, let alone hold, me in her arms the way she wanted me to hold this cold, hard trinket.

How like Cherished Twinklings to not want me to see my own blood, to not want anybody to see blood. "All hail Tina Slaughter, mother of all Cherished Twinklings!" What the fuck does Tina Slaughter know about anything? She's been bleeding life from the world for thirty years, paying

Bora Borans to sweat over molds for her little porcelain people so she can sell them in backlit displays at Nonpareil Bookstores. But that is just what a slaughterer, a butcher does, right? Takes some watery-eyed, hot-breathed, slimy-nosed, grass-eating, muck-shitting cow and scoops out the heart, the lungs, the intestines—all the innards that make a cow a cow—until it becomes nothing but a red-marbled hunk of meat resting on a white Styrofoam tray, wrapped in cellophane for some housewife to buy for $7.82 to take home and cook up with potatoes, carrots, and onions to feed to her family of four. Nothing to her. The meat is nothing but something to fill her family's stomachs, to make them feel pleasantly full until they shit it out and need something more to stuff in their big fat mouths. The meat stopped being a cow a long, long time ago.

At dinner I'd push around the meat with my fork and Mom, who cared as much that we liked how our plate looked as how our food tasted, would stop my hand and say, "Look at what a mess you're making." I'd toss off her hand and smash the meat into the potato, then into the carrot, then into the gravy, liking that if I could not make the cow a cow again, I could at least see that it had a life of its own before my digestive juices struck it down. Mom would fork a perfectly-cooked, petitely-cut morsel into her own mouth and sigh, then frown as though she were thinking that a cow just standing out in the field was no good to us, but look at this fine meal she had prepared for her family from this trimmed roast she had purchased, and look at how little her daughter even cared.

"Eat it," my mom would say then. "It is what it is, now just eat it."

I'd fork the now mashed-together roast into my mouth, chew, and swallow, experiencing a certain satisfaction, but also knowing that while there was nothing wrong with that hunk of meat a slaughterer made from a cow or the roast that my mother made from the meat she had purchased from the slaughterer, it also was not enough for me, never could be enough again, being so far removed from what it once was, and I needed that cow standing in the field every bit as much as I needed the bite of pot roast in my stomach. A hunk of meat can be as hollow as a porcelain figurine.

But the nature of a slaughterer defies thought and sight and feeling. And Tina Slaughter can no more think, see, or feel than the meatcutter whose job it is to turn a cow into digestible parts, disposing of the indigestibles and prettying up what remains. Tina Slaughter may believe she thinks, sees, and feels, may think she promotes her laughing, living, giving mantra, but I don't believe she can. Real living and giving are too hard, too bloody, for almost anybody to do well. I sure as hell suck at it.

"Honey, you feel too deeply."

That accusation branded me from the first time my mother who doubled as my Sunday school teacher spoke it. We were painting pictures for Veteran's Day, honoring the American heroes, but I hadn't even bothered to look at the other kids' easels to see how I should go about it, how what I should have been painting were pictures of flags and gravestones with rainbows bursting through clouds. Instead, I just jumped in, thinking about Uncle Albert, my dad's uncle really, who told me after a Sunday dinner about how he'd lost his right leg to a Vietcong landmine, how losing that leg felt like losing a child. So I had this painting of Uncle Albert in agony, leg blown away at the knee, shreds of flesh and spatters of blood blazing brilliant red against a blood-muddy rice paddy. I wasn't thinking about gore—just reality, the way it must have been and must have felt. When I painted Uncle Albert's face, trying to get just right the feeling that he was losing not just a limb but a child, my fists and my face got all tight and all I wanted was to close my eyes and not see what it was I was seeing, not feel what it was Uncle

Albert felt then and must still feel in the phantom pains of a leg-child that is no longer even there.

So when, in a voice that maybe meant to be kind but sounded only cold and bothered, my mother-teacher said, "Honey, you feel too deeply," I felt ashamed and embarrassed, like I had done something wrong. I tried to change my painting, to even out the ragged leg stump, to make Uncle Albert look like a proud American soldier full of strength and optimism, even to make his blown-off leg look like an angel child flying to heaven. But my picture still didn't measure up, and my mother said it couldn't be displayed in church. I threw my art away and in five minutes painted a cemetery full of uniform white military gravestones. I even wrote Uncle Albert's name on one of the front stones. My mother liked my picture, and it didn't seem to matter that Uncle Albert hadn't died.

Even so, "Honey, you feel too deeply" has always been more true than I wanted, and if anything at Cherished Twinklings is a sin, it's that. I don't know how anybody can keep from feeling deeply when somebody they love dies, but they find ways. That's what Mom did when Joey got struck down by lightning as he took his first swing at the unmoving ball on the T-ball stand. But I didn't. I couldn't. I was twelve. In another week, Joey would have been seven. I slept with Joey's baseball glove under my pillow, taped a circle of Joey's pictures to the wall above my bed with his newspaper obituary and my own handwritten one in the center. Mine gave details beyond him being a "loving son and brother," described the accident as it had really happened, as more than an "act of God with some greater purpose that is not ours to know." I didn't always cry, but I usually did. Sometimes I got angry and punched the walls. Sometimes I tried to tear open my orange shag pillow with my teeth. Sometimes I yelled "Fuck God!" and "Stupid asshole little brother to go die like that!"

"Shit-for-brains Mom making Joey play fucking T-ball!" I screamed once, then turned to see Mom standing in my doorway, her body rigid, her face white, her eyes dropping away from mine to stare at the floor. Mom just stood there saying nothing, doing nothing, not looking at me even as my eyes bored into her. I didn't know what to say or do so I screamed and screamed and screamed without words until it wasn't me anymore in my room, only an unending and indecipherable scream spilling out. When my words found me again and I screamed, "Joey wanted dance lessons, Mom! Not fucking T-ball!" Mom turned from me, shuffled slump-shouldered down the hall. I slammed my door, locked it from the inside, collapsed across my bed empty of screams and tears and feelings, hugged my orange pillow. Hollowed out. That's how I felt.

On the Greyhound, picking at loose threads from the seams of my pillow, I remembered how I had buried my face in its bright orange ugliness. Mom had been so efficient, I had thought back then. So goddamned efficient packing Joey away like she did. I remembered how she hadn't so much as glanced at Joey's six Olan Mills photo portraits as—more machine than mother—she stripped them from the main hallway, placed them face down in bubble-wrap, and wrapped them with precision before packing them away in a huge blue plastic tub. I remembered how Mom had quick-slid Joey's crayon drawings of our family and his imaginary friend Eggy from the front of the refrigerator into a plain manila envelope, licked the seal and flattened the flap. I remembered how she had snatched Joey's AquaFresh tube and bright yellow toothbrush, dropped them into a gaping gallon-size Ziploc, then zippered it shut as though it were some transparent body bag and she were just some worker at the morgue.

I remembered how I had wanted Mom to linger over Joey's worn brown sandals, and how she didn't even turn them over to see where Joey had painstakingly written his name, though it still looked like an uncoordinated scrawl. Mom just absently wiped the dust from the soles onto her pants, then dropped Joey's sandals on top of the other layers in the tub before placing the lid on top, clicking it down like a second casket to be forgotten if not buried.

"If you're trying to get rid of Joey," I had said, watching her from where I sat at the kitchen table not eating the waffles I had made for myself, "get on with it, why don't you?"

Mom said nothing, just bent at the knees, heaved up the tub, and struggled bow-legged to the storage closet at the end of the hall. Like she didn't even care. All that effort packing Joey away, but Mom never could remove him. In Joey's absence, I felt his presence every bit as much as I had when he was alive. Mom had been so goddamned efficient, I thought, and here I was such a fucking mess.

Then there was Dad. Dad who didn't make waves, who never protested a single thing Mom chose to do. But I had seen Joey's kindergarten picture in his wallet—Joey dressed in his fuzzy green kangaroo sweater, "Gotta keep bouncin'!" stitched below in thick purple yarn. I knew that every time Dad opened his wallet, every time he looked at Joey's picture (and Dad always looked at it, never glanced), he remembered Joey putting on that sweater for the first time on Christmas morning and bouncing around the living room like a kangaroo in the Australian outback, unbounded and free. That's what I would have remembered had I been Dad.

But Mom? Remember particulars about Joey? God, no. She never talked about Joey's death or even his life before his death. Never said, "Joey would have loved this spaghetti," or "Remember that time Joey buried all his dinosaurs in the backyard?" or even, "You know, I just really miss Joey today." Instead, she could only talk about Joey as an angel with newly granted wings wearing a snow-white child's robe. She could only talk about how God had needed Joey to play on the heavenly T-ball team. Jesus fucking Christ! Joey didn't even like fucking T-ball!

Mom never talked about Joey as Joey, like he'd been a real person, her son, like his absence in the house made a difference. Mom had always had her Cherished Twinklings, always admired them as trophies, but after Joey died she loved them. She kissed them, held them against her cheek, dusted them, arranged them in story sequences with the little "Laughinglivinggiving.com" girl emailing the not-so-Indian-looking chief with pastel-feathered headdress in "Chief God Gives Us All," weird shit like that. Once I caught her kneeling low before her display, the tips of her shoulder-length hair kissing the floor. Mom keeps her Cherished Twinklings safe behind glass, keeps them good and safe. They couldn't even be broken, not like Joey. But two months after Joey's death, not even Mom's private Cherished Twinklings collection was enough, so she began spending every waking moment in the Cherished Twinklings Chapel petitioning Tina Slaughter to paint Joey into Hosanna Circle. She must have thought if she could just get Joey put up on that wall, could just look at him transfigured into pastels and big eyes, then she could celebrate his passing into eternal life and never again have to picture his limp mud-streaked body fallen over home base. This was her opportunity to have Joey turned into an angel baby.

Do I blame Mom? I don't know. Maybe. Or maybe I blame Tina Slaughter because without Tina Slaughter there would be no Cherished Twinklings. But maybe I can't even blame Tina Slaughter because maybe Cherished Twinklings is just what you have to bury yourself in when you're the sort of craftsman who works in pastels and big eyes and some idiot too drunk to drive straight smashes into your teenage daughter on the highway. Maybe big eyes and pastels are how Tina Slaughter deals with her traumas, but if that's the case, wouldn't she have had to deal first with blood and shattered glass? But with a name like hers, what would you expect? How can I see her as anything more than a slaughterhouse zombie walking away from a spoiled mess she can't make anything out of, can't make whole again, can't hold or hug or even be gentle with, not with all those inside parts on the outside, that bloody smashy mess that's fleshandglass, bloodandgravel, bonesandmetal. There's nothing any skilled cow processor could have made from that.

On the Greyhound bus, picking my pillow's loose threads, I recalled the stuffed Isabel angel doll Mom had given me after Joey died. She thought maybe I'd finally love Cherished Twinklings, but what was I supposed to do with this doll with blonde hair as wispy and wild as cotton candy? What did she think I would make of this pretty girl doll dressed in a glitter-strewn jumper over a pink shirt, and wings protruding from her shoulder blades? Did she think this doll with its big black eyes staring at me from behind enormous diamond-studded glasses could replace Joey? And why the fuck were Isabel's bow and arrow for all tucked under her left wing? Was Isabel up in heaven shooting down angel birds? She wasn't Joey. Hell, she wasn't even Isabel.

I set my pillow next to me on the seat and stared out the window, watched cars and trucks pass each other on the highway but never connect. I thought about Joey getting struck by lightning, and I imagined the Isabel doll getting struck by a car and me asking Tina Slaughter: Did you see Isabel's body? Did you see her sixteen-year-old body broken and bloodied? Did you see it and know she was lost to you forever? Can you see it now when you think back to that day she died? No? Right! Because she's only a fucking DOLL! I really need to know if this is how you see us. Kids have real fucking bodies, and it hurts like hell to bleed.

Deal with it. Then let go. Say that shit is shit, that life sucks sometimes, that nothing you do can bring back the one you loved, that believing your loved one is in heaven watching over you is just fucking not enough to keep you going from day to day.

On the third anniversary of Joey's death, watching my mother prostrate herself before the chapel's Hosanna Circle for yet another day, her Cherished Twinklings Joey now looking down on her from a cloud, I knew I had to break Mom's "Home Run" figurine. Well, maybe not so much break it as change it to how Joey had really been, only I never got to finish the job.

My brother Joey was scrawny as a malnourished cat with standard light brown hair that stood up in patches like a permanent case of bed head. Joey's nose was perfect except for a cat-scratch scar that gleamed white in summer while the sun reddened the rest of him, and he had a smile that melted me even though his lips were often chapped and flaking. Joey looked like the sort of kid who should have worn wire-rimmed glasses and gleaming silver braces, but his sight was clear and his teeth were straight.

When Mom should have let out a batshit crazy scream, she didn't, just stood with one foot on the kitchen linoleum, the other still frozen on the front porch, screen door pushing against her backside. Her eyes became puddles and I saw the sight that had caused her eyes to fill—Home Run Joey spread out in pieces across the kitchen table and me, startled, staring back at her with a tube of Krazy Glue in one hand and Home Run Joey's head in the other. Mom was not supposed to see this. Mom was not supposed to see this at all, but what string of words could I invent to explain how the picture in her head was all wrong? And how could I make her see Joey again as he really had been? She stepped into the kitchen and the screen door squeezed closed behind her. Without speaking, Mom unclasped her purse and pulled out a wad of Kleenex, then wrapped each of the pieces of her cherished boy before nesting them in an empty shoebox.

I knew without her saying so that she planned to ship the dismembered Home Run Joey to Tina Slaughter at her Bora Bora resort for repairs.

"Do you really hate me this much?" Mom said, her eyes filling again with tears even while her hands never strayed from her task. And for a twinkling, for one truly cherished twinkling, I was struck by my need to tell Mom that I loved her, that I hated only her love for washed out big-eyed children that kept her from really loving Dad and me instead of just drifting alongside us.

Why don't you love us? I wanted to say. *You're all filled up with loving them and here I sit, empty.* I wanted—I needed—to say all this, but only one word slipped through my lips.

"Fuck."

As I watched the sun rise high through my Greyhound window, I tried to fight off sleep. See, I have these nightmares, only they're not so much nightmares as memories that strike while I sleep because I've gotten good at blocking them when I'm awake. After Mom traded in our house for an RV and parked us permanently at Bumbly Bunny, she wouldn't go only half-way on anything having to do with Cherished Twinklings. Since she insisted and Dad was out of work anyway, Dad took a job managing the lights for the Gusher of Cherubs show. Dad never talked about the show, never talked about his job, and all Mom could ever say about it was how "inspirational" it all was, what fantastic "evangelism" took place, how just watching the show brought her "comfort and fulfillment." I'd roll my eyes and bite my tongue, guessing that like everything else I'd seen at Cherished Twinklings, Gusher of Cherubs was just a bunch of bull, but I still wanted to see what Dad saw day in and day out, what he endured because of Mom's dysfunction. I didn't know what Dad thought about it all—he never did say—and to him I think a job was just a job, that he could just as well have been renting out porn at Satin Touch or flipping burgers at McDonald's, but I went to work with him once anyway.

My dreams always begin with me sitting in the auditorium at some distance from the true-believer audience that takes up less than a quarter of the available seats. I'm watching the audience as much as I'm watching this dwarf, no taller than four feet two inches and dressed in a plain black tuxedo, stand on stage and sing about "somebody bigger than you and me," that somebody being God—to a pre-recorded track. The song ends and Jolly the Jester jumps out in full Cherished Twinklings garb to join the dwarf who proclaims, "And now, folks, clap your hands and stomp your feet as we welcome Jolly the Jester in his singing debut of Albert E. Brumley's wonderful gospel classic, 'This World is Not My Home.'"

The audience of old people wearing clothes as pastel as the big-headed Cherished Twinklings mascot claps, not even fucking noticing that they are just sitting in this big ass shed, the concrete Gusher of Cherubs looming before them like hungry gravestones. My hands sweat and my head pounds, but when I try to stand, my legs buckle and I collapse. My body fuses to the chair. Stuck.

Jolly the Jester exits with a wave and the dwarf says, "I'd like to take a moment to praise Jesus for the military members who are in our audience tonight. Why don't you veterans stand up so we can see you? Let us give you a hand for protecting and serving our country, from the days of fighting against Hitler in Germany to the days of fighting under the fine God-fearing leadership of President George W. Bush."

So then these veterans—at least a dozen of them—stand, and all eyes and applause turn to them while the gusher turns on, splurting water over half-naked concrete cherubs lit up in purple lights while jets of water shoot for the ceiling. I watch the fountain as the dwarf sings "God Bless the U.S.A."

I still can't stand, so instead I scream, "Wake up!" both to my sleeping self and to the audience. "Wake the fuck up! Can't you see how freaky this is? You're drugged, all of you! This isn't joyful! This isn't cherished! This is a freak show!"

But nobody turns to me because nobody hears me because my mouth isn't moving even though my mind is. I stare at the gusher that doesn't even look graceful, just cluttered with too many delirious cherubs playing instruments and riding fish. Harp music plays like I'm in some deranged heaven, but it's so hot in here, so humid. My head throbs. I'd sell my soul for an Excedrin. The greatest horror of this place is that the rest of the audience with their quietly orgasmic ahs and their tear-streaked cheeks finds this oversized shed with its gusher of water-spewing concrete cherubs fucking inspiring. I want to rip through these walls but I can't even move because just then, these three clean-cut Christian types walk up and stand where the dwarf had stood, and begin singing a southern gospel song about Moses striking a stone to get water, Jonah falling into the depths of the sea only to be swallowed by a great fish, and Jesus walking on water.

The pounding in my head gives way to cruel Novocain injected straight into my brain. I give myself over just to get through this nightmare that I know cannot possibly last forever because it hasn't done so yet. On the edges of my mind, the singers invite the audience to clap along, and my eyes seek out the row of Amish who choose not to. I want to get inside their heads to know what these Amish with their black hats and woven head coverings think of this spectacle, but then the show begins for real. The shed darkens and for a moment all I can see is the glowing red "Exit" by the door. A voice rolls out numbers—hours of construction, number of cherubs, gallons of water—until the numbers give way to the "wonderful worshipful orchestration inspired by Tina Slaughter's laughing, living, giving wisdom," music full of harps and strings.

Above the fountain, a screen descends and a video begins and I watch the beginning of the world—darkness turns to light, water spills forth in tsunami-style waves, fish swim, lamb and lion lie down together, a silhouetted naked man and woman watch a pastel sunset. And then there's the Earth—my planet—hanging in the blackness of space like something to be plucked and worn, "like a jewel in God's necklace," booms the voice. But then it all goes bad, as I know it will. Eve can't leave the fucking apple alone so death and pain enter the world, but…wait…who's that entering the picture at the edge of the horizon on a white stallion like this is some fucking western? *Jesus Christ!* It's Jesus Christ, so pretty with his stunning blue eyes and glossy auburn hair flowing down around his shoulders.

The music swells as Jesus redeems the Earth, but there's not so much as a fucking trickle of Christ's blood, and what kind of redemption can come without furious pain and suffering? I stop watching the video and watch instead the gushers now lit with red and yellow and purple lights that jump nearly to the roof. Somewhere between the movie screen and the statues in the fountain that can't do anything except get fucking wet, water moves, going nowhere, just cycling through the same show time and time again.

And then from beyond the far reaches of the Gusher of Cherubs, I hear the Greyhound toilet flush. My salvation! I race for the flickering red "Exit" sign, but I cannot leave this nightmare before I see my mother sitting alone yet also in the center of this true believer audience, wiping tears—real, genuine tears—from her eyes. As much as I want to deny the tears of a woman I've never seen cry—not over Joey, not over me, not over Dad and the whole fucked-up mess of us—I cannot. Somehow this Gusher of Cherubs freak show moves my mother, and I feel bitter.

I cried then for myself, for desiring what I most despised. What the fuck was wrong with me? Here I was on this bus to a place where I would supposedly get help (a hospital? a home?), be able to work through the hell of Cherished Twinklings, yet I also wished I could be happy in the way Mom was happy. No, not happy. Drugged with sentiment. But she didn't know any of this the way that I did, so she could exist (how is it I can't bring myself to say "live"?) in her Cherished Twinklings fantasy and survive, maybe even thrive. But I couldn't, and if I tried I'd just be fooling myself. Maybe I could never cry my mother's tears over Gusher of Cherubs, could never see the world through her eyes, but did I have to be so cynical and jaded and fucking hateful? Sometimes being right about things just makes me sad.

But all that was weeks ago. Eight weeks full of deprogramming, sorting out, maybe even healing. What I have found here in Florida, Ohio, here in this NATAS hospital, is that I'm not the only one stuck in some weird fucked-up state. I may be the only one whose little brother got struck down by lightning at his first T-ball game and whose mother lives and breathes Cherished Twinklings, but I'm not the only one who has lost someone, not the only one who feels out of place, not the only one who's angry or disillusioned about the influence of some tourist attraction on their life. Not everyone here is like this, though. There is one who, like Mom, continues to believe that where he comes from is best, that he is one of the few fortunates who knows how things really should be in this world. That's how it is with Ezekiel. And, fuck, sometimes I just don't know.

Look, I know I can be outspoken. I know I've got a big mouth. When I look in the mirror, the first thing I see is my mouth, my big fat mouth that everybody hears. But when I look at my mouth, it's closed, unspeaking, and I wonder what it's like to see it open and yelling. I'm sure Ezekiel could tell me but I don't think I'd want to hear it from him, to hear anything more from him than I already have.

Ezekiel and I, we're both in the Survivors Without Islands group that meets Thursday mornings at ten. It's meant to be a place to go just to talk and be heard, to sort things out, to feel less alone in our fucked up states. Dave, the counselor, keeps things even-keeled, makes sure everybody who wants to talk gets to talk, heads off problems before they arise, typical counselor shit. This isn't usually a problem since most everybody knows they're fucked-up in some way or another, and if they don't know it when they arrive, they figure it out real fast. Most everybody except Ezekiel, that is, who has been here a record seven months and still hasn't figured out a single fucking thing. Ezekiel's an intervention case, rescued from the Old Testament exhibit of this fucking bizarre Living Bible Museum in Mansfield, Ohio, which always makes me think of Charles Manson. Ezekiel refuses to accept that he's here for any reason other than as a martyr sent by God to this wicked place to convert all us heathen since we're so obviously going straight to Hell. It's one thing to be fucked-up and know it, but it's another to be fucked up and believe you're the only sane—or in Ezekiel's case, righteous—person among a bunch of crazy sinners racing each other down the wide highway to hell.

Ezekiel's always causing trouble in Survivors Without Islands because he never talks about himself, only about his buddy God. And if he's talking about his buddy God, you can bet he will be aiming his talk at somebody in the group who is sinning against God in some horrible way as we all are except, of course, Ezekiel. So last week, this new guy Nikos came into group. And before Nikos started talking, things were going really well—Ezekiel wasn't saying much, probably reciting the Ten Commandments in his head and checking off his list every commandment he'd kept. Wes had been talking about his collection of jackalopes back at Wall Drug, how he missed them, wished they were here, how he knew he didn't really need his jackalopes to be happy, but still desired to have them near. Wes had talked about this in every Survivors session since he arrived five weeks ago, and I listen because he needs to talk this out, but I didn't focus as well as I did at first, mostly because Wes is only talking and never working towards recovery, keeping jackalopes hidden away in his closet which everybody except the staff knows about.

But then from the seat next to mine, Nikos, who's this round kid from Spongearama with permanently tanned Florida skin (and I mean fucking *Florida* Florida, not Florida, Ohio) started sharing, just letting his story pour out to anybody who would listen. So I started to listen, really listen, because all of us Survivors except Ezekiel have been in that place of needing somebody to listen just as much as we needed to talk. Nikos could have been talking about anything and I would have listened, almost all of us would have, but he just so happened to be talking about love, about falling into it, about missing his "beloved" who was now so many states away. Now nobody would be so fucking stupid as to call me a softy, but I can be moved by something genuine, something real, and Nikos was nothing if not real.

When Nikos started to cry, I reached for his hand and held it, and he returned a slight pressure as if to keep himself going. I could have said then that I knew what it felt like to be so far away from a beloved, could have spoken of losing Joey and all the weirdness of Cherished Twinklings that I had been working through, but even though his story sparked fragments of my own, over two months' time I had learned that sometimes it is best to just shut the fuck up and listen to somebody else's story rather than throw out my own again. This being one of those times, I just held Nikos' hand as he went on talking about his beloved—going diving for sponges, accidentally kissing for the first time underwater through his diving mask, speaking at last of their shared attraction over a plate of spinach pie at Hella's. It took Nikos a long time to let slip his beloved's name was Pete, but once he did, his grip on my hand tightened and I didn't even have to look across the circle to feel that Ezekiel had stopped tallying his obedience to God and was making ready to stand judgment on poor Nikos.

Ezekiel may be a too thin, too pale, too pasty kid who wheezes when he breathes and has the phlegmy smell of an eight-year-old on his way to Vacation Bible School who is allergic to everything, but, man, can he turn red with rage! Righteous rage, mind you—that's what he'd call it—but righteous or not, it's scary. The rest of us Survivors knew what was coming—we'd all been attacked, some of us repeatedly—but Nikos, he was something entirely new for Ezekiel to condemn, and I could have predicted what Ezekiel was going to say before he ever said it, even as the catch phrases started spilling out.

Sin is sin.
Marriage = 1 Man +1 Woman.
God created Adam and Eve, not Adam and Steve.
Remember Sodom and Gomorrah.

And then—the real fucking clincher of clinchers—"I stand on the Holy Word of God, and as it is written in Leviticus 20:13, 'If a man also lie with mankind, as he lieth with a woman, both of them have committed an abomination: they shall surely be put to death. Their blood shall be upon them.'"

We all watched, bodies tense, breathing shallow. Nikos' hand went slack in mine as his body sagged and his color drained. Nikos wasn't believing this, was he? Wasn't really taking Ezekiel fucking seriously, right? But he was. Nikos fucking was, and I hated then about Ezekiel what I have always hated about my mother and hate myself for hating—how right and certain they were, how they both made God so fucking small, so easy to use.

Sitting in Survivors, I struggled to stay afloat as the undertow slammed me back to being seven years old. I'd come home from school to find Dad and Joey in the kitchen while Mom was away at a Cherished Twinklings collectors convention, her display case left uncharacteristically unlocked. Fucking unlocked! With Dad boiling macaroni and Joey eating Cheerios in his high chair, I managed to slide open the glass doors, pick up the little "My Love for You Has No Measure" girl with her arms outstretched, and feel in my fingers her coolness, her not-quite-smooth body, a texture like silk sandpaper. With the tips of my fingers, I traced her body from her top-knot of hair down her blue jumper and around the jumper's pink heart, all the way to her pure white shoes. I turned her upside down, exposing at her base the Cherished Twinklings logo and two small holes on either side that opened to a hollow cavern I knew was at her center. For reasons my second-grade self could feel but not explain, disappointment washed over me when I placed my pinky tips in the holes but could push them in no further.

I returned "My Love for You Has No Measure" to her center shelf, then moved to pick up the other figures—only twenty-six of them at that time—from "Mom, You Flower with Love and Compassion" to the honeybee "Beelieve!" girl, to the flag-waving "God Loves America" boy with his dog. I know now that I had desperately needed to fill those hollow figurines, fill them up with my fingers, stuff them for good with cotton, tape shut the holes, and return the figures to their shelves under Mom's hand-calligraphied "Laughing, Living, Giving" banner. Then I imagined Ezekiel's fucking wax heroes, Jonah and Lot and all the rest still hollow in the center, and above them a banner that read "Judging, Damning, Burning." To me, it was all the fuck the same. Would Ezekiel fawn over my mother's Cherished Twinklings collection and cry at her Gusher of Cherubs?

Would my mother fill with rage against the burning Sodomites at Ezekiel's beloved Living Bible Museum?

The churning in my stomach told me yes.

This whole time, Ezekiel hadn't stopped shouting, shaking, and pointing like some spastic fevered preacher, Nikos the center of his wrath. The acid in my stomach rose to fill my mouth with words, but before I could spit them out, I was on my feet, walking the three long steps across the deck of this storm-tossed ship and feeling my open palm strike Ezekiel's fish-damp face. Ezekiel turned to look at me with a "get-thee-behind-me-Satan" glare before resuming his mission. When Dave asked Ezekiel if he had even heard what Nikos had said, Ezekiel proclaimed, "Oh, I heard, all right. Nikos said he flagrantly disregarded God's infallible Law against homosexuality and loved another man, an abomination in God's sight."

"God!" I seethed, my words breaking free in a full force gale, "You are the fucking asshole of assholes!"

"Blasphemy of the Holy Triune God will be held against you," Ezekiel declared, turning from Nikos to me, his raised fists clenched so tight his knuckles showed white and blade-like beneath his fiery red skin. "And you, Becky, are breaking one of the Big Ten: 'Thou shalt not use the name of the Lord thy God in vain.'" I looked away, and the storm ended.

While the rest of us tried to patch up the splintered mess that had been Nikos, Dave escorted Ezekiel to the Thinking Room to cool down as Ezekiel quoted Scripture, this time to himself and not to us. "Ephesians chapter six, verse eleven," Ezekiel began. "Put on the full armor of God so that you can stand up against the devil's schemes."

Since Survivors, I'd done what I could to avoid or at least ignore Ezekiel, an easy enough task. Sure, he sits at the edges of everybody's conversations, euchre games, and meals, but I always know I could be rid of him with a sharp nudge from my elbow, that it would be easy enough to make him crumple and fall away. When Ezekiel's not preaching, he's annoying in a chapped lips kind of way—unattractive but no great pain so long as he doesn't open his mouth.

Today we'd all gone in a big NATAS van for on an out-and-about-afternoon of pizza and fresh air at the Gessner Family Park—this dinky run-down park along the Maumee River, not far from the Center but far enough to feel a measure of independence which I appreciated. As usual, Ezekiel had started witnessing, annoying Nikos with his "Good Person Test," fucking rigged for everybody to fail and ultimately see their need for God. I'd gotten rid of Ezekiel by telling him to go off and witness to this unsuspecting stranger with a mutt for a dog. I wouldn't normally wish Ezekiel on anybody, but this guy with a pierced ear, open-toed sandals, and "Visualize Whirled Peas" t-shirt looked secure enough in himself to handle and maybe even be amused by Ezekiel, and for an hour and a half, he must have been because Ezekiel didn't rejoin us until we were all piling back into the NATAS van, Ezekiel sitting in the backseat, quiet and pale in a way he usually wasn't after a fervent bout of witnessing.

Back in the dayroom, the counselors and staff had put together a table with white-frosted chocolate cupcakes and a stainless steel tub filled with ice and pop in celebration of Wes' fifteenth birthday. After we all sang "Happy Birthday" and Wes had blown out the single candle on his cupcake, I stood there, weighing my options. The cupcake was a no-brainer—they were all the same—but the pop was a different matter, even though there were only two choices: Sprite or caffeine-free Coke. It should be an easy fucking decision, right? Nothing to it, so what was my problem? But what I wanted was Coke—*real* Coke—but they never had real Coke at the Center, only that caffeine-free stuff. So that was my choice. Sprite or caffeine-free Coke, both sitting in a stainless steel tub surrounded by ice, and I knew it wasn't a flavor I craved but a charge, a jolt, and Sprite not only had no charge, no caffeine, it also had no fucking color like it was pretending to be water but wasn't.

Maybe with caffeine-free Coke I could fake it, pretend I was drinking the real thing, but I knew too fucking well that pretending never worked for me and that, at least where pop was concerned, the Center wasn't so different from home; Mom never bought the real thing either, though she did have a "Jesus. He's the real thing" t-shirt for awhile, bought from the Cherished Twinklings gift shop. But I never knew what real Coke was meant not just to taste like but also to feel like until eight weeks ago when I drank my first can on the Greyhound bound for NATAS. So I stood at the corner of the table, ready to give up and walk away from the whole fucking thing when I saw a hand reaching out from a polyester-blend blue plaid sleeve, and I didn't have to look down to the hand or up the arm to know whose it was.

You're breaking the third commandment, Becky. Blasphemy of the Lord your God will be held against you.

I could have been angry back in Survivors, but what would have been the point? Instead I had shrugged it off as proof of the impossibility of communicating with somebody who doesn't listen, something I'd gotten used to doing with Ezekiel. Still, when Ezekiel wasn't actively pissing me off, I sometimes wished I could get through to him in the same way I often wished I could get through to Mom. I wanted to say, "I don't hate you. I just think maybe you'd get out of here sooner if you could open up a little."

As Ezekiel walked around the table to the other side of the pop tub, I didn't look up. I let my eyes follow his wrist with its tightly-buttoned cuff, then watched as his wrist lifted and plunged into the cooler, then stayed there for too many seconds as though trying to prove endurance. *What the hell?* I thought, but I'm glad I didn't say anything because from below the ice, all the ice, buried deep beneath the Sprite and caffeine-free Coke, the hand pulled out a real Coke, the fucking good stuff! Ezekiel's sleeve was wet from his wrist halfway to his elbow, the blue plaid darker, heavier, clinging to his skin like cellophane clings to a supermarket steak. Ezekiel's hand was always so fucking cold and clammy, yet here it was, holding this Coke, holding it out to me. I took it and let my eyes travel the length of his blue plaid arm until the fabric ended at his tightly-buttoned collar.

"Fuck!" I said. Ezekiel stiffened. I stared at the red and white can. "How did you... I mean, did you know that Coke was fucking in there?" I asked.

His shoulders rose slightly against the taut fabric, then fell. I lifted my eyes to meet Ezekiel's before he dropped his eyes again, and for a moment I noticed something I'd never noticed before, never having thought to look at Ezekiel's eyes which looked like Joey's, hazel with specks of green. Ezekiel was human—so human—and he had done me this small kindness when he didn't have to. I reached out my hand to take the Coke and saw that we both wore the same watch—digital, blue, sporty, waterproof. On me, I always thought my watch looked cool, but on Ezekiel, well, maybe before today I wouldn't have thought so.

"We're not that different," I said, feeling that this could be the moment we moved past that gap between us, between Ezekiel and the whole fucking rest of the world beyond the Living Bible Museum. "I mean, we see things differently, a lot differently, but shit... sorry, but shoot... we both come from religious tourist traps." Ezekiel bristled. I backtracked.

"OK. You don't see it that way, but we're not all that different. Or maybe what I mean is that maybe in some other life we might have ended up as friends." I watched Ezekiel for a response that would let me continue, but I couldn't read him, and not being able to read Ezekiel was odd. He didn't exactly relax but he also didn't look any more uptight, his eyes still lowered, his arms just hanging at his sides. I thought of a story I could share, something I thought would be familiar to him, that maybe he could understand, the first planks of a bridge across the chasm that separated us.

"When I was eight," I said, trying to catch his eyes and bring them up to my own, "Tina Slaughter, you know, the lady that started Cherished Twinklings, came to speak at my church one Sunday night. And as she talked about growing up poor yet still discovering God's love, the beauty of innocence, and the whole laughing, living, giving thing, the whole congregation got to crying, and when I heard this uniform sniffling, I stopped picking the scab on my elbow and listened just long enough to feel like I was the only one in the whole church, maybe even the whole world, that didn't have whatever it was that they had. See, I was more afraid in that moment to be the only one who maybe had it right, so I went forward and prayed to laugh, live, and give more, then went home and threw away all the crayons in my Crayola 64 box that weren't pastels and drew my first and only angel baby."

Ezekiel didn't get it. I could tell he didn't get it by the way. Just the way he looked at me—blankly, no spark of recognition, looking only at the can of Coke still in my hand. I hadn't opened it. I suddenly didn't know if I could. His shirt sleeve was still wet and I could see prickled goosebumps on his wrist from the cold. We looked down then, both of us, embarrassed, me feeling awkward in the way I had during sixth grade gym class when everybody knew before I did that my very first period had started, and him feeling awkward because he had been the first person to see.

Fuck. What was I thinking? Ezekiel was more like my mother than like me. Had I really forgotten that?

I could only have ever been like Ezekiel if I had slid easy out of my mother, her clone with an innate disgust of colors except pastels. Even when I was eight, I knew better, knew I had abandoned my bold crayons by force of will, not because I wanted to. I could not color with pink, lavender, and baby blue. When Dad bought me a new Crayola 64 box, Mom was disappointed; she had liked my one drawing of an angel baby on a cloud, kept it framed in fake gold on her dresser next to her bed. Mom loves a lie, but I'm the one who invented the lie. Maybe she would have loved me if I could be the real me. Then again, maybe not. Besides, I had to draw what I saw, what I fucking felt, no matter how deeply I felt it. It was not in me to do otherwise because even if nobody else ever knew, I always would. Life would have been easier had I been born caffeine-free, but I hadn't been and I couldn't fucking fake that to myself.

Out of planks. Halfway across the bridge I was building to Ezekiel and I had run out of planks while he was left standing on his cliff unable to trust the stack of wood beside him, waiting to be used. I stopped my story. I didn't tell Ezekiel I hadn't lasted long as a convert, that I never had fit Cherished Twinklings the way he still fit the Living Bible Museum. Sure, we both came from religious traps, but for me, Cherished Twinklings always had been a trap while for Ezekiel, the Living Bible Museum had always been his home. We both knew that. He couldn't find a way to get past that and neither could I. And maybe that was ok. Maybe sometimes things just had to be okay that way, with me and Ezekiel, sure, but also with me and Mom. Sometimes life just is what it is and has to be what it is until with any luck it doesn't have to be that way any longer.

Ezekiel wasn't angry. I would have preferred Ezekiel be angry with me, to scream that I was wrong and a blasphemer, to condemn me to Hell. But he didn't, and I didn't know—couldn't know—why.

Ezekiel removed his glasses and wiped them on his shirt. "I'm sorry," he said, putting his glasses back on. "I, we, can't talk. I mean, you confuse me, and I've, well, I've had enough confusing conversations for one day. I know confusion is of the devil but. . ." He shook his head like he was trying to unsettle some doubt that had already begun to take root but didn't know how. "I'll pray for you," Ezekiel said, looking at me but differently than when he usually said that, like he wasn't looking down on me but looking sideways, even upwards a little. Did he want me to say thanks? To tell him I'd pray for him too?

I watched Ezekiel walk down the hall away from me—shoulders rounded, head bent, arm wet and hanging at his side. Ezekiel hadn't taken a can of pop or a cupcake for himself, just walked down the hallway away from the birthday party and from all of us.

"Fuck," I said under my breath.

And the space after the word filled with a familiar deep sadness.

All filled up with such wanting.

I'd used all my planks and stood midway across the chasm on the last solid board, a vicious drop below me and the wind hungry for something I couldn't give. "You confuse me," Ezekiel had said, and he said it like somebody who'd been unsteadied. Yeah, I got that. I knew Ezekiel wasn't able to trust the story he'd been given to tell, wasn't able to trust his own planks to be strong enough to hold him or, even scarier, that he couldn't trust what it might mean to step foot onto the planks I had laid down. I understood that. Still, I wanted, fucking *wanted* him to turn back around, pick up one plank and bolt it to the chain that was waiting to connect us to each other. Maybe if he could just spill out his story we could close that gap between us.

Such wanting, and all filled up with it.

But wanting does not make things so. It if did, Mom would not have kicked half her planks into the chasm when Joey died. I had to admit, my own intensity had burned up some of the planks I had been given for bridge-building.

Such wanting.

Now I was angry because I couldn't fix what would always be broken. I plunged the can of Coke down in the cooler, soaking my sleeve up to my elbow, holding my arm below the ice long after I'd let go of the can. Like the plate glass door that had sliced me open when I was five, the cold cut my nerves even as my arm grew numb. Who the fuck cared who was right about Cherished Twinklings or God or Joey or the Living Bible Museum. Who the fuck cared about any of that head stuff when all that mattered was the deep ache, want, and hollowness at the center of me that yearned to be filled. How could we ever have each other? Know each other? Love each other? Not even Dad and me, sitting side by side had been able to bring ourselves close enough to touch, afraid we'd burst into flames.

I pulled my arm out and looked at it, a shade of purple-blue I could see but couldn't feel. Not permanent. I knew there'd be no damage; my arm would dry and warm up and go back to being a normal part of my body, not like a limb that had been severed. Still, I wondered about me and Mom and Ezekiel and Dad and Nikos from Spongearama and Wes from Wall Drug with his jackalope fixation. We had to fucking get the words out and begin, that's all. We just had to start. Stories were everything—I knew that, and felt a sudden rush of sadness for all the stories people were unable to tell.

Fuck.

Around me everybody was eating cupcakes and drinking pop. I picked up a Sprite that showed itself above the surface of the water, thinking maybe I should drink something that blended in with everybody else, thinking maybe it would be easier to drink from a can that didn't stand out. But I wanted Coke, not Sprite. The others could drink what they liked—drink what worked for them—but I needed the real thing. I put down the Sprite, pulled the Coke up from the bottom of the cooler. I wiped the ice and water from the top of the can and rubbed my thumb against the top tab. I liked the feel of sharp and jagged metal against my skin before I pulled back the tab to drink.

Afterword by the Editor

Becky Appleton's account of the Cherished Twinklings Encouragement Retreat takes place at the height of glory. In June 2008, Cherished Twinklings cited a reduction in senior citizen bus tours as the primary reason for park closings, and no longer features the Gusher of Cherubs or Bumbly Bunny RV Park central to Becky's story. Only the chapel and main visitor's center with gift shop remain open as public attractions.

Cherished Twinklings figurines continue to be sold around the world.

© Mary Jane Pories

Taxidermy Tabernacle

> *"Just as God's love and concern was demonstrated in the miraculous ways in which He delivered His people, so was His wrath and judgment executed by the destruction of the corrupt and disobedient."*
>
> —*Living Bible Museum, Mansfield, Ohio*

Editor's note: NATAS intervention. A painful but necessary first step for separating acute Tourist Attraction Trauma cases from their attractions. Following separation, these cases are taken for treatment at the NATAS Hospital for Research and Recovery in Florida, Ohio. Some are released after a few days, some after weeks or months. The young man whose story you are about to read has, as of this writing, been a patient in the Youth Resources Center for a record eleven months, extending, to date, four months past the time of this account.

* * *

This morning I woke up knowing the day was Thursday. I knew it was the day I had to roll the trash bins to the curb, to go to Survivors Without Islands for brainwashing (they call it "detoxing," as if I've ever been high on anything besides the Holy Spirit), the day to wade through to get to Friday which would then lead to Saturday and a break from all the day-to-day at this "Hospital for Research and Recovery." That name still gets me. I woke up knowing the day was Thursday in the way that I know my name is Ezekiel William White, but then I stepped outside into the chilly, still-dark, mid-April morning, and there stood the trash bins. Empty and waiting for Janitor John to wheel them back inside the fenced enclosure behind the back kitchen door.

My first thought was that Becky had slipped up and wheeled out the trash bins two weeks in a row, when this was the week for me to show my service to the Lord through this task meant to humble me, then thought that the trash men must have come extra early this morning, and that Becky just happened to be out when the trash men came so wheeled the bins back in, not caring that she's robbed me of my opportunity to be a witness through my good and selfless works.

My second thought was that the National Association of Tourist Attraction Survivors hadn't thrown anything away in a week, but while NATAS recycles like crazy (pointless, since Jesus is coming back so soon that it won't matter, and that what really matters—their eternal souls—aren't getting the attention they deserve) there's just no help for some things but to be thrown away.

My third thought was that it wasn't Thursday at all. And when I wondered whether it could have been Wednesday, the empty trash bins told me no. And when I realized it had to be Friday, I felt so confused, so cheated. A whole day. How could I have missed a whole day? Did I go through Wednesday thinking it had been Thursday? Would tomorrow still be Saturday or a second Friday? Maybe God took Thursday away just to humble me, to remind me that He (not NATAS) is in control. God can do that, you know. God can mess with time and space, will and purpose, reality and everything else. God can't be stopped if He wants to do something, not by me or you or all the counselors and psychiatrists in this evil place.

Seven months I've been held here against my will. My so-called "parents" are at fault. My "parents" who, seven and a half months ago, showed up out of nowhere claiming my real name was Patrick Reilly and that I had been stolen away from them fourteen years ago when I was only two years old. But I don't believe them, and I don't call them "Mom and Dad" as they would like, just Lucy and Earl. A week after finding me, with DNA "evidence" (and I know how unreliable DNA is, given that evolutionists manipulate it to promote wrong thinking) of their parentage, Lucy and Earl got the law on their side. They brought in NATAS for what they call "intervention," but what I know is kidnapping, meant to "save" me from the only home I've ever known—the only home I ever care to know.

By the grace of God and the Diamond Hill Cathedral of Mansfield, Ohio, Nan and Bill—my true God-given parents—raised me faithfully in the Word, the Living Word of God and of the Living Bible Museum. The sudden appearance of Lucy and Earl (my would-be parents who are not even saved by the blood of Jesus) changes nothing. In fact, when Nan and Bill told me the true story of how God had delivered me into their loving arms, I rejoiced. Prior to my coming to them, they had—for two years—been praying for a child but Nan's womb had been unable to bear fruit.

Then one day while they were vacationing and soulwinning for Christ on Florida's beaches, I toddled over to them, stretched up my arms, and said "'ome! 'ome!" giving them the only sign they needed that I was a gift delivered by God to be taken into their home. So Nan took my left hand and Bill took my right, and together the three of us walked down the beach together as a new family. I was too young to remember any of this, but having since met Lucy and Earl, I can only marvel at how great God's wisdom is, and how great Nan and Bill's courage was in taking me home to Mansfield!

I'll tell you what, life with Lucy and Earl would have been different. It would have led me down the wide road to Hell rather than through the narrow gate to Heaven, and I can say that with absolute certainty, because both Lucy and Earl are Catholics. Lucy writes me letters every day, saying that she's praying for me to come back to the Catholic Church I was baptized into as an infant, but I just write back and say, "Mary's an idol, Lucy, you're an idolator, and praise the Lord Catholic baptisms don't count in the Kingdom of Heaven."

For fourteen years at God's decree, I have been a son to my true parents, Nan and Bill White. For fourteen years I have worked with them and the entire Diamond Hill Cathedral congregation to transform Old Testament stories into dioramas of God's great love and great wrath for people, depending on what they'd done and whether they proved their love for God by following all His many commandments.

Taxidermy—squirrel resurrection as I like to call it—is my particular calling, my gift from God. When I was eight, I became the youngest licensed taxidermist in the state of Ohio, using my God-given gift to populate the greatest Bible stories ever with squirrels. I've also stuffed my share of ducks to the glory of God and for the good of the Living Bible Museum, but squirrels, squirrels are my true passion. Squirrels in the Garden of Eden. Squirrels with Abraham at God's calling. Squirrels in the 23rd Psalm. Squirrels with Noah after the flood. I had even designed a group of charred squirrels running away from the fires of Sodom and Gomorrah, but Bill told me that since God was only angry with the people, not the squirrels, they couldn't stay. I was real disappointed that day, but I obeyed my earthly father and put the squirrels away. Maybe someday they'll still come in handy for something.

Here in the NATAS hospital—a spiritual prison really—I cannot practice my craft. I cannot meaningfully contribute to the Kingdom through my primary calling. Instead, all I can do is tell people about God, and about God's judgment unless they turn to Him and seek forgiveness for the evil they do. Witnessing doesn't bring the same joy as squirrel resurrection, but every Christian is called to go soulwinning in this way, even me, even if it's not my primary calling. And if there's one thing I can talk about besides squirrels, it's God. Not everybody likes to hear what I have to say, but everybody needs to hear it. So long as I am here and so long as God calls me to do it, I will preach and I will be a witness for Him. To say the least, I have had some flack, even had a death threat slipped under my door one night. But I'm loving it. That's just more treasure for me up in Heaven.

See, when I preach the Gospel, I'm hardcore. I preach straight up. During last week's Survivors Without Islands group, Nikos, this new guy from Tarpon Springs, Florida—a hurricane-ravaged state thanks to God's judgment against all the immorality down there—started talking about how he missed his "beloved" Pete back home at Spongearama, how the two of them used to go diving for sponges to sell to the tourist shops, and before they even knew they were in love they had "accidentally" kissed for the first time underwater, their diving masks clacking against each other in the middle of a "wrestling" match.

Nikos just went on and on about how he had never thought he would fall in love with another guy, but when he fell in love with Pete, it was the only thing in his sponge-worshipping town that made any sense. I couldn't believe how everybody was falling for Nikos' story, patting his hand, even crying with him. Counselor Dave encouraged Nikos to "share his pain," to "talk it out," to go further and talk about how he "might find ways to help Pete also leave Spongearama for a more normal life than one centered around sponges."

Well, I knew what God would say about all that, so I just cut in. I cut right through Nikos' tears, right through everybody's sinful encouragement of his defiling lifestyle (undoubtedly a result of his not having had a masculine father) and I said what had to be said. I preached that sin is sin, that God created Adam and Eve not Adam and Steve, that Marriage = 1 Man + 1 Woman. I even told them how I had helped build Sodom and Gomorrah and had watched it burn over and over again, and how I knew Nikos would not want to be subjected to God's wrath that way, that nobody—not even squirrels—would want to go through that for a few moments of sinfully corrupt "pleasure."

When Nikos started bawling like a girl, Becky, who had done most of the hand holding, walked across the circle and slapped my face. Dave reminded me that Survivors was about listening to each others' stories with empathy and without judgment. He asked if I had even heard what Nikos had been saying. Of course I had heard what Nikos said, and I repeated it for the whole group—"Nikos said he flagrantly disregarded God's infallible Law against homosexuality and loved another man, an abomination in God's sight."

"God!" Becky seethed, "You are the fucking asshole of assholes!"

"Blasphemy of the Holy Triune God will be held against you," I said straight out. "And you, Becky, are breaking one of the Big Ten: 'Thou shalt not use the name of the Lord thy God in vain.'" To this, Becky spat out a string of curses so vile it was hard to believe she came from the wholesome, laughing, living, giving place that is the Cherished Twinklings Encouragement Retreat. It was like all the demons inside of her were rising up against me and against God, just like the demons used to do with Jesus.

"For having the joy of the Lord," said Becky, "you really are a miserable bastard."

"I don't think God would approve of your language, Becky," I said, "and I—the son of a righteous, holy, powerful King—do have the joy of the Lord. I also have sorrow over the souls that go unsaved, the souls I can't reach, the souls like yours."

"You forget," Becky snorted, "where I grew up, what I'm learning to leave behind. 'Laughing, living, giving,' and all that shit Cherished Twinklings preaches, draining Christ of every last drop of blood. That's not what God is all about."

That just gave me the go-ahead to preach even more hardcore, to milk the Gospel for all I could, and I laid into those kids good, laid into Nikos for his defiling lifestyle, into Becky for not honoring her mother and for blaspheming God, and into Wes from Wall Drug for hiding graven images of jackanapes in his closet. Even as counselor Dave dragged me away from Survivors, I laid into him for his NATAS work, which is the work of Satan, and how it would be better for him to be drowned with a millstone around his neck than to continue leading all of us astray, or trying to lead us astray as I, for one, was not going down Satan's path, only God's.

"God's a whole fucking lot bigger than you think," Becky yelled after me, but I know God well enough to know He would not want His name used in the same sentence as the f-word.

For my "disruption," I spent the night alone in the Thinking Room, a room with pale-pink padded walls, floor, and ceiling. It's not such a bad place to be—the room, even the floor, is heated—but I would have preferred to have at least had some good Christian literature with me. "This is not meant as a punishment," Dave told me as he walked out of the room and closed the door, "Just for thinking."

I was still full of righteous godly anger when Dave left, so the first thing I did was pound the soft walls and cry out to God over the sins of my company in this place, and over having been placed in the midst of unrepentant sinners to try me. But after who-knows-how-long of pounding and pounding and pounding at walls, I started to give out, to slow and soften inside. "Justice against my enemies, oh God!" I called out with the last of my strength, dropping to my knees and raising my hands to Heaven.

It's just that I get so angry when I see the sin and evil in this world. I tell people they need to repent, turn from their sin, but they don't. I am so tired of having to tell people they're going to Hell, so tired of having to say that they—even those who despise me—need to accept Jesus so they can escape the eternal fire. I am so gosh-darn tired of having to be responsible for all the souls around me. It's a hard place God has put me in, here at the NATAS hospital. A hard place to have to talk to people, to preach to them, to tell them of the judgment that is coming their way if they don't repent, and if they don't turn from their wicked ways.

I am not supposed to be in this hospital where I must use words to confront people with the truth. I am supposed to be home, at the Living Bible Museum, working with squirrels to create dioramas—God's stories of truth that will change the lives of the people who see them. Jonah and the whale. Daniel and the lion's den. Noah and the flood. Naaman and his leprosy. I know these stories inside and out, backwards and forwards, sideways and upside down. I know these Bible stories better than I know my own.

So I told God about all this during my time in the Thinking Room. I even suggested He might have been wrong to have stuck me here in the NATAS hospital when my real work was back in Mansfield, back at the Living Bible Museum, back with Bill and Nan and Pastor Diamond. My real work was resurrecting squirrels to place in dioramas so as to more accurately represent Old Testament stories and thus lead sinners to repentance. Lying on my back on the pale-pink padding, looking up and around at even more pink padding in the Thinking Room where I might as well have been on the ceiling looking down, God didn't speak. Instead, a deep, quiet, dreamless sleep came. This sleep was so different from the fighting for God I'd been doing all day that I awoke feeling peaceful and content, but when I started thinking about how I felt and how I should feel, I was guilt-stricken for not keeping uppermost in my mind the struggle constantly being waged between God and Satan. I'd taken a break. I'd slept on the job. I'd allowed the Enemy to seduce me with false peace in the midst of unending war. "Forgive me, Great King of Heaven," I pleaded.

Over the past seven months I have thought a lot about the so-called "intervention" that brought me here, and I don't approve of it anymore now than I did when I arrived. For starters, who has the right to intervene in what God has called good? Does NATAS, who ripped me from the loving arms of Nan and Bill, my true God-given parents? Do Lucy and Earl, who may have physically given birth to me sixteen years ago but had nothing, absolutely nothing, to do with my spiritual birth? I am not some computer with no mind of my own that can be "deprogrammed" by force of will of an organization.

See, I've got NATAS all figured out. They call themselves the National Association of Tourist Attraction Survivors and say they're all about saving people from tourist attractions. While that might be a good thing for Artie, raised in the gambling pit of the MGM Grand in Las Vegas; Clyde, nursed since birth from the Budweiser bottle in Saint Louis; and especially Dawn, raised by the demon-possessed mannequin of Belle Gunness in LaPorte, Indiana, I am NOT a victim of a tourist attraction. I am washed in the Blood, saved by an Awesome God, committed to living a sin-free life, so that I might be accepted into God's Great Heaven when I die. It's hard work, this business of Grace, but I'm well on my way, and being tied down here for the past seven months is just getting in God's way.

NATAS may think they have intervened, but I have infiltrated. NATAS *thinks* they're in control, but I consented to coming here. I didn't have to. I could have stayed at the Living Bible Museum. Nan and Bill could have taken NATAS to court, prosecuted them for religious persecution and kidnapping. I wonder sometimes why they didn't, how they could so easily let me go, but I know that they too understand that God works in mysterious ways and this surely is just one more of those ways, part of God's plan for my life. This hospital is a mission field, ready for the harvester (me!) to bring in the harvest, separate the wheat from the chaff, and at the end of it all, bake a holy loaf of communion bread to be served with the unfermented fruit of the vine. Still, I have to play along with this intervention stuff somewhat, answer the counselors' questions honestly and without shame, for there is nothing I am ashamed of—especially not the infallible and everlasting word of God.

Two weeks before the intervention, I left my home with Nan and Bill and moved into the Living Bible Museum. I left out of obedience to God, not disobedience to my parents; Nan and Bill, they knew that. Even Pastor Diamond knew it and appointed me as the "Keeper of the Old Testament" for as long as God called me to stay. You see, I'd caught a glimpse of what God was doing in and through the Old Testament Walk with my help, how He was moving in Mansfield to save one soul at a time. All I wanted was to be more completely a part of it, to live—really live—the reality of the Old Testament day in and day out. Here was where God spoke, His holy words of Scripture broadcast over the loudspeakers, His holy truths embodied in the larger-than-life Moses, Abraham, Joseph, David, Jonah, and other Old Testament heroes.

By the time I moved in, there wasn't much work remaining at the Old Testament Walk. Pastor Diamond had announced that we now had enough Bible dioramas to rotate throughout the year, keeping the Bible Walk fresh and exciting for returning visitors. Bill had told me they had enough of my squirrels for the exhibits, including an extra twenty in storage, not even counting the charred squirrels of Sodom and Gomorrah. Bill told me that Mrs. Mulloy would rather I stop trapping the squirrels that came to rob her birdfeeders. But I couldn't just walk away from squirrel resurrection because when I thought about God and His plan for my life, squirrels were an inescapable part of it. I don't know, but maybe David felt that way too when God called him away from his sheep to go kill a giant and then become a king. Maybe there were days David would rather have been out tending his sheep. If so, I hardly blame him. The only difference between King David and me is that God did call him to something else when he called him first to slay Goliath and then to rule over Israel. Me? I just don't know.

For two weeks before the intervention, I lived in the Old Testament Walk of the Living Bible Museum, seeking to live and breathe the Old Testament and desiring God's direction about how best to use my squirrel resurrection gift even beyond the Living Bible Museum. During the day I stayed out of sight, sleeping behind the burning cities of Sodom and Gomorrah, in the shadows of the serpent in the Garden, in the belly of Jonah's whale. Day in and day out, I half-slept, half-listened to the words of God telling these stories of other people's faithfulness and wickedness, of God's power and dominion.

At night when there were no visitors, I was free to roam the dioramas, to live the Old Testament journey myself. The lighting, controlled by the same system that controlled the sound, restricted me to staying in one scene for as long as God was talking, as long as the words of Holy Scripture were being broadcast. I'd lie down on the kindling set up for Isaac, wait for my father Abraham to lift his knife to slay me and wait for God's voice to break through and rescue me from death by sending a ram in my place for the sacrifice. Then I'd stand alongside Abraham and pretend God was calling me to leave for a new land, to be the start of a new nation. Then I'd move to lie beside Samson, draping his hair over my head, never believing Delilah would do such a thing as cut my hair even while knowing that she would.

I inhabited story after story, every story but one—always choosing to remain in the dark with Elijah and the widow of Zarephath and her sick son instead of moving into Job's story as the lights came on and the voice of Holy Scripture spoke. Was it Job's boils—pus-filled and red-rimmed and covering him from the top of his head to the soles of his feet—that held me back? Yes, it was the boils, but it was also more. God let Satan cover Job with boils, let him take away everything Job had just to test Job's love for Him. But why? I knew that God could do and did whatever He wanted, and I knew Job's story turned out ok. Job was a hero for standing firm and taking it, for not cursing God and dying like his whiny wife told him to. I knew it but I still couldn't fathom it. I sure didn't like it, and I didn't really want to understand it.

In all the Old Testament Walk dioramas, Job was the only one I pitied. He wasn't lucky enough to get thrown to lions or into a fiery furnace or swallowed by a whale. Job wasn't rescued by God from certain death but had to suffer miserably from boils and had everything—lands, servants, children—taken away. Everything. How could anybody recover from that? Even with lands and fortune restored, what could Job ever think, ever feel but that he'd been some powerless pawn played by both God and Satan? And how could he ever trust that it wouldn't happen again?

The night of the intervention, I was with Elijah and the widow of Zarephath and her son, eating the bread of promise. Just as God had promised the poor widow that the flour would not run out nor the oil run dry so long as Elijah stayed with them, so I felt He had promised me the same.

This story—not Job's—was mine. Indeed, even though I had brought no food with me into the Living Bible Museum, I never went hungry on all those nights.

But then they came: Lucy, Earl, three NATAS so-called counselors, and one Mansfield police officer to make it legal. The story of Job was underway, but I stayed behind with Elijah, climbing into bed with the widow's son and praying for God to hide me. I heard Earl first, pleading, "Come home, Patrick Reilly. We love you. We love you as much as when we lost you at two when you went walking down that beach and never walked back."

"We know you cannot see it now," Lucy pleaded, "You're too close to everything. You're sick. You need help."

I did not speak then, and perhaps I could have kept from speaking, but then Lucy and Earl invoked God's name, said that they had been praying to Jesus and Mary for fourteen years, and that God had led them to Mansfield to find me. That's what got me. That's what made me angry. That they could act like *they* knew God! That they could act like God had spoken to *them* to drag me away from the place where God had raised me up, the place where God had given me my gift. I knew that Satan could speak and make his voice sound like God sometimes—that another name for Satan is Lucifer, Angel of Light—and that Lucifer, not God, was speaking through Lucy and Earl.

"Patrick Reilly," Lucy pleaded, "please come home to us."

"I won't come with you," I shouted. "My God-given name is Ezekiel William White, and what you see as sickness is the wisdom of God! I am home and I am loved. In the holy and righteous name of God, get behind me, Satan."

Then they found me. Three NATAS thugs with fingers like bleached slugs lifted me from the sick son's bed even as I called down the wrath of God upon them, even as I shouted, "Get thee behind me, Satan." In my enemies' struggle to keep me under their control, my feet kicked over the urns of flour and oil, leaving the widow Zarephath, her son, and God's prophet Elijah to starve.

I stopped fighting. I let myself be led, like a lamb to the slaughter, out of the Living Bible Museum and into the NATAS van. A straightjacket lay on the backseat in case I made a fuss, but I didn't. I just climbed inside and sat beside it, guided by a white-coated NATAS worker with a long blonde ponytail who smelled of peppermint and woodsmoke which both frightened and intoxicated me, smelling like I had always imagined Hell to smell even though Nan had told me that Hell smelled like sulfur. "Like rotting eggs ablaze," Nan had said. The NATAS woman pulled my seatbelt around me, clicked it in place. She smiled, said, "You'll be ok. It takes awhile, but you'll be ok." She touched the back of my hand, the tips of her fingernails feeling like spikes going into my flesh. I stiffened but stayed silent as fear gnawed at my core.

I pressed my face to the window, read "Live for this life alone and you will miss the next one" on the Diamond Hill Cathedral sign. The van lurched forward, and I thought about how the one thing I know for certain is that I don't want to live for this life alone. I had always been pretty good at that, I thought, always keeping my eyes on Heaven and heavenly things. I didn't even like much in this life except for squirrel resurrection and the Living Bible Museum, and those things weren't really "for this life" anyways, but for the next—my ministry to gain entrance into the heavenly life to come.

The NATAS van headed west on U.S. Highway 30 with me in it as the sky in front of us filled with dark clouds that I hoped meant the Rapture was coming, that Jesus would split the sky and take me Home, not to Lucy and Earl or even to Nan and Bill, but Home for real which was in Heaven where a room had been prepared for me in God's mansion. Maybe that's not quite how the Rapture was going to happen—I'd watched *Megiddo* and *Left Behind*, God-glorifying movies that preached Truth to the world—but I prayed that it was ok for me to imagine being swept up to Heaven and rescued from this world's hardships.

"Live for this life alone and you will miss the next one."

So true. I thought about how Kirk Cameron—as the left behind journalist Buck Williams—really made me consider how the next life isn't far away, how there will be hard times after the Antichrist takes power, but how even those who are saved after the Rapture will ultimately be victorious in Him. Wasn't everything in the end about living for the next world? Wasn't that the message of *Left Behind*? Wasn't that the message of God? That's what I was thinking about on the bus when the woman who smelled like peppermint and woodsmoke said in her slippery, slithery voice, "I know you don't understand right now, but this intervention is for the best, and you are going to a good place where people can help and you can recover from Tourist Attraction Trauma and then be able to figure out what's next for your life."

Because I knew better than to talk with the Devil, I said nothing, but I thought again about Kirk Cameron and how he went from being a TV star to joining up with Way of the Master, this awesome ministry to help Christians "seek and save the lost" the way Luke 19:10 says that Jesus did, and I thought that if I ever did leave the Living Bible Museum of my own free will, and going to NATAS which was against God's will did not count, I'd like to join Kirk Cameron out in California, see if he could use my squirrels to help Christians witness more effectively.

Outside, thunder rolled, a spear of lightning pierced the sky, and water poured through the clouds. I wish it could have been Jesus coming down through those clouds, but even when I yearned and prayed for the Rapture, I got rain. But that didn't surprise me because God never makes things easy. The windshield wipers screeched and scraped as the NATAS van bounced down the road and the driver turned on the radio to a secular station. I prayed that God would intervene and change the station so I could hear Casting Crowns because they are really good, seriously dedicated and anointed, and their music might have helped me right about then, might even have saved somebody else in the van, but God continued to work in mystifying ways and He didn't change the station so I had to block out "What if God was One of Us" because that song sure wasn't about the God I knew. I thought about what made me happiest instead which was God's being awesome and people getting saved and how I was called to be a part of that both by resurrecting squirrels and also by sometimes writing columns for the Diamond Digest about how sin is sin, how sin has no place in the presence of a holy and righteous God.

There in the NATAS van—somewhere between Mansfield and Florida, Ohio—I didn't know what God had in store for me, and I wasn't sure why God had not intervened on my behalf. I wasn't a Jonah running away from what God would have me do. I was ready and willing to prophecy, to declare God's judgment, to live for the next life alone and not this one, but when we arrived at the hospital the last of my tracts which were essential to my witness were confiscated during a degrading and unholy strip search, making me feel a little of what my brothers and sisters in Christ in the underground churches in Russia and China must feel.

When I asked why I couldn't keep my three favorites—"Are Roman Catholics Christians?" "Allah Had No Son," and "Doom Town" (which would have been really useful for teaching Nikos the truth about homosexuality)—the woman who had sat beside me in the van told me I could not keep them for the same reason that Weeki Wachi survivors couldn't keep their mermaid tails, that South of the Border survivors had to give up all their Pedro paraphernalia, that World of Coca-Cola survivors had to switch to drinking Pepsi. She told me my tracts kept me "too close to my illness," kept me "bound" to the tourist attraction I came from, kept me from "seeing," as if I—not they—were blind.

"I have new eyes," I told my persecutors. "These tracts by God's humble servant J.T. Chick help me to see the truth in comic book form, and they help me communicate that truth in a dramatic and life-changing way to those who really are blind." That was when I noticed that the man overseeing the strip search from a far corner of the room was wearing a crucifix on a gold chain around his neck, no less a slave to the papacy than Lucy and Earl. I understood then the greater plot behind my persecution and imprisonment, but still I prayed that he might read "Are Roman Catholics Christians?" and that it might save his soul. I got to keep my Bible, but the tracts all had to go, down to the last "This was Your Life." I tried not to take this too hard, though, and to remember that children of God will be persecuted in this life but will reign forever in the next. I tried to pity my persecutors, not hate them. After almost seven months in this place, I think I've learned how.

After last week's time in the Thinking Room, I had begun to sense God telling me the time had come to turn my back on those around me in the hospital. They had already made their choice for Hell, and He knew that just as well as I did, having given them over to their vile natures. This morning, while staring into my usual bowl of Alpha-Bits, I saw God's will spelled out clearly before me: "G OOT." Never had anything made more sense to me than those four letters, God's personal revelation that my real mission field wasn't NATAS but the larger Hell-bent world. I needed to "GO OUT" ("G OOT") to the total strangers I had never met and would never again meet—people who might well never hear about Him if I didn't do the telling. If I didn't tell, they wouldn't know, and if they didn't know, the weight of their souls would rest heavy on my eternal soul because I could have told them but had chosen not to. So during today's Out and About Afternoon (OAA), I went witnessing.

On Out and About Afternoons, those of us who have reached Level 3, which means we are no longer considered at risk for either suicide (yes, this unholy act is a consideration for some) or running away, get loaded up in a big blue van that announces our status as patients at the National Association of Tourist Attraction Survivors Hospital for Research and Recovery (NATASHRR) in blocky white letters across both sides. As if that isn't enough, two stickers on the back bumper read, "NATAS: When you're tired of being part of somebody else's attraction," and "Boycott Wall Drug." Because of where we've all come from and the problems NATAS has with any sort of tourist attraction, we don't go anywhere interesting. Mostly we just go to parks, eat brown bag lunches or five dollar pizzas, throw Frisbees, sit in big circles for "guided discussions" about how much better it is to be out in the open than in somebody else's attraction (though the truth is, I miss my home and I know I'm not the only one). Out and About Afternoons are hard for me, though, especially since most every other survivor has turned not only against God but also against me, God's messenger. So on OAAs, I mostly walk around on my own, avoiding Frisbees thrown at my head.

For today's OAA, we'd driven the road that runs along the Maumee River from Florida through Independence and on to Defiance so we could pick up pepperoni pizzas at Domino's. Then we drove all the way back to Florida to eat lunch at the Gessner Family Park which is nothing more than a couple picnic benches, metal monkey bars, and a swing set on the Maumee riverbank. I tried one last time to witness to the NATAS crowd, this time trying out the Good Person Test by asking the nonbelievers (which was everybody but me) if they thought they were good people and then—after they'd said yes—asking if they'd ever lied, stolen, or taken the Lord's name in vain. Everybody had to admit to having told even a little lie, and I'd gotten Nikos to go so far as to admit he was a liar, thief, and blasphemer ("well, technically," Nikos had said) when we all saw this real shaggy homeless-looking guy with a Heinz 57 type of terrier.

We all watched the man as he fed the dog treats out of a Milk-Bone box, and I kind of felt something inside—a restless kind of feeling that I took to be the Holy Spirit. Becky must have seen me watching him because she said, "Get your ass over there, Salvation Boy! He's the one that needs saving."

I hesitated, but then when she said she and Nikos and all the rest were going to Hell anyway, I knew she was exactly right. So, remembering God's "G OOT" message in my Alpha-Bits and not wanting to disobey God, I said, "Well, ok, but I'm taking the rest of this pizza." Then, forgetting for a moment that everybody around me was going to Hell, I turned back around and asked them to pray for me.

"For fuck's sake, Ezekiel," Becky said, "I pray for you every day," sounding so sincere in her own profane way I almost believed her.

I could be wrong, but this guy, well, he was watching me the whole time I was walking towards him, like he was waiting for me. It's hard to strike up a casual conversation with somebody who has been watching you, but I gave it my best shot.

"Hungry?" I asked, opening the pizza box with three remaining slices and pushing it towards him. "My friends and me," I said (which wasn't so much a lie about my peers as an exaggeration) "we ate all we wanted and thought you might be hungry."

The man leaned over and peeked into the box. His scruffy terrier stood on its hind paws to look at the pizza too.

"Pepperoni?" he asked.

"Yes," I said, "Pepperoni." And then I added, as a way of introducing God into the conversation, "God's gift to pizza."

The man smiled but said, "No thanks. I don't eat meat. God would have done better to let the pig keep the pepperoni and to have gifted the pizza with olives. I like olives."

This caught me off guard. Who doesn't like pepperoni? And how would I continue the conversation now?

"Have a seat," the man said, scooting over to make room on the bench. "I could use the conversation. And you just go right ahead and eat the pizza yourself. I'm not one to judge and you look like you could use some extra padding."

I sat down on the edge of the bench wondering whether I should stay there or scoot in closer like he wanted me to, like we'd sit if we had been friends for a while. I asked myself, "What would Jesus do?" but when I didn't get a clear answer, I scooted in just a little from the edge and placed the opened pizza box between us. That seemed natural enough, even if he wasn't eating any pizza.

"Are you from around here?" I asked, lifting a slice of pizza, thinking it would be impolite not to eat since he had said I should.

The man snorted and laughed. "Do I look like it?"

I studied the man. In Florida, Ohio, most everybody dressed in wholesome and unsurprising ways, but this man was wearing open-toed sandals, cut-off jean shorts, and a green t-shirt with white lettering that read "Visualize Whirled Peas." Around his neck hung what some call a peace symbol but what I know to be a broken upside-down cross used in Satanic rituals. His long hair was halfway down his back, streaked with gray, and tied in a ponytail. What's more, he had shiny silver studs in both his ears, making me think of Pastor Diamond's sermon, "Body Piercing Saved Us," but I knew this man's body piercing did not save him and only defiled his body, a temple God had given him to use. From his appearance alone, I could tell God had a lot of work to do.

"Guess not," I said, then asked, "Where are you from and where are you heading?"

"Well, I started out in Los Angeles and meant to end up in Florida, as in the state, but MapQuest took me to Florida, Ohio. I'll get down to Florida—the state, that is—eventually, but destinations are overrated," the man said, stretching his arms high and linking his fingers. "The journey is what I live for."

"You think so?" I asked. Pushing to what was really important, what I was really in this conversation for, I said, "Well, I'm heading to Heaven. I can tell you how to get there if you want to go with me."

I'd reached my hand into my back pocket to pull out a copy of Jack T. Chick's *This Was Your Life* before remembering NATAS had taken all my tracts, but the man put his hand up and said, "Save it for somebody else. I've already found my way."

"Is Jesus your way?" I asked, not missing a beat because when it came to evangelism, I was the best soulwinner around. "Because if Jesus isn't your way, then your way is only going to land you in Hell."

I thought for sure this would get him, that he'd soon be begging to hear the Four Spiritual Laws, but he just smiled and said, "Oh, sure. But I also listen to Buddha, Mother Earth, Krishna, even myself." Was this man mocking me? Surely, he was mocking me and mocking God (and the Bible says in Galations 6:7, "God will not be mocked"), but he didn't have a mocking tone, so I decided to ask him the hard questions to draw out his beliefs.

"Well, sir," I began, "do you mind if I ask you a few questions?"

"Only if I can ask you questions in return," he said, moving the Domino's box to the ground so he could pull up a knee on the bench as he turned to face me. Not having the box between us made me nervous, but I was quick to pull my red Gideon's Bible out of my back pocket and set it between us just as the man's dog scrambled onto his lap.

"Mind if I go first?" the man asked, "Seeing as how you've been doing most of the asking so far."

"Sure," I said, but I didn't feel sure at all. This man was good at the game he was playing, and I was worried he'd put me on the defensive, make it hard for me to ask any more questions. If I'd learned one thing about witnessing, it was to not be put on the defensive, to stay in control and argue the case for Christ all the way through. But I prayed a quick silent prayer that God wouldn't let this man get the better of me and of Him.

"But first," the man said as he leaned across the bench, reaching his hand out to shake mine, "allow me to introduce myself. My name is Charley, what's yours?"

Good move, I thought as I reached out my hand to shake his, feeling cheated that I hadn't thought to ask his name first. What a way to gain somebody's trust, and I hadn't even thought of it! Granted, his soul mattered most to me and to God, but here in this life, people do like to feel known through their names. And I hadn't even thought to ask.

"So what's your name?" Charley asked again.

"Ezekiel," I answered. "My name's Ezekiel William White."

"Like the prophet?" he asked, and though this was his second question, I let it slide.

"Yeah, I guess so," I replied, embarrassed that I'd never really thought about my name before. Nan and Bill had never told me how they'd come to give me my name and I'd never thought to ask. The Old Testament Walk had no diorama of Ezekiel, so I didn't really know much about him except that he was a prophet. And now that I didn't know how to answer, what to think of my name, I felt all twisted-up inside.

"Relax," Charley said, like the matter of me not knowing how I got my name could just be shrugged off. "Ezekiel was clueless until he was twice your age. And that," he leaned over and whispered in my ear, "is when things really started to get weird. Wheels in the sky and all." Charley tossed back his head and laughed. "Ah, forget about all that, Zeke," he said. "I can call you Zeke?"

"No," I said, feeling tightness in my mouth and remembering how certain Nan and Bill had been about me being Ezekiel and only Ezekiel, how they'd put a stop to my kindergarten teacher calling me Zeke and pulled me out to be homeschooled after that unholy incident. "My name is Ezekiel, not Zeke. My turn," I said. I was worried that if I didn't start witnessing now, I would lose my chance to deliver Charley's soul to God.

"Sure," Charley said, folding his hands behind his head like this was the start of some everyday conversation of no real importance and not at all about his eternal soul. "Go for it!"

Where to start? I'd never been in this kind of situation before, a complete stranger's soul in my hands, waiting to be won for God. And if I botched it up, Charley would keep traveling the wide and fast highway to Hell. I knew the questions that really mattered, the questions that would let me know what Charley believed, and how to turn him onto the right path—God's Way—so I launched out with the best of my knowledge, knowing that with men like Charley, cold hard facts would turn him to God. With the Bible Walk's Eden diorama firmly in my mind, I began at the beginning.

"Evolution or creation," I began. "Monkeys or an intelligent, loving, Creator God? Which do you believe?"

"Well," Charley began, scratching behind his ear, "it's hard to say since I wasn't there, but I think science shows us evidence for evolution, don't you?"

"No!" I shouted, though I hadn't meant to. Charley's dog startled out of sleep, lifting his head to look at me. "I didn't come from a monkey. And I'll tell you this—"

"Whoa, partner!" Charley said, holding up both hands as if to hold me back. "Wait a minute. I know we're taking turns here, but give me a minute to explain, if you don't mind."

I could lose Charley completely now, and I knew that. My soulwinning training had stressed the dangers of allowing the destructive spirit of anger—even anger for a righteous cause—to take over when witnessing. *Forgive me for the weakness of my flesh, O God*, I prayed as Charley told me he thought evolution or creation was "not necessarily an either/or scenario," and how he "couldn't say for sure," but that God—"if there was a God"—"could have used evolution."

Locked back into calm detachment, my anger at bay, I told Charley that was impossible, that according to biblical record, the Earth wasn't old enough for evolution to have taken place, but he didn't believe the Bible (didn't believe the BIBLE!) was "necessarily literal historical truth."

I was ready to take him on then and there, ready to prove the Bible on the spot, remove the confusion from his mind and help him see the truth of God. God loved Charley and God had delivered his soul into my hands—I couldn't lose it now. Charley was nicer to me than anybody I'd met at NATAS and I wanted to let myself like him, but I knew he could be an Angel of Light masquerading as a friend but speaking the Enemy's lies. If I let my guard down now, I would lose his soul, maybe lose mine too. Whatever work it took to redirect his soul to Heaven, I was going to do it, and I had to do it now.

Charley held up his hands again as though to push me back. "Hold on there," he said. "Relax! It's my turn to ask a question."

I thought for sure Charley would pull out some obscure "fact" from evolutionary theory, attack me with language I didn't understand and therefore couldn't easily argue against even though I knew it was untrue, but he sidestepped evolution altogether. "Tell me something about yourself," Charley said. "What matters most to you?"

"Saving souls," I said, feeling that for Heaven's sake, the answer should have been obvious to him by now. "Saving souls from the fires of Hell and redirecting them to the gates of Heaven."

Charley scratched the gray bristles under his chin. "Yes," he said, "I can see you're zealous about that, but that's not quite what I was asking. Mind if I revise my question a bit?"

I looked first at my watch and then back at the NATAS van. I didn't know how much time I had, but then NATAS wouldn't leave me behind. I looked back at Charley, so relaxed like he had all the time in the world. "Sure," I said. "Go ahead." To tell the truth, I was worn out from thinking about evolution and didn't mind a little break. If Charley wanted to waste his question to find out some detail about me, let him.

"I want you to look me in the eyes," he said, "and tell me about a time when you were happy, really happy. Don't speak right away, not until you're ready."

I knew I should tell him about when I was saved at the Diamond Hill revival when I was five, how the Power Team had come to Diamond Hill and broken concrete blocks with their heads for God, how they talked about Satan having dominion over the unsaved and how only by being saved could we break Satan's dominion just like they had broken those concrete blocks with their heads, how I had gone forward and gotten saved. I knew that's what I should have told Charley, but I didn't recall feeling happy so much as relieved. Relieved that I didn't have to go to Hell and burn forever and ever. Relieved that I had the truth of God and nobody could take it away from me. Relieved that God had saved me from a life of sin and that if I just obeyed my pastor and my parents, didn't swear, didn't drink, or smoke, or look at dirty magazines, I'd stay on God's good side.

I knew that's what I should have told Charley, but then Charley said, "Forget looking in my eyes and just close yours, ok? You'll remember." So I closed my eyes, and the first word to enter my mind when I thought the word "happy" was "Obadiah," and I knew without even looking that Charley had seen my smile before I had even opened my mouth.

"Now," Charley said, and all of a sudden I felt his hand on my shoulder which should have made me jerk but didn't. "Now we're getting somewhere."

I don't know why I relaxed then, why with this guy who believed in evolution, New Age, all kinds of weird stuff, I relaxed and started to talk about Obadiah, about a time I hadn't even known to have been the happiest until I began to share it.

"I like squirrels," I began. "I've always liked squirrels, and my first and forever favorite squirrel was Obadiah." I opened my eyes and looked at Charley, wondering whether I should continue. Since everything in his face said I should and since God chose not to stop my tongue, I let myself keep talking.

"Nan—she's basically been my mom for as long as I can remember—Nan says that even when I was two years old, I used to sit on a big black Holy Bible pillow in front of the living room window and watch the squirrels. I don't really remember back that far, but I do remember sitting on that pillow when I was a little older, watching. I remember once as Nan and I sat together watching our favorite squirrels—Obadiah (my squirrel) and Nebuchadnezzar (hers)—running in circles up the tall oak in our front yard, Nan told me that God created those squirrels for us to watch, and even though I already knew all sorts of things about God, that just made me love Him, that He would create squirrels just for me to watch. I couldn't have been older than four."

"Can you tell me more," Charley asked, "about this Obadiah?" And just thinking about Obadiah flooded me with joy and sadness in equal amounts.

"Obadiah was scrawny," I sighed. "His tail was twice as thick as the rest of him. But let me tell you, Obadiah had style! He'd never run straight up a tree but would always circle around and around in a spiral, all the way to the top. He was a Christian squirrel too, I'm sure of it. When Obadiah would get a nut, he'd never just bite straight into it, but always prayed first, bowing his head for a moment of squirrel thanks before setting his teeth to work. That Obadiah," I said, closing my eyes and remembering him in his living glory, "he was a squirrel worth keeping around."

Charley nodded. Said nothing. Scratched his dog behind its ears until it stretched its head forward so Charley could scratch under its chin.

"I spent enough time watching Obadiah that he came to know me," I said, "recognize me. Nebuchadnezzar never paid me much attention, but Obadiah, he'd take time out from gathering acorns, chasing Nebuchadnezzar, and grooming himself to come up to the window while I was sitting inside, watching. He'd scratch on the window with his tiny claws, press his face full against the window so that with his nose on one side and mine on the other, we were practically touching. Then he'd stand straight up and chitter-chatter, as if I could understand what he had to say."

"Could you?" Charley asked.

"Maybe," I said. "Maybe I could. I'd imagine conversations anyway, us talking back and forth about the weather, Obadiah asking me to come outside and play, me saying I'd like to but couldn't. See, Nan was always real concerned about the dangers of the world, especially the dangers of our neighbors who had all these weird Native American feathers and symbols around that we knew were really demonic, so I told Obadiah that. I even told him I wasn't much good at climbing trees, though I'd never even had a chance to try. Obadiah, he understood. I'm sure he did."

"What happened to Obadiah?" asked Charley.

"Oh, he's in the Garden of Eden now," I said.

"You mean Heaven?" he asked.

"No, not exactly," I started, wondering how best to continue in a way he could understand. "I mean, yes, Obadiah sort of died, but then I, um, resurrected him and placed him in the Garden of Eden, the one I helped build."

Charley looked at me like he didn't know if I was telling the truth or making this up, but he should have known enough about me by then to know I wouldn't lie because that would be a sin.

"You know," I continued, "the Living Bible Museum. It's just a couple hours to the south and west of here, over in Mansfield. It's a real ministry to the lost, representing Bible stories through beautifully crafted dioramas." Then, remembering what I had gotten into this conversation for in the first place, I added, "You should go. Check it out before you leave Ohio. God speaks to people there."

"Thanks. Maybe I will," Charley said, and he sounded like he meant it. "Can you tell me more, please?" Charley asked. "Tell me more about Obadiah and the Garden of Eden?"

"It's true," I said proudly. "Obadiah really is there, right next to Eve, and all thanks to me. See, I was six when I received my calling. Everybody at Diamond Hill—my church—was hard at work on the Old Testament Walk, and Pastor Diamond was talking every Sunday about people using their gifts to the glory of God. I didn't understand entirely what he meant as I was so young, but then Obadiah died and I set to work on him, not knowing what I was doing but feeling I needed to do something, and in doing what came naturally to me, I began to understand what my gift might be."

"Back up a little," Charley said. "Can you back up and tell me how he died, this Obadiah of yours?" I hesitated, looked away from Charley and down at his sleeping dog. I'd never talked about this before, not to anyone except Nan and Pastor Diamond, and even that had been a decade ago. Looking back up at Charley, part of me wanted to run, or turn the questions back on him, to get back on track with our conversation about God and Hell and Heaven and other more important things. Part of me recoiled at the thought of telling this unbeliever about Obadiah, but I'd never met anyone before—not even another Born Again—who made me feel like whatever words came out of my mouth next would be okay, so I kept talking.

"Obadiah was attacked," I began. "Attacked by this big black tomcat that sometimes ran out of the house with all the ungodly Native American idols to come slinking around our place. I saw it happen. Sitting in front of the window, I saw it happen. Obadiah was in his prayer position under the bushes by the narrow gate leading to this heavenly squirrel palace Nan had created out of split cobs of corn, and all of a sudden there was this blur of black, then a tossing circle of black and brown, fur flying everywhere. Not even thinking that I could be running straight into the evils of the world, I rushed outside with a broom to chase the tomcat away, and I whacked him good across the back, scared him enough to go running away. Obadiah, he was hurt, but he wasn't dead. Still, I didn't think he could make it, not without help—my help. His black eyes pulsed with pain, and he wasn't moving much except to twitch and shiver. I lifted him up and turned his body over in my small hands. Obadiah's body was hot and damp with blood, blood that flowed out of the gash in his side.

"I had never touched Obadiah before—I'd only watched him through the window. I had imagined conversations with him, imagined chasing him up trees and being chased by him, imagined us as friends who would collect acorns together and then pray over them before setting our sharp hard teeth to break through the hard shells so our tongues could taste the soft, buttery insides. But now I held Obadiah in my hands, and I didn't know whether I was his friend or his enemy, whether I loved him as much as I always believed I had, or whether I hated him—hated him for stopping to pray under that bush before heading straight for squirrel Heaven, for letting that old tomcat attack him, but most of all, hated him for making me come outside and pick him up, for making me see the fleas hopping in his fur, for making me care about him and then for maybe dying on me."

Too much? Was I sharing too much? I didn't even fully know what I was saying, I didn't even know whether it was true. I tried to pray that God would guide me, but God seemed absent, and that only made me talk more to cover up His absence. I looked at Charley, but Charley didn't say anything, only watched me, still listening, waiting for me to continue. So I did.

"Nan doesn't even know about all of this, about my feelings especially," I said, "nobody does." Was I warning Charley that he had better not repeat any of what was to come? As if he'd ever meet Nan or Bill or Pastor Diamond or anybody else I knew. Was I telling him he was special to be hearing this? What was I telling him, and why did I keep talking?

"I'm not even sure about all of this, how everything unfolded, but I do know how it all ended. I had resurrected Obadiah, discovered my calling, found happiness." Charley just nodded and listened. I rested my hand on his dog's head, feeling the shape of skull beneath skin, knowing without even thinking what it would take to stuff and mount Charley's dog for the bit of Proverbs wisdom about a dog returning to its own vomit like a fool to its folly. Beneath my hand, the dog's ears twitched. The dog took a deep breath and exhaled a whimper before settling back into sleep. I had never resurrected a dog and I never would. Dogs were not my calling.

"Nan was sleeping," I said, removing my hand from the dog's head. "When Obadiah got hurt, Nan was sleeping. I didn't want to wake her, so I wrapped Obadiah in some K-Mart fliers I found in the mailbox and rushed him into the house. My Heroes of the Old Testament plate from breakfast was still on the kitchen counter, and I laid Obadiah across the plate, his tail and head hanging over the edges, his bloody hurt middle stretching across the heroes from Abraham through Daniel. Fleas hopped off Obadiah and bounced on the counter. They were not my greatest concern, even though I prayed that Nan would never notice them, that they wouldn't fill the house like the plague of locusts in Egypt.

"At the kitchen sink I scrubbed my hands with Dawn dishwashing detergent until my hands were free of Obadiah's blood, then found a pair of Nan's sewing scissors, a needle and some brown thread, rag strips from Bill's old Petra *Never Say Die* concert t-shirt, and a container of yellow Play-Doh. I didn't know what I would need or what I was going to do, let alone how to use a needle and thread, but I had to help God heal Obadiah—that much I felt certain about—so I headed out to the garage with him. Looking back to that day, I know that God was leading me, that God showed me what to do, that God guided my hands and my mind to do what I had to do, that God was working in me and through me to do what I had to do."

I closed my eyes and rubbed my forehead, trying to think, to remember details. What came were flashes from patching up Obadiah in the garage, trying first to heal him and then to preserve him. Rolling Play-Doh, thin and snake-like between my hands, cutting off the ends so that its length matched Obadiah's wound. Placing Play-Doh in the wound to stop the bleeding, the blood pulsing through the Play-Doh, softening it, turning the yellow to orange. Sealing up the wound with the sticky blood-orange Play-Doh, smoothing it down with my fingers across Obadiah's side, but not fast enough to save Obadiah. Twitching. Whiskers, nose, tail, paws, chest, abdomen—twitching. All of Obadiah's body twitching. Slight shuddery chitter-chattering from Obadiah, as if God was speaking through him, guiding me, telling me what should and should not be done, and telling me too how we could have been the best of friends, how we could be still.

"I listened to God," I told Charley. "I listened to God and God gave me my gift. I listened, obeyed, and created for and from Obadiah a squirrel that will never die, never rot, never be different from how he was meant to be. Obadiah's new body is a resurrection body—no fleas, no tomcat scar. Obadiah's coat is sleeker, softer, more majestically squirrel than it had been in life. He has no stomach, no liver, no brain, no heart, nothing internal that can decay. In the garage of my earthly home, over the course of a week, it just came to me what to do. How I should split the skin, remove the blood from the coat with alcohol and cornmeal, scoop out the brain with a melon baller and the intestines with a small slotted spoon. I somehow knew to cure the pelt with heat from a space heater, to create a new skeleton from discarded clothes hangers, to stuff Obadiah with the insides of my toy Psalty Sing and Dance Bible. And by the end, when I had mounted Obadiah in climbing position to the highest cross of corn in a new squirrel heaven and enclosed him in plexiglass to protect him from the elements, Obadiah looked more gloriously alive than he had all those days I watched him through the window. And though I couldn't see him so closely, I knew that even his fleas were gone."

I looked at Charley who was looking at me—neither out of curiosity nor judgment but clear-eyed and straight-on and open, like his whole body was listening and he wanted to hear about the happiest moment of my whole life. "And Nan and Bill?" Charley asked, "What did they think? And where were they that whole time you were working on Obadiah?"

"They knew," I said, "that God was at work with me in the garage. I didn't know at that time what they were thinking, but when I was awarded my taxidermy license at the age of eight, Nan stood up at a special Diamond Hill Cathedral ceremony for me and said she had known from the first that God was at work, that I was being gifted and she just needed to stand back and let God work. Bill, he took that moment to make clear that my gift would be used to God's glory, that from then on, every squirrel I had ever resurrected and ever would resurrect would have a place in the Living Bible Museum. Kind of amazing when you think about it," I said, "especially when you consider how they might have responded when they discovered the empty hide of Psalty, which had been my favorite of all my Christian toys at the time."

"That's when you were happiest?" Charley asked. "With Obadiah?"

I thought again before saying anything. I thought about how much I had delighted in Obadiah in life, about how difficult that day had been, seeing Obadiah attacked, how embarrassed and angry I had been seeing Obadiah close-up like that, how I had hated his fleas, his yellow teeth, his mangy fur. I thought about how, led by God, I had restored—no, perfected—Obadiah, combing out the fleas, coating his yellow teeth with White-Out, evening out his fur with clippings from my own hair. Maybe Obadiah could not breathe anymore—didn't even have the organs to do so—but he was permanently beautiful now, and that would never change. I thought about how, there in the Living Bible Museum's Garden of Eden, Obadiah was even more real than Adam and Eve whose skin was wax.

And then I answered.

"Yes," I said, "That is when I was happiest. With Obadiah."

But what did that mean? Was I happiest when Obadiah was alive and running around out in squirrel-heaven where I could not go, when I could only imagine what it would be like to run with him, to touch him, to be his friend? Or was I happiest as I was trying first to save and then preserve Obadiah, working to perfect God's small creature with my own small hands? Or was I happiest after I had found my calling and had it acknowledged and praised by Nan and Bill and Pastor Diamond, after Obadiah was stuffed and mounted to the glory of God in the Garden of Eden? All three times I was happy, I supposed, but in different ways. I pushed back any separation between Obadiah's life and death, pushed back the unspokens of Charley's question that would only open more questions I could not answer. I did not say any of the other things I felt just then. I did not tell Charley that the other squirrels—dozens of them over the years—paled in comparison to Obadiah, that even though they were mounted to the glory of God for the salvation of sinners in the Living Bible Museum, that even though I had perfected their imperfect bodies, they were never like Obadiah.

I did not say that I missed my first friend.

"Yes," I said again, this time more firmly. "That is when I was happiest. With Obadiah." Then before Charley could ask any more questions, before I could be foolish enough to open my heart and mind even more to this stranger—because that's what Charley was—I took my turn at asking questions, got things back on track where they needed to go, telling Charley that the most important thing—right now, right here, on this park bench—was the state of his eternal soul.

"I like you, Charley," I said, "but right now you are headed straight to Hell."

Charley tried at first to draw me back into talking about Obadiah and happiness, but something inside of me had shifted, and I decided I had better lock up anything else that might get out if I kept talking. Instead, I stuck to what I knew God had wanted from me all along, truths about Heaven and Hell, about being saved or not, about there being only one narrow and certain way to get to Heaven and that I knew it and Charley didn't. Charley started telling me about what he called his "faith journey" and how in 1989, three years before I'd even been born, he'd been bankrupted both in faith and finances by Heritage USA—"a kind of Christian Disneyland in Fort Mill, South Carolina," he'd told me it was—and how he'd had to rethink God and life and everything. I'll admit I was drawn in at first by his story, but when he told me his wife had left him and she'd been right to do so, I knew I had been drawn in by a Lucifer, an Angel of Light who had made me trust him long enough to almost unsettle my God-given sense of how things are. I knew because God didn't allow for divorce any more than He allowed for homosexuality, both being abominations in His sight.

Across the park, Becky and the others made their way to the van. My soul-saving time was up and I had not only failed both God and Charley, I had also been nearly drawn into confusion by an Angel of Light.

"I've got to go," I said, standing up too fast and stepping on the leftover pizza. "But I'll pray for your soul, Charley," I said, peeling the pizza from my shoe and dropping it back in the box.

Then Charley stood so I reached out my hand thinking we should shake hands, but my fingers were smeared with pizza sauce so I wiped them on my jeans as Charley pulled me into a hug, wrapping his arms around me while my arms dangled limp like the boiled turkey hot dogs Nan used to make for me. Charley's stubbled cheek scraped against my smooth one and his lips brushed against my ear.

"Be yourself, man," he whispered, "Just be yourself." Then he peeled himself away and looked at me again, this time his hands on my shoulders, "I'll think of you as I find my way to Florida. And maybe I will stop off in Mansfield, stop to see this Obadiah of yours."

Then Charley turned away and walked off, his dog following, yet even when my eyes could no longer see him, his spicy-sour hippie smell remained.

Sitting alone on the backseat of the NATAS van, I felt mighty uncomfortable thinking about Charley seeing Obadiah, like I was naked and needed to cover myself back up, like somehow I'd let God down by being so full of pride that all I could do was share stupid stories about Obadiah and me instead of just preaching the Word of God like I was called to do. And I didn't know what Charley meant by, "Be yourself, man. Just be yourself," though I knew better than to fall into that trap when it wasn't about me being anything but about God being who He is and me just being God's instrument. All that confusion in my head, and so hard to fight, because I had liked Charley even if he was an Angel of Light, and what did God want me to do with all of that anyway? So I bowed my head and repented, then prayed for Charley's soul, feeling desperate that Charley might see Obadiah and be led to understand.

© Mary Jane Pories

© Julian Norwood

Under the Sign of Sleepytime

> "A Celestial Seasonings herb tea is meant to be more than just a hot drink. It is 'religion, science, philosophy and humor' sifted through a teabag, claims Mo Siegel, Celestial's founder, quality control expert and co-president."
> —Frank W. Martin, "Mo Siegel Was Blending Red Zinger When He Knew Celestial Seasonings Was His Cup of Tea," People Magazine, *September 13, 1976*

Editor's note: Few Tourist Attraction Trauma survivors are as articulate and forthcoming as Bud Blackenberry about the complex interplay between a life and a tourist attraction. Since its inclusion in *Tourist Attraction Travesty: Tales from Tourist Attraction Trauma Survivors*, "Under the Sign of Sleepytime" has helped hundreds of patients at the National Association of Tourist Attraction Survivors' Hospital for Research and Recovery grapple with their pasts and transform their futures.

To understand Bud Blackenberry's story, or "life blend," as he calls it, one must begin with Kitty Morgenstern, Bud's Boston landlady who entered his apartment after the rent went a week overdue and found Bud submerged in a cold peppermint bath, forty bags of Celestial Seasonings Peppermint tea floating at the top. According to NATAS hospital records, this moment was "the lowest imaginable for anyone afflicted by Tourist Attraction Trauma," an assessment Bud has neither confirmed nor denied.

Given Kitty's personal familiarity with Tourist Attraction Trauma from her childhood upbringing at Atlanta, Georgia's, World of Coca-Cola she immediately knew to call the National Association of Tourist Attraction Survivors. Kitty recounts:

I dialed 1-800-555-TATS straightaway, told NATAS I had an emergency on my hands and asked if they could please send someone quick. Then I went back to be with Mr. Blackenberry, my heart torn up from not having taken the time to know any more about him than that he'd grown up at Celestial Seasonings, but knowing I now had to do for him whatever I could. I sat there on the side of the tub and pulled one of his hands—cold and dull green and smelling like the peppermint tea he had steeped himself in—from the tub. I held his hand between my own two hands, rubbed it warm and felt his wrist for a pulse. That's how I knew for certain he was alive, even though he was unconscious. "Everything will be alright, Mr. Blackenberry," I just kept repeating. "Everything will really be alright. Help is on the way."

Hours later, two strong young men in white NATASHRR uniforms came in. They rolled up their shirt sleeves and slid their arms under Mr. Blackenberry's naked body, lifted him from the tub and onto a gurney, which was when I saw the words at the bottom of the tub, wobbly at first then becoming clear as the water settled, the same words I could have read a hundred times on the candy-striped Peppermint tea boxes lining Mr. Blackenberry's bathroom wall: "Settle into an intimate cove and while away a few moments on yourself, letting the delectably sweet taste of peppermint pour over your thoughts." I didn't know what to make of those words just then or of what Mr. Blackenberry had done or tried to do to himself—I just didn't understand it at all—so I plunged my hand into the bath and moved the tea around in a slow circle, first in one direction and then the next until I'd made the cold tea all wavy again and unsettled the look of those words that had first unsettled me.

* * *

I know this much. Every story's beginning begets a different ending.

I was twenty-eight years old when my landlord Kitty Morgenstern found me submerged in a bathtub of peppermint tea, and I had been living alone in my one-bedroom apartment in her building for the last seven of those years. I call the building "hers" but the apartment "mine" because during my stay I had truly transformed and made it mine, lining my walls with various "families" of Celestial Seasonings boxes—some empty, some in the process of being emptied—and pinned to my refrigerator a handwritten list to remind me what belonged where:

Bathroom: Peppermint, Mint Magic, Grandma's Tummy Mint, Tension Tamer, Chamomile

Kitchen: Red Zinger, Lemon Zinger, Wild Berry Zinger, Raspberry Zinger, Tangerine Orange Zinger

Bedroom: Bengal Spice, Cinnamon Apple Spice, Mandarin Orange Spice

Hallway Closet: Roastaroma, Morning Thunder

Living Room: True Blueberry, Black Cherry Berry, Peach Passion

My list made sense to me, provided scaffolding for my world, for my life. But though I was in my own home, I never felt truly at home. I blamed Celestial Seasonings with their unrelenting growth and change as they discontinued old teas and churned out new ones based on seasons and sales. Just when I would think my list was complete, I'd have to cross-out Waikiwi Peach and Cranberry Cove, and then the winter holidays would roll around and I would have to add in Gingerbread Spice and Candy Cane Lane, only to cross them out again months later. Regardless of how restful and secure I believed a life filled with herb teas must be, the reality never matched my philosophical ideal.

Then there were the complaints.

Larry Mullins who lived in the apartment below me was the first to complain to Kitty about the smell, said it gave him headaches and affected his sense of taste. Then Gwen complained. Then Karin. Finally, Tahir. While they all complained about the smell, only Karin also expressed personal concern for me, waiting in the hallway each morning just so she could say, "Good Morning, Mr. Blackenberry. Are you doing alright?" I would nod and smile before grabbing my morning paper and slipping back inside my apartment.

I guess you could say I kept to myself, not uncommon for somebody who grew up getting knocked down, who had learned early on to distrust everybody, distrust the whole world. I didn't know my neighbors as people so much as complainants, which is what I'd come to expect so much that perhaps I had by then become a self-fulfilling prophecy. In hindsight and with the help of the National Association of Tourist Attraction Survivors, I now understand my neighbors' complaints and concern and have faced my own dysfunction, even recognizing how the co-mingling of Peppermint, Wild Berry Zinger, and Bengal Spice must have driven my neighbors crazy, my obliviousness proof of my own self-delusion. NATAS says that Tourist Attraction Trauma can manifest in a multitude of ways, each highly specific and particular to the attraction itself. My manifestation remains for me less a source of shame than of mild embarrassment. We have to forgive our limitations, be gentle with ourselves, and work towards healing whatever form healing might take.

To her credit, Kitty never did evict me for my strange and odorous ways; she only contacted NATAS after she found me submerged and unresponsive. After all, Kitty knew I had been born and raised in Boulder, Colorado, and she recognized Tourist Attraction Trauma when she saw it. Still, Kitty did not know—and how could she have known?—that I was an unreliable narrator of my own life story? That's just how life becomes when you start with a mistaken premise and then build your life upon a lie. Kitty could not have known I grew up believing I was the love child of my mother Althea Blackenberry and Celestial Seasonings founder Mo Siegel, and that I believed this fiction for no reason other than that Mo had taken it upon himself to be kind to me, to watch over me like a father because my own father—whatever the reason—was absent.

In the end we are all characters in each other's stories, aren't we? Each of us playing roles—major, minor, all mixed up—in each other's lives. Part invention, part fact. One-of-a-kind and wanting to fit. We can be so terrified we might change, might dissolve, that we package ourselves and each other into four-sided boxes, shelvable by external design. Maybe this both-and of our mingling, shifting, unknowable stories and selves is what we fear the most.

Half-lived.

Half-invented.

My life story. My reality.

And when all of everything came undone, I moved through the world more shadow than body, unable to regain the substance I had once taken to be so very, very certain. I am learning that I can create for myself a new story, blending old ingredients with newly milled ones, creating a one-of-a-kind life-tea that I don't intend to package and sell but only live, really live, as best I can. I won't promise that this new blend will be 100% organic and free from all contaminants. Why should I? Sometimes the best teas come about quite by accident, and sometimes the worst are the most intentional. All the same, I am Blendmaster of my own life story, and what you are about to savor I call Bud's Blackenberry Brew.

I was conceived during a Sunrise Break. My parents, full of sunshine and smokes, retreated to the coolness of the barn loft filled with drying peppermint. Herbal infusion at its best. "And then," my mother told me, "your dad and

I fell fast asleep because nights of packaging teas by hand were exhausting."

On May 26, 1971, I was born an unrefined bud, and so I was named. I would, in my lifetime, go through the same three stages—Mill, Blend, and Package—herbs pass through before they are sold as Celestial Seasonings teas. But unlike a hopper of hibiscus, those stages of my life were not so clearly distinct, not so easily identified.

I have pleasant—if scant—memories of my early childhood, that milling period essential for maintaining freshness and flavor. For what could be better than to be raised in the birthplace of the Sleepytime Bear? In the early days before production was beyond what Mo Siegel, my mother, and the merry band of herb packers could handle by hand, I tottered around the floor of the building at 47th and Pearl, tied to my mother by a long length of hemp. When I would tire of roaming, I, like a tether ball that wraps itself round and round a pole, would circle round and round my mother until I had wrapped her up tight and she would have no choice but to be still and let me hold her until I decided it was time to unwind.

The outside world never smelled so good to me as that building where my mother spent her days sewing tea bags with her sleek silver Singer, a gift from Mo essential to her work. Some days, the odor of blackberry leaves permeated the building; other days, hibiscus dust coated everything, including me, pink. But on any given day, my favorite place to go, my favorite place to be, was a room that never changed and was always kept closed—the mint room. Stepping inside, my eyes burned, my lungs filled with cool fire. I knew, without yet having words for it, that this was as close as I could get to the moment of my conception—the womb before my birth. I have always imagined that when my mother's water broke, it was not some bland amniotic fluid that went spilling over that worn wood floor, but peppermint tea. Gallons and gallons of steaming hot peppermint tea.

My first memory. Thick black hair that smells earthy-sweet. I am prickled hot and crying and my mother has lifted me to her shoulder. Around me tumble waves of blackberry hair, soft and sweet and blanketing the whole of me. My trembling stops and I breathe in, out, in, out, in, out. A song. Hers.
Hush-a-bye little Blackenberry, hush-a-bye my love.
I am hushabyed and held. From behind I feel another body. His. Arms like vines wrap around us both. A song, hers, with his voice an overlay.
Hush-a-bye little Blackenberry, hush-a-bye my love.
The vines loosen and drop to the gates through which I first swam into this world. A groan. His. Whispered not into my ear but hers. "Oh, Althea. My rose hips." Pulled away from blackberry hair, I lie swaddled tight in soft cotton, nestled inside a hollow of drying yellow flowers that prickle but smell sweet and soft and safe.

Love. Peace. Equality.
Using herbs of all kinds for a healthy, harmonious life.
That was Celestial Seasonings, and that, to me, that was Mo Siegel.
Only once do I remember feeling those vines wrapped around me, and only once do I remember hearing that other man's voice, but as Mo was a constant presence in the building at 47th and Pearl and a constant presence in my life, he came to feel like family and to be in a way my true father if not my real one. But then sometime during the period in which I'd been taught to raise two fingers when asked my age, the age when children begin to notice not how long somebody has been around but rather when they first begin to leave, I sensed Mo's absence as he began to travel, flying all over the world to buy his herbs instead of picking them himself in the Colorado countryside. And by the time I was raising three fingers in answer to the most frequently asked question, Mo had made his first million and established an

office for himself eight blocks away. I did not understand and because I did not understand, I felt abandoned. I wanted him to be a man whose voice could join my mother's in singing me a lullaby, so I told myself that once upon a time he had, replacing an uncertain memory with an unprovable yet undeniable truth.

We are all characters in each others' stories. So it was that I made Mo the father in mine.

All children make sense of the world with the details available to them, no matter how fragmented and incomplete. So as I perceived that growing distance between Mo and Mom and me, all I could figure was that the grand celestial Blendmaster had gotten something wrong. Maybe the money ingredient was too high. Maybe there should have been a trial run before it was put out on the market. But there wasn't, and the "Mo, Mom, Money, and Me" line flopped. When we were all working so closely together at the building at 47th and Pearl, Mo would spin me in circles until I was dizzy, walk me around on his shoulders like I was the prince of herbal teas. I loved him as my father, and for many years it seemed he loved me like a son. The three of us—we would have made a good blend—but money pulled him away, or so I believed then. But I'm getting ahead of myself, using terminology only Celestial Seasonings insiders would understand without offering an insider's explanation. Back to the Blendmaster

At Celestial Seasonings, the Blendmaster is the person who dresses up in a white lab coat like a scientist so he can spend his days putting milled and blended herbs into clear glass beakers, pouring boiling water over them, swishing them around, and then letting them rest for four to six minutes before tasting the resulting brew. Of everybody at Celestial Seasonings, the Blendmaster wields the greatest power in determining the product line. When I was growing up, the Blendmaster's name was Bob.

Now, things went wrong for Bob the Blendmaster all the time. He tried all kinds of crazy combinations like his infamous Pep-o-Nilla-Scus (peppermint, vanilla, and hibiscus) and Cozy Creosote (Sleepytime's lesser cousin), but fortunately, most of these never made it to market. The one notable exception was Nutcracker Sweet, released in 1995 as a tribute to Bob the Blendmaster who choked and died during the taste trials.

As business thrived and profits really kicked in, it felt at first like Blendmaster god was saying to himself, "A little money tastes pretty good in here, so a whole lot must be even better." But Blendmaster god was wrong, the Mo, Mom, Money, and Me blend was a flop, and in the end, Mo and money both pulled out, leaving behind the basic blend of Mom and Me. Still, with her shared profits from Mo's 36 Herb Tea, Mom bought us a two-bedroom house. I was thankful we had a roof over our heads, but I watched my mom struggle to pay the bills, budgeting down to the last nickel so she could keep the heat and lights on and still shop at Alfalfa's for wholesome, organic food.

I felt the growth of Celestial Seasonings much like a blackberry leaf must feel itself drying in a heated tumbler, turning brittle and crumbling at the edges. I began to see more faces than I could recognize or name, and I listened to Mom talk about how Mo was "selling out," how his "ideals and values were slipping," how he was "changing who he was to turn a better profit." I did not understand all my mother's words, but I applied them to my experience at a company picnic when I was six, watching Mo serve hot dogs and hamburgers for the very first time while my mother stuck to her tofu and sprouts. Mo offered me a hot dog with ketchup, and I, trusting him, took it. I had taken just one bite when my mother grabbed me up and made me spit out the bite of half-chewed hot dog into her hand. She squirted fresh water into my mouth, made me rinse and spit, rinse and spit, until all the meat was gone while Mo stood beside these men in black shiny suits who laughed between their bites of hamburgers. Mo didn't laugh, though. Just stood there, watching in a way that seemed to me even then as not unkind, though still my mom scolded, "Really, Mo! Can't you leave just one thing uncorrupted? If you want to sell out, sell out. Eat hot dogs for all I care, but can't you at least leave Bud out of it? Let him decide what he wants to do, who he wants to be."

And there I stood, ketchup down the front of my "Happiness is a warm puppy" t-shirt, my mother moving for the bean sprout and tofu salad she'd made and scooping a spoonful onto a reusable plastic tray for me. Mo bent down and wiped the ketchup from my shirt, but I don't know whether he smiled at me because I only looked down. I felt a gentle hand between my shoulder blades push me towards my mother, and when I turned around Mo had turned away. I felt so ashamed, but I didn't know why. Had Mo not shooed me towards Mom, not turned away from me, had he even just said anything to me, perhaps I would have set aside Mom's salad and gone back to try another hot dog, maybe even a hamburger, but I didn't. In that moment, everything pointed to Mom being more right, more pure, more committed. She was, after all, my mother, the woman who had brought me into this world and who took care of me day after day after day. Without my mother, I could not survive.

Since I've always liked the simple varieties best—Peppermint, Chamomile, Sleepytime—Mom and Me came to seem like a pretty good blend. After that company picnic, she never said or did anything to turn me against Mo and I continued to visit the factory he was building, though I seldom came into contact with him. When I did, he was always kind, but never close. "You look out for your mom now, Bud," he would say. "She needs your support."

Because Mo always gave me new teas to try and had even granted me a special pass into the mint room, I believed I was special, was more than just a kid who liked tea and whose mother was a Celestial Seasonings employee, working as a quote finder. In a secret place deep inside me, Mo was Daddy to me; I had nobody else to fill that hole. After school while my classmates played baseball, rode bikes, and traded cards, I went to the mint room, the holiest of Celestial Seasonings holies, the place I felt was as close to Mo as any other. This suited me. I preferred solitude over chatter, steeped myself in the intoxicating aroma of mint that cleared my head of all the world's clutter.

You know how there's always that one kid in school everybody wants to avoid? The kid who smells funny? That was me. Most days I smelled like peppermint, but some days, after lounging on a fresh cutting of spearmint, I exuded a sickly sweet aroma. Add Celestial Seasonings' Mountain Herbery shampoo and Mom's campaign against antiperspirant (she was certain it would clog my pores and I would die) and I must have smelled just awful. I knew I was different because I smelled different and liked different things. Even so, I was friendly to everyone, even if they weren't always friendly back to me.

I remember third grade especially well, for I had high hopes that year. I didn't have any friends, and to tell the truth, school was rough, but I decided I could make things change on Valentine's Day and made sachets of herbs and spices my classmates could turn into original one-of-a-kind cups of tea. Ever tried to come up with twenty-five never-before-been-tasted tea blends? It's not easy! For two weeks before the Valentine's party, I spent my afternoons with Bob the Blendmaster, blending and tasting, getting myself so full of tea that I couldn't help but wet the bed every single night.

Mom went with me to a fabric store and helped me pick out fine netting, the type used to make birdseed pouches for weddings. The night before the Valentine's Day party, I finished my twenty-fifth blend and stayed up until the sun rose tying tea sachets with pink ribbon and inventing names to go with my classmates' names. Sweet Sue Spice. Zany Zed

Zinger. Minty Matthew. Hibiscus Hugh. Won't You be My Lemon, Linda. Because I Clove You, Clara.

The morning of February 14th, I left the house with a red heart-shaped basket full of individually wrapped and labeled teas. Oh, what high hopes I had! Mom, with tears in her eyes, hugged and kissed me and said, "I'm so proud of you, Bud Blackenberry." At the time, I believed the tears rose from her great pride in me, but now I wonder if they were tears for what she knew I would have to face in school that day.

When I walked into the classroom, my classmates turned to look at me, wrinkling their noses as they always did. Hugh sneered and pointed at my basket. "Whatcha got there, Bud?" he asked, then let his wrist go limp and said, "It's real puur-rty, whatever it is you got there." The class, the whole class, laughed. I made my way to my desk and sat down, putting the basket of teas by my feet and telling myself that, when the time came for the Valentine's Day party, they'd understand.

Stapled to the back bulletin board were twenty-five construction paper mailboxes, one for each of the twenty-four students in the class and one for our teacher, Miss Makechatter. When I squinted my eyes and looked at the wall, all those twenty-five mailboxes turned into one beautiful pink blur.

Before first recess, Miss Makechatter set aside twenty minutes for us to put Valentine's cards in mailboxes, and I watched as other students put their cards in the boxes, even putting cards in mine. Miss Makechatter had a rule that everybody had to give cards to everybody in the class, not just the favorites, so I was assured twenty-four cards in my box just like everybody else.

While everybody was scurrying around the back wall, Miss Makechatter leaned against my desk and said, "Why aren't you joining your classmates, Bud? Don't you like Valentine's Day? Have you nothing to share?"

"I-I'm waiting if I can, please, Miss Makechatter," I stammered. "I'm w-waiting until everybody goes out to recess,"

I said, trying so hard to be confident through my quavering voice. "I just w-want mine to be a surprise."

Now, I wouldn't say that Miss Makechatter was a mean teacher, but I don't believe she ever had control of herself. She was a coffee drinker, and even then I had a sense of the sort of poison coffee could be. Her right hand always held her "#1 Teacher!" coffee mug that had apples, ABCs, and 123s on it, meant to make it look friendly somehow. In her classroom, she was always brewing a pot of coffee, and she was forever drinking the stuff. Her skin had the color and texture of a used coffee filter, brown-streaked and warm-damp. Her teeth had bathed in so much coffee, they were not only stained but had taken on the shape and color of whole black coffee beans which clung tenuously to her coffee ground gums. Perhaps they had even become coffee beans that could be plucked and ground into a final cup of coffee if the world should ever run out.

"And what have you got that's so special, Bud?" she asked, her eyes darting about the room like startled hummingbirds as she questioned me.

"Please, Miss Makechatter," I said, "I want it to be a surprise. Even, ma'am, for you."

She leaned down to look at the basket beneath my desk, and before I could bend down to cover the tea sachets, she must have guessed what I had. "If you must, Bud Blackenberry," she harrumphed, "you can have the room to yourself for the first five minutes of recess, but that's all. I need to walk down to the cafeteria to pick up my new shipment of coffee—they order Folgers in bulk for me—and then I'll be back so you'd better be done with whatever it is you're putting in those mailboxes."

I was happy. So happy! Five minutes wasn't long, but it would be long enough. Miss Makechatter dismissed the class and there I was, in the room, alone. I dropped the tea sachets into the mailboxes with care, making sure they were right side up and on top of all the cards and red heart-shaped suckers. I even had a special one for Miss Makechatter—Miss Makechatter's Morning Thunder—which I had endowed with that ingredient she most liked (or so I thought) in coffee, caffeine. Of all the teas I made for that very special Valentine's Day, only this one, with no less than Mo's blessing, made it to market.

I had just slipped Miss Makechatter's Morning Thunder into her mailbox when she opened the door and walked in, carrying a twenty-five pound bag of coffee beans over her shoulder. "All right, Bud Blackenberry," she said as she opened her slim closet and heaved the bag inside, "go outside. There are fifteen minutes of recess left and you need to go out and get some fresh air." She was right about that. The smell of coffee was making me sick.

I sat on my usual swing on the far end of the playground, waiting anxiously for recess to end and for the Valentine's Day party to start. The party would, I had convinced myself, be grand. When the whistle blew, we all—even me—raced to get in line.

Within the short time I had been outside, Miss Makechatter and several mothers had taped red, white, and pink streamers from one end of the classroom's ceiling to the other. On our desks were red Valentine's Day search-a-word sheets with words like "heart," "love," "chocolate," and "kisses" printed at the bottom. Miss Makechatter's desk was cleared of its usual stacks of papers and books, and in their place were tinfoil pans filled with red-sprinkled cupcakes, cupid cookies, and heart-shaped finger Jell-o. Even my too-cool-to-care classmates came unglued at the sight of sugar in its many guises. While I have always preferred honey and carob to white-death sugar and chocolate, even I was tempted.

Miss Makechatter gave us a "ready, set, go" and we started on our search-a-word sheets. The children whose mothers had come received extra help, and it was no surprise when Hugh and his mother, who had been hired by Senco, Inc. after their delivery truck full of sewing needles plowed into a JC+ Ranch trailer hauling irrigated pasture grass, found all the words first and won a giant chocolate heart.

Finally, the time came that I had been waiting so hopefully for. "Before you have treats," Miss Makechatter said, "you can take your mailboxes down from the wall and read your cards."

While everybody rushed to the back bulletin board and ripped off their mailboxes, I sat on my sweaty hands, more tense and excited to see what they thought of my gifts than to care about the cards they had given me out of obligation.

Hugh got to his first and read my note aloud: "'Hibiscus Hugh: Here's a little hibiscus to see you through. From Bud Blackenberry.'" Hugh screwed up his face and held my tea sachet out at arm's length, letting it dangle between thumb and forefinger. "What is this crap, Bud?" he asked, but before I had time to explain, he dropped the tea sachet on the floor and stomped on it like it was a roach. As red hibiscus powder poofed out on the floor and over Hugh's white canvas shoes, I heard a high-pitched shriek and turned around to see Hugh's mother, red-hot. "You freak! How dare you stain my son's new shoes!"

"B-but he wasn't supposed to—" I started to say, but she was hitting me about the head, and nobody, not even Miss Makechatter, tried to stop her.

Between the blows, I made out my other classmates' reactions to their gifts and saw my creations, my one-of-a-kind blends, die a variety of deaths. Sue spat on Sweet Sue Spice. Zed zapped Zany Zed Zinger in an electrical outlet. Matthew masticated Minty Matthew. Clara took her scissors and cleaved in two Because I Clove You, Clara. Linda left Won't You be My Lemon, Linda, floating in the toilet. And Miss Makechatter? I watched Miss Makechatter most intently, knowing she was my final hope, knowing that she could make all the difference in my world if she would only respond in kindness and understanding, could even just say thank you.

I watched as Miss Makechatter opened the card on which I had written, "Miss Makechatter's Morning Thunder: For picking you up in the morning and helping you go all day long," and I watched her read those words silently. Miss Makechatter did not stomp on the tea like Hugh, nor did she drown it like Linda. For a moment her face was unreadable, but then a crooked smile spread across it and a decidedly cruel laugh percolated like bitter coffee from between her lips. She walked to her closet, her too small closet with the huge bags of coffee beans, ripped open one of the bags and began throwing coffee beans at me. She didn't have to say why she did it; that much was clear. Miss Makechatter wanted nothing to do with herbs—hearty, healthful herbs. Miss Makechatter wanted nothing to do with herbs, and she wanted nothing to do with me.

I ran out of the classroom feeling the sting of cruelty and coffee beans. I ran towards home, not knowing how or if I could run that far, just knowing that I needed to get away, as far away as possible. Four blocks from home, I saw my mother kneeling on the pavement with her arms outstretched and called out "Mommy!" as though I were still a toddler. I ran into her arms and buried my face in her blackberry hair, and even though I reeked of coffee, my mother lifted me up in her strong arms and held me close. As she picked coffee beans like little black beetle from my hair, I could not speak and she did not. I was past the age where mothers carry their sons. I knew that. Still, she carried me all the way home.

Inside the front door, my mother knelt again before me, this time taking care to unbutton and remove my shirt, my pants, my shoes, everything. Standing naked before my mother, my eyes met hers, then dropped to the tile floor. I could not reconcile my feelings of wanting to be held and needing to hide my body, both from my mother and from myself.

"I love you, Bud Blackenberry," my mother said. "Will you be my valentine?"

She smiled, but I still could not speak. I tried on a smile that was less than half of what I had worn on my way to school that morning, but even that faded and disappeared. Mom stood and took my hand in hers, walked me to the bathroom door. "Go inside," she said. "I promise you will feel better." She turned and I watched her walk down the hall, bending down along the way to pick up my discarded clothes. Turning towards the bathroom, I caught my reflection—distorted and disproportionate—in the shiny doorknob. I wrapped my fingers around the knob, obscuring my reflection, then turned the knob, pushed open the door, and walked into the embrace of hot peppermint steam. I let myself be pulled inside and inhaled.. The pure peppermint blaze burned away the bitter stench of Miss Makechatter's coffee beans. I closed the door behind me, feeling the tingle of peppermint's healing powers even before I stepped into the tub.

My life can be summed up in that Valentine's Day. I always believed the best in people and I always believed that drinking herbal tea leads to healthy, happy lives. As far as I could tell, the only reason Miss Makechatter and the rest of the world were so out of sorts was because they didn't drink enough herbal tea. I'd taken to heart my mother Althea Blackenberry's philosophy which was all wrapped up in that of Celestial Seasonings.

At home, Mom had done everything she could during my early years to make life hopeful and secure, as true to the vision of Celestial Seasonings as she possibly could. As one of Celestial Seasonings' first quote-finders, she extended her talent to writing inspirations on our walls and to tucking tiny paper scrolls into my lunch bag alongside an egg salad sandwich on whole wheat bread, yogurt cup, and carrot sticks. I'd unwrap, "If you give love, you get love," her personal favorite, and feel a special warmth. True to my mother's favorite saying, I gave love again and again and again, believing beyond reason that someday my love would be returned by people who were not just my mother.

One week after that third grade Valentine's Day party, I found myself sitting at a desk in a different classroom in a different school, a private school run out of the spacious attic of Ms. Starshine Spangles, a friend my mother had met in her early herb gathering days who had appointed herself principal. This school was not legally recognized by the city of Boulder or the state of Colorado, but it felt right in ways beyond legalities. Along the left wall, rabbits pushed wheelbarrows full or peaches; from above the chalkboard in the front, the Sleepytime Bear smiled drowsily down at us; along the right wall, two children picked blackberries in a forest; and behind me, the bulletin board was covered with laminated quotes my mother had provided. "If you give love, you get love" was the umbrella quote under which all the other sayings rested. I was one of four students in my class, but for the first time in my life as a student, I was neither ridiculed nor mocked. My classmates—Celeste, Starlight (Ms. Spangles' daughter), Aurora, and Adam—were as much unlike my public school classmates as they were like me.

Amongst likeminded peers I became even more committed to the Celestial Seasonings vision. In fifth grade we were called upon to collaboratively write "The Celestial Seasonings Story" and I am to this day proud to claim as my own the closing line about goodness, purity, and inspiring art!

How steadfastly I believed in the superiority of Celestial Seasonings' art! I scoffed at Picasso, scorned Van Gogh, made fun of Chagall. They could not compare to Beth Underwood, Catherine Deeter, Robert Giusti, and—my favorite—Braldt Bralds. My teacher Ms. Chamomile Teague praised my passion, my use of language, my vision for the world. Ms. Teague said I could do anything I set my mind to, and at that particular fifth grade moment, riding high on optimism, on love that I both gave and got, on the glory of Celestial Seasonings as both a producer of fine quality teas and also of a promoter of life-as-it-was-meant-to-be-lived-naturally, she might have been right.

Then came 1986, the year Celestial Seasonings introduced their Gourmet Black Tea Line, the year Mo Siegel decided to quit the company and travel the world helping people, the year I turned fourteen. In 1986 my sunny Celestial Seasonings herbal tea world collided with the cold commercial reality that caffeinated black teas were to be sold under the same name, and I could not find a way to repackage and sell back to myself this new vision for consumption. Lacking words for this imbalance of realities, I could not even allow myself to consciously acknowledge the irreparable schism occurring in my psyche. When faced with two worlds that one cannot reconcile, I did what so many are compelled to do; I chose to live even more fervently inside my Celestial Seasonings tea box world, this time in defiance of reality.

At home with Mom, we had for years kept the artwork of Celestial Seasonings' domestic fantasies in our living room: a woman picking apples; a woman with wind-blown hair drinking a cup of tea atop a rocky hill, a black and white dog by her side; a family dressed in starched white clothes of an earlier era picnicking in a park. Before I reached my teenage years, my mother and I would act out the scenes that surrounded us, drinking teas and engaging the characters in conversation.

Some nights we draped green silk over two coat trees and played our apple picking game, talking to Blossom while we drank Cinnamon Apple Spice. "What beautiful apples we have this fall, don't you think?" Blossom would say to us, and my mother would reply, "Lovely," while I blushed and hid behind the tree, peeking out occasionally to catch Blossom giving me a sideways look. Other nights, when we were feeling bold, we would pile blankets and pillows in the center of the floor and climb them together to meet Evelyn with the wind-blown hair and her faithful dog Blaze. From the northernmost corner of the room, a fan would blow, and our hair would flare out to one side. We would sit and sip with Evelyn, and Blaze would nuzzle me under the chin. Then, together, we would look out to sea. "You're so strong, Evelyn," my mother would say, pulling a blanket around her body to protect her from the wind's sharp chill.

My favorite nights were those when we spread a checkered blanket over the green shag carpet and joined the family in the park. My mother would recline in the arms of a gentle man in white, and I would climb up on their laps. My brothers and sisters would come with hoop and stick, wanting to play, but I could not be bothered.

I had my own private places, my own private fantasies, too. When I was a child, my bedroom had been decorated with the same pictures that were still painted on the walls of my classroom—rabbits wheeling peaches around in wheelbarrows, children gathering herbs in a fairy tale forest, the cozy cottage of the Sleepytime Bear—but by the age of thirteen, I was too old for all that and redecorated. Mina, the Mandarin Orange Spice woman with her black hair pinned back and slices of orange in her outstretched hands, occupied the wall above my bed. Before sleep each night I would stand on my bed and press my lips against Mina's so I could taste a hint of citrus. And every morning when I opened my eyes, I saw Trina the Tension Tamer, dressed in red and sitting comfortably upon her dragon. Mina and Trina filled my dreams, charging the air with odors both familiar and new. After nights of sleep and dreams, a thick spicy-sweet fluid—secreted from every pore of my body—glazed my bedsheets.

It's embarrassing to think about my adolescence, let alone write about it, let alone share it in this way, but to get beyond it, I must go through it. Last night as I was sorting through the physical artifacts of my existence, I discovered a box of notebooks I had kept beginning at age fourteen, handwritten pleas to the "Maker of Herbal Delights" for a more sustained devotion, a greater understanding for others, and the self-control to stop doing "obscene things" in the mint room. Such small traumas they now seem, anguish over common things! And all my idealism about changing the world soured like damp spearmint when Mo banished me from all Celestial Seasonings properties at fourteen years of age.

"Quality control," Mo said, then turned his back on me as I, fumbling, pulled up my underwear and green corduroy pants.

"I'm s-s-sorry," I stuttered, my face aflame with shame.

I wanted to say, "Please let me stay."

I wanted to say, "It won't happen again."

But Mo's back was to me and I knew he couldn't look at me, knew he could not say even a word. I paused on the border between the mint room and the factory floor, closed my eyes, inhaled. Mint behind me. Fresh-cut blackberry leaves mingled with machinery oil before me. I longed to slip back under the spell of mint, but that moment had passed and I stepped forward into the factory Mo had built, this place that milled and blended and packaged nature so that people might drink it from teacups. The door to the mint room clanged shut behind me, and with it went all but the memory of mint as a whole-body experience.

At fourteen years old I was cut off, adrift. And so I set about trying to do things right, trying to get things natural. Too ashamed to return to the Celestial Seasonings school, I quit school altogether and even though my mother didn't know why, she accepted that it was all for the best. I started staying in my bedroom for days at a time, making the two-dimensional worlds of Celestial Seasonings paintings three-dimensional through sculptures, creating an atmosphere where Mina, Trina, and all the others might truly come to life. My mother homeschooled me, more determined than ever that I could succeed, that I would hold fast to the pure vision of Celestial Seasonings, that I would keep money from messing with the mix, which was easy enough to do since we had none. With Celestial Seasonings needing fewer and fewer quotes, Mom's income dropped and even shopping at Alfalfa's for anything but chickpeas became a challenge.

Deep inside, I knew I was the impurity—the thistle in the blackberry leaves, the pebble that could stop the gears, the pervert polluting the mint room. But what could we do besides live as we always had? We drank Celestial Seasonings teas by the gallon, adored tea box artwork, and preached its philosophy. We weren't sure about anything else that made up life and the wider world, and I was less sure than ever about me.

Distanced now, I watched the changes in my presumed father's company as it was sold first to Kraft, had a near-merger/monopoly with Lipton in 1988 (the year I "graduated" from homeschool), then moved to 4600 Sleepytime Drive in 1990. Mo returned as CEO in 1991, and though I tried many times to get back to the mint room, to regain Mo's favor as though I had some inherited right to it, it was no good. I wanted to remain a part of the Celestial Seasonings story as I felt I always had been, but Mo could no longer allow this and even told me in a letter—one of those serious this-is-how-life-is-son type letters young men should get from their fathers—that he was not my father, that he, "had only wanted to do right by you and should never have let you believe this thing that is not true." This rejection, this new distance without any explanation of my true paternity (did I even believe him?) confused and hurt me. I did not know what to believe. When my mother, Althea Blackenberry, may God rest her soul, fell asleep from an apparent overdose of Sleepytime laced unnaturally with valium and didn't wake up, it became too hard to live so close to the center of the Celestial Seasonings world.

At the age of twenty-one I moved to Boston for no other reason than it was far from Boulder, to an apartment of my own. I didn't work—all my attempts at securing a job failed—but lived off the allowance Mo, who continued to care about me beyond any obligation to do so, doled out every month. The modest sum was enough to cover rent, all the tea I could drink, and food from a local food co-op. I began to build walls around myself inside my own apartment, walls of Celestial Seasonings tea boxes that insulated me from the world. Though I still believed herbal tea could change the world, my few attempts to share my passion with others ended badly. I still smelled funny, after all.

But I could only build tea box walls around myself for so long, and after five years when my landlady Kitty Morgenstern found me steeping in my own personal Boston tea party of peppermint, I had no choice but to begin rebuilding my life with the help of NATAS. In 1999, the year Celestial Seasonings took to poisoning prairie dogs and two years into my recovery, I returned to Boulder, Colorado, when Mo sent me a personal invitation to take the Tour of Tea with his usual Christmas card. Even seven years after I had left, a part of me—a central part of me—yearned for the world Celestial Seasonings had created on their tea boxes and through marketing to promote their products. With my still-believing heart, I at first found on the Tour of Tea what I longed to be true.

Bright and delightful. What better words exist to describe the new visitor's center? Windows aplenty and yellow galore, graced with women and young children waiting around for the 11:00 Tea Tour and only three men, all accompanying women. Children gathered around and hugged the stuffed Sleepytime Bear wearing his red cap and sleeping in his huge overstuffed chair.

"Hello, old friend," I whispered, resting my hand briefly on Sleepytime Bear's soft brown paw before moving to make way for these children who seemed to love him as much as I always had. I watched, smiling, as three generations of women—a grandmother and mother holding the hands of a young girl—experienced Celestial Seasonings together. I read the quotes on placards, some the same as those on the tea boxes I knew and loved, some new even to me. Above my mother's old Singer sewing machine on display for all to see was a line from Shakespeare: "How far that little candle throws his beams. So shines a good deed." I couldn't help but think, couldn't help but believe, that Mo—be he Daddy to me or not—had chosen this one quote in remembrance of my mother.

I walked over to a wooden cupboard displaying a variety of teas, all open and available for tasting, with mate teas and chai upfront. Disdaining the caffeine content of black teas including chai, I chose the mate whose caffeine, unlike coffee and tea, enhances mental alertness without causing sleeplessness or jitters, a fact I remember from creating Miss Makechatter's Morning Thunder with Bob the Blendmaster. I took a Tropical Mate Zinger bag from the box, dropped it into a paper cup, and added hot water.

I sat and sipped, looked around, noting above the Art Gallery entranceway an old friend, the Bengal Spice tiger I had created in my bedroom during my last days in Boulder. Though I wondered how they had acquired Colonel Spicey, as I had named him, I was glad to see him looking as strong and alert as ever and gave him a small salute.

The tour guide announced the start of the tour, so I refilled my cup with iced Lemon Zinger and shuffled into the art gallery along with the tourists. The guide, Mica, a pretty woman about my own age with brown curls, dimmed the lights so we could watch a video that told how Mo Siegel had gathered herbs from the surrounding Colorado countryside at the age of nineteen and began drying them and selling them as tea. "We're looking to herbs to keep us healthy with the power of nature," the voice on the video said. And as pictures ran across the screen of the young crazy-haired Mo and his happy band of herb grubbers, my mother among them, I couldn't help but think how lucky I was to have been even a small and unknown part of it all.

But then I took the tour.

Maybe I wanted too badly for everything to be natural, even though I knew it wouldn't, couldn't be. Maybe I wanted to walk inside the new factory and have it not be a factory but instead be fields full of people picking and drying herbs under the heat of the big red sun. I knew it wouldn't be like that, but knowing does not stop wanting.

I took note of the order on the processing and packaging side of the factory—so different from the days my mother sewed with her Singer—and read the signs above the machinery: "Double Package Maker," "Tea Bagging," "Straight Line Closer," "Overwrap," "Case Packing," "Robotic Palletizer." A handwritten sign on a pallet of boxed teas read, "Leave here for Robot Programmer. Thanks!" Forklifts zipped in and out, and Mica was careful not to let anybody walk in front of her for fear, I think, of being run over. She was bright and eager, executing her lines flawlessly, gesturing dramatically to our group, saying things like "this factory runs 5—7 days a week," and "During the winter months, Celestial Seasonings experiences its highest productivity due to high demand for teas," and, "When in full swing, we produce 8 million bags of tea each week," and "All the machinery in the factory is made in United States, except the Tea Bagging machine which came all the way from Italy."

She pointed to an area above the main factory floor—"the mixing room"—and an elderly woman asked if the group might go up there to see all the herbs being mixed into teas, all computer monitored so each batch is precisely alike. "Oh, no, ma'am," Mica said kindly. "We never take tours up there. It's too dangerous." I nodded, thinking less of herbs than of that early mix of Mo, Mom, Money, and Me.

At the exit, Mica handed out sample packs of Wild Berry Zinger, then ushered us through a door above which hung a placard with a picture of a woman I recognized as Evelyn looking out to sea and the Ralph Waldo Emerson quote, "Nothing can bring you peace but yourself." Like a pump handle that's been rusted through and so breaks in the hands of a thirsty man, something broke inside me. Nothing fit. Not Emerson's words, not Evelyn, not me. With everything on the factory floor behind me clanking and humming, with all the workers wearing earplugs and the forklifts and pallets full of case upon case of tea, with all the noise and the production and the contradictions that I had never been able to hold together in myself and in the world around me, "Nothing can bring you peace but yourself" did not fit in my world where I had for so long been trying to secure my own peace but had never found it for long or without constant vigilance—which is not in the end any sort of peace worth having.

With sweaty fingers I pulled from my head the hairnet I'd been given to wear, focused all my energy towards dropping it in the metal wastebasket half-filled with hairnets that sat there, waiting, at the factory exit door which I stumbled through only to enter a gift shop. Flashes of merchandise burned my eyes: "Wings of Love All-Natural Lipstick," "Burt's Beeswax Lip Balm," "Jelly Belly Fruit Bowl Flavors," "Jelly Belly 39 Flavors," "Jelly Belly Tropical Flavors." T-shirts. Mugs.

Woozy. I felt so woozy as I steadied myself against a postcard rack for a moment before a pigtailed girl with braces and the first pimples of youth gave it a turn. I staggered, then steadied myself on my own two feet. I saw in front of me a wall of Celestial Seasonings teas neat and perfect and tidy on shelves, and on the boxes the inspirations and the art I had grown up loving and believing multiplied so many times as to be meaningless to me now. A hundred Minas and Trinas. A thousand quotes by Emerson. The Sleepytime Bear asleep in exactly the same posture in hundreds of the exact same chair. I shut my eyes tight against the endless repetition and saw my mother's pale face, her eyes closed, her hair writhing and rearranging like blackberry snakes made of the same words in constantly shifting orders over and over and over again. *If you give love you get love if love*

UNDER THE SIGN OF SLEEPYTIME • 203

you give love you get you get love if you give love love love you give you get if you give love if you get love. My mother's eyes opened. Her lips moved. Her voice sang again. *Hushabye little Blackenberry, hushabye my love.*

The broken pump handle inside me did not repair; even so, tears gushed forth. When I opened my eyes I saw in a corner of the shop bushel baskets that brimmed with reject teas in dented boxes. Their covers were imperfect—the boxes had gotten caught on the line during packaging, mangled unmercifully. Around those bushel baskets women, men, and children grabbed and snatched at the teas, loading up their arms and their baskets, fighting over the last 40-count box of Lemon Zinger as they yammered about cheap prices, not caring if they couldn't read the quotes, not caring if the artwork was wrecked. Over their shoulders I glimpsed one box of Peppermint, machinery claw marks through its candy-striped lid. *This box matters,* I felt more than thought as I reached down and rescued it from all the scrabbling hands and took off running past the children being fitted with Sleepytime Bear T-shirts, bumping into the postcard rack that crashed beside an awkward pre-teen, not even giving a backward glance to the cashier who yelled "Stop, thief!"

I ran and ran and ran, out beyond Celestial Seasonings and cars and buildings and parking lots and road signs until at last I stood before the foothills of the Rocky Mountains. I threw off my long-sleeved shirt and shed my shoes and socks. My toes stubbed on rocks and thistles lashed my ankles, but I kept going on and on, out into this big world that was so much bigger than Celestial Seasonings or Boulder or Boston or NATAS or me. I ran until I smelled a smell that was unlike the great big world, that instead smelled soft of chamomile, spearmint, and lemongrass, that smelled like that building at 47th and Pearl that had once been my everything, where once my father's arms had vined around my mother and around me, where once I had been laid in a nest of chamomile, where once I had wrapped myself around and around my mother with a long length of hemp and would not let her go until I was ready to do so.

Inside my head I heard a voice that was not my mother's and was not Mo's and was not the one I recognized as mine but was somehow me all the same but more me than I had ever before been: *Were I younger, I would be called Hora; were I older, I would be called Ra; as it is, I am Bud Blackenberry and that is enough.*

That is enough.

Bud Blackenberry, somewhere in the middle with nothing much to recommend me to anyone as anything all that special. That was enough, and I had neither to believe nor disbelieve for my enoughness just was, so I kept walking out into what remained of the unmilled, unblended, unpackaged wildness where chamomile, spearmint, and lemongrass still grow. I gathered what I found, stuffed first my pockets and then my shirt full of it. This was different. Unprocessed, undefined, unboxed. In all my life I had never once gone herb picking myself, and now here I was wishing I had done this with my mother before she died, wanting to have done this too with Mo whom I no longer believed to be my father but who had in his own way been family, watching over me after my own father had slipped away to wherever he had gone.

It was enough just to be me—Bud Blackenberry at the foothills of the Rocky Mountains—and it was enough to breathe in the open air, smell spearmint on the breeze and feel the hot sun on my bare back.

Did Mo miss this after he started traveling far and wide to buy his herbs? Did he ever hunger to feel the sun's warmth against his skin, to feel the weight of his gunnysack slung over his shoulder? Did he trade in the wonder and uncertainty I now felt, truly, for the first time, or had he found a way to carry it through his life moment by moment, ever changing? Was there a way to do just that, or, rather, to let it be? I wondered.

I picked a stalk of peppermint, plucked a soft leaf which I rolled between thumb and forefinger, then breathed in the spicy soothing scent, far richer than even the mint room had ever been.
Inhale.
I didn't know a thing about Mo.
Exhale.
I didn't really know a thing about me.
Inhale.
The moment flavors me.
Exhale.
I flavor the moment.
Inhale.
Peace.
Exhale.
Grace.
I am Bud Blackenberry.

© Mary Catherine Harper

The Thing Is

"Death in the Desert," *Arizona Range News*, June 23, 2005

The body of sixteen-year-old Arabella Buena Cosa was discovered in the San Pedro desert on Tuesday evening, June 22, by Cochise County detective Lucian Romero.

Cosa's parents, Isabella and Bill Cosa, reported Arabella missing the night of June 21. Bill Cosa told police that Arabella left at sunrise that morning, telling them "'I'm just going to commune with the desert,' which sounded kind of odd to us but, well, that's just Arabella for you."

Isabella Cosa declined to comment.

In a press conference this morning, Detective Romero described the body of Arabella Cosa as "reverently mutilated." When asked what that looked like, Romero said, "Parts of the body had been cut off, but very purposefully. They just were not there anymore." Cosa's face, Romero said, was "placid, almost holy" despite the body's mutilation.

Further investigations, Romero said, will focus on "a letter to an unknown 'dear one'" found in the "neatly folded pile of clothes" near the body. Romero declined to comment about the cause of death, other than to say, "no evidence exists of an outside perpetrator."

Arabella Cosa was born in Dragoon, Arizona, on December 21, 1988. She attended Dragoon High School where she was a member of her school's National Honor Society chapter. She worked at the family business, "The Thing? Mystery of the Desert," 2631 Johnson Rd., Dragoon.

* * *

My Dear One,

Once, just once, I would like to keep a friend for more than forty-five minutes. But I live at the home of "The Thing?" and people just keep moving on, moving through. Men, women, and children, all pay their dollar to walk through my dad's long metal sheds, enduring all the weird stuff he collects, enduring the bad "The Thing is" jokes, enduring it all so they can get to "The Thing," The Thing of all things that has been waiting for them at the end. And when they reach that Thing they are always disgusted, every one of them. I have seen them recoil, have listened to their conversations, have heard the same conversation repeated over and over.

"Disgusting!" the man says, looking down through the plexiglass case.

"Great God in heaven, what is that thing?" the woman beside him asks.

"What on earth would possess a man to own such a thing, let alone display it?" the man says, turning away. "It's so shriveled up, so ugly."

"Why," says the woman, "I can't even tell if it's a man or a woman." She leans in for a closer look, then looks away before leaning in again. "Honey, do you think it's real? A real person?"

"Oh, it's real, alright," the man calls back, walking towards the exit. "Only a real freak would fake such a thing."

The woman takes one last long look and follows.

And then they are gone, having spent a dollar to see The Thing they do not like, The Thing they do not want to understand.

Everybody who has ever stopped to see The Thing while passing by Dragoon, Arizona, on I-10, has walked through my backyard. In the rectangle of land surrounded by my dad's corrugated metal sheds are trailers; I live with my parents in the pale cream-colored one with brown shutters shaded by three spindly trees—one with half its limbs missing and a couple off-balance branches of green. When families pass through the sheds, I "Psst!" at the kids and sometimes get them to leave their parents and spend a little time with me.

"Do you live here?" they ask wide-eyed, and when I say that I do and ask if they want to meet my pet snake Molly, they always say yes because the ones that come over and talk to me are the ones brave enough to stick around.

Though it's nice to have a little company, I know that I am just a freak show for these would-be friends, something to talk about when they go back to their schools at the end of summer. For the kids who live around me, the kids I go to school with, I am not a freak show, just a freak, and my whole family with our boa constrictor Molly and our alligators and Dad's "Very Special Exhibit depicting ancient methods of torture" is a freak family. It's kind of fun being a freak show in the summer because tourists like freaks in small doses and I'm good at putting on a show, but during the school year, being a freak in a bigger freak family is no fun at all.

At school, I'm either teased or avoided. Though I've hardened myself against responding, the teasing still bothers me, and I hate the names my classmates call me—names designed to humiliate me and my family. Trailer trash.

Mummy fuckers. I eat my lunch alone, and after lunch I sit alongside the other misfits on the gym bleachers and read books about other times and places than Dragoon, Arizona, in 2005. Sometimes I even create new places in my head, places where nobody gets left out of basketball games or lunch table conversations, sword fights or dragon racing.

Nobody. Not even me.

More than being teased, I hate being avoided, overlooked, invisible. This is less the case with my classmates than with my teachers and has been for a very long time. My second-grade teacher Mrs. Stumpt was the first to tell my mother that I was smart, "gifted" even, the first in a long line of teachers to send me to the library when I had finished my class work, the first to leave my education up to me. I liked going to the library, liked reading everything I could get my hands on, liked feeling connected even if only to characters in books. Though I never did like that I had no one with whom I could share these experiences. I understood Wonderland's madness, wept with Jess when Leslie's swinging rope snapped above an icy surging creek, puzzled over the giantess in a sad café who longed to be loved by a hunchback dwarf, and ached to feel with Parker the tiniest hint of wonder in the presence of a tattooed man.

But in the summer when there is no school, no library to hide myself away in, none of this really matters. I have no history with the tourists, no risk I must take, and so I can, if I want, play up being a freak in ways that may not be entirely true but that give the tourist kids—ages six, sixteen, or somewhere in between—something to remember me by. So the kids who pass through during the summer, who follow me to play Frisbee in my yard or even come into my trailer, they give me somebody to talk to and to listen to, if only for a little while. And when they leave I can, if I want, imagine what it would have been like if they could have stayed longer, if I could have counted them as friends. Most times I don't bother since few leave much of an impression and more are coming through all the time. Most times this not-keeping-a-friend business doesn't matter so much to me. Most times I'm ok with forty-five-minute friendships.

Last Wednesday, though, last Wednesday was different.

The Thing is, I loved you and you left. I understand you didn't have a choice, that your parents moved you on. I understand that even if you had been in control, you still would have left, because leaving would have been the best thing for you. Dragoon, Arizona, has nothing to offer a teenager from Cleveland, Ohio. I understand all that. But, still, The Thing is, I love you.

The Thing, this Thing, is a monster. Had I never met you I would have been relatively okay with who I thought I was. I took a certain pride in belonging to a family that by choice of location and occupation set themselves apart as freaks. I took pride in being set apart in that way, and maybe that unusual pride helped me to explain to myself why I was always so out of place, so out of sync with the rest of the world. My pride was my defense, to be sure, but most days it kept me from despair. Within my family I at least thought I had a place—surely, I could play the role of freak as well as they—but had you asked, I could not have said what that place was exactly, how I fit into this attraction my parents maintained for all the world to see. But as I had never thought about all these things, never really thought about them until I met you, my life was not so very bad. Instead, my life felt unnatural and abnormal in an almost comfortable way, like the life of a child whose parents run a tourist trap should feel.

But then you came walking through my backyard, catching my attention before I could catch yours. You smiled at me and waved; I smiled and waved back. We sat beneath the half-tree beside my trailer, and there you read to me a story you had written about a queen who ruled a desert from her palace of bones, and I swore I could have written it too. My too-small world shifted two feet to the left, all my defenses fell away, and I loved you more deeply than I love my parents, more deeply than I love my snake Molly, even more deeply than I love all the characters in all the books I have ever read. Within minutes of meeting, even before the start of your story, my heart lurched and I knew, just knew, that this was it, this was The Thing for which I'd been forever waiting. And I loved you. I just didn't know how much until you left.

Once there lived a queen in a palace of bones in the middle of a desert.

So began your story. Now I must tell mine. And I love you more than ever, but I hate you, because you are not here to hear my story.

When you left and my mind wandered to think of you, I felt this deep ache and thrill all at once, like I had been punched in the gut with something I'd always wanted. I could not have you. That much I knew. I could never even find you again as I didn't know your address, your phone number, your email, not even your name. You had said you would give me those, but your parents snatched you away from me there by the half-tree in front of the door to my trailer. They had seen The Thing at the end of it all, and I knew from their pale unsettled faces that they had hated what they had seen as much as they claimed to love you. And you were gone.

When I went back to my trailer and slumped onto the couch in front of the turned-off TV, knowing my life would never be the same, knowing I would surely die in this desert place all alone, all my mother could say was that I needed to get off my butt and get busy cleaning Hitler's car before the lunch hour was over.

Even though I am one in a family of supposed freaks, since meeting you I can put words to at least one thing that sets me apart as a different sort of freak. I want to create other lives, other worlds, out of words. I want to imagine worlds greater than my own, live lives that have both more and less promise. I want to escape into somebody else's mind, body, and soul, if only for a short while. I think I've known this for a long time, but since meeting you I can put words to this longing. I can say that, whatever else I may be, I am also, by my very nature, a writer.

But who I am is not acceptable to my mother who, I can see now, is not really a freak at all but only puts on a freak show from which she can profit. I watch my Desert Mystery Goddess mother at work in her flowing tie-dye skirts and her glittery gold-plastic bangles, watch her being all mystic and spooky with the tourists as she sells dollar tickets to The Thing, as many as three hundred on a good day. And then I watch my just plain Isabella Cosa mother at rest in our trailer, stretched out on the brown velvet couch wearing her threadbare gray sweatpants and bright pink "Bite Me!" t-shirt, smoking Camels, drinking Coca-Cola, reading *Redbook*.

Who I am is also not acceptable to my father who believes the only lives and worlds worth knowing and living are the ones we have been given, the physical ones grounded in the here and now. In my father's view, the only worthwhile way to be a freak is to collect freaky objects and display them for people to look at and say, "Wow! Whoever runs this place must be a real freak!" Until I met you, I never saw my father for what he really is, an ordinary businessman with unusual merchandise.

It's not that I can't appreciate my father's decision to buy The Thing years ago, that I can't appreciate his interest in preserving curiosities and oddities. I can appreciate his interest; I just can't maintain his distance. While my father can keep from seeing his desert wood monsters with their contorted forms and blazing red lips as anything more than strange pieces of desert wood with faces painted on, I can't. I see the monsters in my nightmares, see them take on lives of their own and use their big red mouths to devour all that I love. Sometimes I even think I understand them.

As for Molly, Dad likes her because she's a big boa constrictor and people like to look at big boa constrictors. Mom likes Molly because drawing people in draws in more money. I like Molly because she can do what I cannot—she can swallow other creatures whole. I feed her live wriggling rats and watch as she swallows them down. Sometimes she curls herself into a tight circle, mouth resting on her tail. Lately I have wondered what would happen if she took to swallowing herself whole. Sometimes I withhold her feeder rats in hopes that she will try.

Devour myself. That's what I am forced to do. You are gone and I am starving; there is nobody here to feed me. Because I cannot do what I imagine Molly could if she only had the will, I will instead carve up my flesh and swallow the pieces down bit by bit, fill my belly to gain the strength I need to leave my body. I need nothing but for myself to become no Thing.

I want to disappear, to absolve myself of loving you too much and myself too little. I have taken small cuttings from unseen places—my thighs, my buttocks, my breasts—have tasted my own blood, and have felt on my tongue the smooth slick texture of my own flesh. Cannibalism? No. This is communion. Flesh becomes bread, blood becomes wine. The ultimate feast. I forgive my own freakishness even as I devour it. The ultimate sacrament. My only salvation.

I recognize pain is an impediment, but pain can be conquered. Certainly, there are ways to numb the nerves, but I must be open to the pain, to experiencing the full reality of what I am doing. I will confess, too, that such a communion raises practical concerns, that at some point I can't help but fail, and will be unable to surpass my humanness. Even if I start with my skin and move on slowly towards the vital organs, at some point I will die and leave part of me behind. Maybe at the moment of eating my own heart. Maybe at my brain. At some point, this communion feast will fail and I will die, leaving flesh and blood and brain and heart, unable to eat any more. As I commune upon myself, my body will war against me, seeing to its own repairs, its own regeneration, even as I long for, work for, my own end.

This reality frustrates me beyond reason. I have tried and tried to think of some method by which I can have everything end up even with, at best, only my jawbone remaining as evidence of my former existence. Like in IQ where you jump pegs with pegs in an effort to end up with only one, the rest cleared off the stubbly board. Even when you win the game, there's still always one damn plastic peg left standing alone.

This much I know: In this communion feast, I must be alone. No sharing of body and blood. No passing of bread and cup. No public declaration that I'm part of any greater body, that I'm sharing this meal with anybody but myself. It must be me alone, in private, in a closet or under stairs or hiding in my locker after school has ended—someplace where there is room only for me and a blade. Even better, out in the desert, the blazing sun my only companion, drying me out even as I bleed myself dry. Nothing to hide me from all who will not pass by. For my communion, there can be no separation of body and blood, no separation between blood shed and body broken. Instead, there is only bloodandbody, inseparable, indivisible, both for me and from me for never and ever, amen.

I look at The Thing in my father's shed and see a shriveled body, blood and fluids gone, leathery flesh stretched tight over brittle bone. Somebody long ago sucked life from it somehow. Such an end is not for me. I want all of me gone, especially flesh and blood—that's the only way to make communion work. If anything must remain, let it be bone. Let it be that skeleton frame on which rests all that matters least to me.

And what has any of this to do with you? You whom I love? Nothing. Maybe nothing. But maybe, just maybe, everything. I must believe this has everything to do with you. I must believe you would understand what I am saying, that you would have thought the same thoughts, felt the same feelings, that you would not turn away, not run away. In that deepest part of me that not even I can know, I am convinced this must be the case. I just want the pain of loving and losing you to go away.

    I am more than just a freak. I read what I have written and I try to wrap my mind around this self-communion thing, and I know that I am sick with no chance of a cure. I am a freak in the way the rest of my family is not. I cannot sell my freakishness or turn it into a sideshow or advertise it on billboards, and as much as I'd like to, I cannot take it on and off to suit business hours. I know that at my very core, I am a terminally sick freak in a way that my family could not even begin to comprehend. Because I cannot return to the way I thought things were. Because you made me see this. Because I used to think it was just them, but now I know it's me alone. Because of all of this I must devour myself, must practice self-communion until nothing remains. Oh, that I could only succeed! That such a Thing were possible!

    The Thing is, I love you and you left.

    The Thing is, I cannot exist alone in this world as the freak Thing that I am.

    The Thing is, I am also glad you left. Your leaving was best for us both. For what if I had wanted to devour you instead of me?

And so I am writing you this letter you will never read because I must. Maybe it doesn't matter that you will never read it, that I will never again see you. Maybe what matters is that I am writing, that I met you, that I have changed—no, not changed, become aware—because of you. But right now I'm in this awful stuck place; I can't move backward, I can't move forward, and all I can think to do is consume my own flesh and blood in hopes of becoming sun-bleached bone.

* * *

Editor's note: Arabella Cosa's experience of life (and death) at "The Thing? Mystery of the Desert" may well disturb its readers but her experience is by no means exceptional. Alienation accompanied by an innate sense of difference, even freakishness, are common traits of Tourist Attraction Trauma. What does distinguish Arabella's letter from other accounts gathered by the National Association of Tourist Attraction Survivors, is her acute self-awareness as brought on by and verbalized to a tourist outsider.

NATAS believes that without this person, Arabella would never have reached this self-awareness, would never have shared her story, and would never have died. Tragically, this letter was found alongside Arabella's body in a remote desert area fifteen miles from her home.

In researching Arabella's case, NATAS discovered I.M. Luvlee's story "Songs Sung in the Desert," published in *The Cleveland Quarterly*'s annual "Youth Make a Difference" issue (Spring 2004, Volume XIV, Issue 1). It is believed that I.M. Luvlee (a pseudonym, we presume), was the "Dear One" addressed in Arabella Cosa's letter.

* * *

"Songs Sung in the Desert"

by I.M. Luvlee

Once there lived a queen in a palace of bones in the middle of a desert.

Queen Dessicada ruled over dry things and dead things, over cacti and corpses. This, though, was not as it had always been. Ages ago she began her reign as Queen Succulent, and she ruled over a verdant rainforest full of roaring waterfalls, flowering trees, and loving subjects—animal and human alike. Queen Succulent reigned with such kindness and generosity over her subjects that they loved and trusted her and each other. They linked arms and legs, mouths and belly buttons, breasts and elbows, and became a living, breathing palace of flesh surrounding their Queen.

All was well in Queen Succulent's lands for many a year until one day a Wanderer, whose vision was poor, entered the land. Where everybody else saw a palace whose very walls pulsed with joyous life, Cadavera the Wanderer saw only a magnification of what stood every morning in her own bathroom mirror. She saw embarrassingly naked bodies that weren't at all pretty but that had moles and scars and parts that were too fat and parts that were too lean, eyes that were too small and feet that were too large. Like waves lapping up a sandy shore, rolls of cellulite undulated out from the palace, flesh that longed to pull Cadavera the Wanderer into itself. And just as she did every morning before her mirror, Cadavera avoided looking at the palace. She looked down at her feet, up at the sky, and when she thought she was safe enough to walk forward without tripping, closed her eyes in self-imposed blindness.

From far away, Queen Succulent spied this Wanderer with a penchant for running into and tripping over all manner of objects. And while the Queen could tell that the Wanderer was not actually blind, only shutting her eyes tightly against the sight of the palace, she could not for the life of her imagine why. When Cadavera the Wanderer reached the palace gates, Queen Succulent met her outside and welcomed her in, just as she did every traveler. The linked arms that made up the gate parted and ushered in the Wanderer before linking again, and a multitude of voices chorused a welcome cacophonous to her ears. Cadavera did not respond.

From her moment of arrival, Cadavera questioned Queen Succulent about her palace of bodies and her welcoming ways.

"Don't you know better than to take in strangers?" asked Cadavera. "Who knows what a stranger might do?"

The Queen was taken aback by the Wanderer's reaction, so new it was to her, because she had only in all her life met friends, never enemies, and so did not recognize Cadavera as such. Queen Succulent persisted in showing Cadavera kindness, in offering a bed for the night, a bowl of warm lentil soup, a goblet of cool strawberry wine. But Cadavera the Wanderer shrunk further into herself, pulled her thistle-weed cloak tighter, and glowered at the Queen. Still, when the Queen left, the Wanderer guzzled the strawberry wine, slurped up the lentil soup, sprawled in the bed, and grumbled under downy covers that all she was given and all she consumed was paltry.

Days went by and the Wanderer was made welcome in the palace. She ate more soup, drank more wine, slept more nights in the bed. Queen Succulent watched and wondered over her—never had she seen one so sad, so alone, so in need of touch, companionship, love—yet Cadavera would have none of it. Cadavera the Wanderer also watched Queen Succulent, but rather than wonder over the Queen, the Wanderer despised her. Not only was her palace made of people, but people surrounded her all the time, smiling at her, singing to her, touching her in ways that made Cadavera terribly uncomfortable, made her itch to even think of such contact.

Never could she imagine smiling at or singing to others, let alone touching and being touched. Being in the presence of people who wanted to do all three just made her pull her thistle-weed cloak tighter around her. Should any try to touch her, they would soon regret it. Though the Wanderer could have left at any time, she stayed. She couldn't help but watch Queen Succulent with her subjects, even as she despised their mutual desire to touch, to love, to protect each other with their own flesh.

One morning Cadavera the Wanderer approached Queen Succulent's throne and demanded that people stop touching, that the palace of flesh be disbanded, that jagged rocks and sharp glass be used for the palace walls instead.

"Walls are for keeping people out," Cadavera hissed. But Queen Succulent, puzzled, asked why people should be kept out when walls could grow big enough to let all people in.

"No they can't," snapped the Wanderer whose mind was so dull she could not see and understand that the walls were indeed growing as more people, even she herself, entered into Queen Succulent's domain. And though Cadavera told the Queen that she could make her regret her ways, the Queen, compelled by her very nature, could not do otherwise.

Queen Succulent was a good woman, a kind woman, a woman whose heart longed only to give and receive love. And just as the Wanderer had been watching the Queen, the Queen had been watching the Wanderer all these many weeks of living in the palace. She had seen how Cadavera cringed when she and her subjects drew near. She had seen how Cadavera used her thistle-weed cloak to keep everybody away. She had even seen Cadavera in her private quarters put her cloak over the mirror before undressing. Everything she had seen. In all of this, the Queen desired only love for this Wanderer. And though she sensed great risk to herself, Queen Succulent knew what she must do.

The Thing Queen Succulent sensed but could not heed was this: Cadavera carried within her flesh a Curse that made everything she touched wither and die. Even had she so desired, Cadavera could not be touched, could not be held or loved or comforted ever. One night after Cadavera had cast her thistle-weed cloak over her mirror, Queen Succulent went to her. A candle burned on the mantle above the cold fireplace, enough for a little light but no warmth. The Queen shivered, and in so doing announced her presence wordlessly. The naked Wanderer spun around, arms and hands flailing to cover her body for her cloak still covered the mirror. Exposed. She knew she must be naked before either the Queen or herself. Having so long ago learned not to look at or desire or touch, the Wanderer left her cloak where it was.

Before her, Queen Succulent saw what she had seen every night. She saw a body. A woman's body. A body no more and no less beautiful than any of those in her vast and tender lands. And then Queen Succulent, doing what she knew she must, embraced the Wanderer. As Queen Succulent's great love flowed out of her and into Cadavera, Cadavera's Curse crept inside the Queen. Breaking free of the Queen's embrace, Cadavera snatched her thistle-weed cloak from the mirror, as angry and unloving as before. Still, she had no desire for touch or for love; still, she despised Queen Succulent. The only effect the Queen's embrace had on the Wanderer was to send her fleeing from the palace of people, cursing and spitting as she sought shelter in the jungle.

All in vain. Such was Queen Succulent's realization after the Wanderer went running from the palace, refusing love, shielded by her own force of will. This saddened the Queen who couldn't help but feel the loss, but still she was grateful for all the others who did love her and who allowed her to love them in return. Joy came from them. Life came from them. Love came from them. But Queen Succulent had only a moment to feel this before everything and everybody began to dry up and die.

One touch. One touch was all it took. One touch of her hand to the shoulder of the child whose body helped make up the doorframe of the Wanderer's room. One touch and the child sighed, wilted away, shriveled up, skin turning to powder beneath Queen Succulent's hand. Where hand touched flesh, it now touched bone. And then this Thing, this Curse spread. The doorframe. Then the door. Then the walls of the room. The palace shuddered, sighed, sank in on itself, bones locking around its Queen. The green forest turned brown, a blazing sun rose, and soon all that remained was scorched. Grief gripped the Queen and she cried out against the Curse. That her subjects, all her subjects, should die, and by her hand! This was the most bitter truth of all.

All had withered. All but one. The one who had ventured beyond. Sestine the Singer.

Though Queen Succulent loved all her subjects equally, she had a special fondness for Sestine, the young Singer who entertained her with songs and poems. Sestine was away on a tour of the Queen's outerlands when Cadavera arrived at the palace gates. On Sestine's return, she saw her Queen through the tangle of bones that now imprisoned her. The Singer's impulse was to break through and rescue her Queen, but the Queen warned, "Come no nearer! I am cursed!"

"What has happened, my great Queen?" cried Sestine, overwhelmed by the vision of her Queen in a palace of bones.

"I have been cursed," howled the Queen, so great was her despair. "Cursed by a Wanderer. See what has become of my palace of people?" she sobbed, motioning with her hands, "they have become a palace of bones. From now on I shall be Queen Dessicada for everything under my touch withers and dies."

The heart of the Singer went out to her Queen, "Please, let me come to you," Sestine pleaded. "I bring in my pack peaches from the Freestone orchards and water from the fountains of Afar. Just as they sustained me on my long journey, they will restore you."

Though the Queen wanted nothing more than to let the Singer enter, to let Sestine bring water and fruit and poetry and song, she could not bear to destroy the one person who was most dear.

"Go!" Queen Dessicada wailed. "Turn and run from me! I cannot bear to have you bring such pleasure to my soul only to destroy yours."

Still, Sestine stepped forward.

Her Queen implored, "No! Please! If you must give me something, then grant me but one wish. Go and deliver your water and fruit, your poems and songs to another. Enrich another's life instead of mine. If I know you are beyond the Curse of me, doing what I so long to do, then I will have some small measure of joy in this domain of the dry and the dead."

And so Sestine, the Queen's beloved Singer, went away heartbroken but with a mission, knowing what she must do.

Sestine delivered water and fruit to the Queen's now-deserted lands, singing poems and songs to the air around, the sky above, the sand beneath. Around Sestine sprang up the most unlikely of plants—fleshy giants with haphazard prickles and razored spikes that warned the Singer they were death to touch. And though this saddened Sestine, still the Singer took joy in their company and was sustained.

© Bex Miller

"Writing in Clay: Discovering a New Language"

A Case Study in the Therapeutic Benefits of Pottery with Tourist Attraction Trauma Survivors

"Beautiful, but Bizarre!"
—*Winchester Mystery House advertising slogan*

Editor's note: The two sculptures shared here in photographic form are the result of Layla Manjun's collaboration with Steve Smith, potter and Defiance College art professor who worked as a volunteer with Tourist Attraction Trauma survivor Layla Manjun at the National Association of Tourist Attraction Survivors' Research and Recovery Hospital in Florida, Ohio.

Layla Manjun, a NATAS rescue, was discovered on October 13, 2009 when eight-year-old Sophia Luz strayed from her family during a Mansion Tour of the Winchester Mystery House in San Jose, California. After an hour's disappearance, young Sophia found her way back to the tour and her family, saying she had "opened a window and fell into a room" that had "walls covered with words" and found a woman with "words written into her skin."

Immediately, Winchester Mystery House staff contacted the NATAS San Jose chapter and Layla Manjun was rescued, though not without initial dismay, disorientation, and screams of, "Leave me lost. Please, leave me lost!" Manjun, while not the first NATAS rescue from the Winchester Mystery House, certainly is the most memorable.

What exactly draws people, particularly women, to claim the vacant rooms in the Winchester Mystery House as their own?[1] A sampling of Manjun's wall writings from the room in which she was found casts light on this phenomenon:

> *I was lost long before I decided to lose myself in this place. Lost in my own past. Lost in my own delusions. Lost in my own consciousness. I just needed a place where I could lose myself, where I could come undone—completely undone—and never be found. I have found that place here in Mrs. Sarah Winchester's house, this room not visited by the tours and free of any easy escape. It is to me a great comfort to have no escape, and a great relief to have no visitors, for human connection—an exquisite joy for one brief and shining moment in my life—has become too painful to bear.*

While the wall writings are made up largely of Manjun's reflections—efforts to explain herself to herself—the writing on her body tells a different story, a story, she says, of "what I had been told and what, in turn, I told myself even through years of doing everything right, obeying all the rules that had been laid out for me from birth—like getting married, having two kids, and going to church on Sunday mornings and Wednesday evenings."

These words, beginning in tight cursive script at her left wrist, coil around her arm up to her shoulder, the ink so black and so deep the words have become permanent: *You feel too*

---

[1] As of October 13, 2009, the date of Layla Manjun's rescue, six out of seven recorded cases of "found" Winchester Mystery survivors have been women.

deeply. You look *so normal. You're just fucking crazy! You are a sinner damned to Hell. If you ever...I would kill myself from shame. You are a disappointment to me. I will never understand you. You are too much for anybody to love.*

Five months and thirteen days into Manjun's six-month hospitalization, Steve Smith entered the lobby of the NATAS Research and Recovery Hospital, inquiring specifically about her after reading *The Crescent News* article about people diagnosed with Tourist Attraction Trauma Survivors in Florida—a ten-mile drive from Defiance College. Smith had been particularly struck by Layla Manjun's story of writing into her skin.

Smith shared that he had previously worked with a group of abused women whom he had instructed to make "simple pinch pots, then take pencils and draw or write how they felt people saw them on the outside, then on the inside draw or write who they really were." Said Smith, "Afterwards, when we went around the table reading, we all cried, and one woman said, 'My children are going to laugh at this little pot, but you have given me back my childhood.' That moment leveled me," said Smith, "Art was saving them, as art had saved me."

At the end of a private conversation with Manjun, Smith handed her two unfinished bell-shaped sculptures topped with trees. "Carve words into these," he said, "anything you want. Don't overthink it. You're working in clay now."

When Manjun expressed anxiety about the new artform, so different than the words she was accustomed to, Smith said, "It's just mud. You mess it up, you smash it down, you start over again. Relax about yourself," Smith told Manjun.

Provided by Smith with basic carving tools, Manjun, in six hours' time and writing a mere fifty words she said came to her "in a dream," made more progress towards recovery than she had over her extended stay and 317 pages of personal journaling, to say nothing of the writing she had done while lost by her own force of will in the Winchester Mystery House.

"In carving these two pieces," Manjun told Smith when he returned to pick up the sculptures for firing, "my spell of madness—a madness that multiplied with my many words—broke."

NATAS has speculated that, like the widow Sarah Winchester who kept building onto her house in an attempt to outrun the ghosts of those killed by the Winchester rifle, perhaps Layla Manjun had also been trying to outrun ghosts, though she used words instead of wood to do so.

Dr. Liz Miller, a graphologist and forensic psychologist brought in to analyze Manjun's writing, concluded that the writing on the walls in the room where Manjun was found was constructed like a "linguistic labyrinth," looking random at first glance and navigable only after "one gave up any hope of doing so."

Support for this claim can be found in this passage written by Manjun hours before Smith would hand her the sculptures and carving tools with instructions for how to start:

> *I think about Sarah Winchester sometimes, how she also had to hide, how she, a widow who had also grieved the loss of a child, had a harder time of it than me. For her, this house was not a destination to move herself into like I had done that cool September afternoon having run away from everything and everybody—my husband, my two young children, my church. No. Sarah had to create these rooms, these spaces, these doors while fretting over the ghosts hard on her heels. Sarah had to keep moving, keep hiding, keep thinking about how to outwit ghosts who by their nature can only be slowed, never stopped.*

As the final step in her healing, Manjun wrote, "Writing in Clay: Discovering a New Language," which she has described as "the place I put my ghosts to rest." The last words she wrote before leaving NATAS to restart her life are published here.

Writing in Clay: Discovering a New Language
by Layla Manjun

Writing in clay, my words take on new texture, new depth, new meaning. I commit unconditionally to my words, invest myself in new and surprising ways. Some slip like small snakes, thin and fluid, sliding with the motion of my meaning. Others scream out from raw scrapes, embarrassing in their need. I want to cover them—erase them even—but I cannot. They are as they must be.

No longer afraid, my pencil curls back the surface of the clay in abbreviated spirals like garden snails. Swipe tip against dry sponge, rest pencil, lift silver tool—delicate like a dental instrument. I slip the pencil tip inside my letter furrows, flick out the afterbirth of words.

Pencil raised, I begin to trust my hands as they partner with my imagination, my lines wedded to my letters. Shift from feeling to thought and my fingers fumble, breaking off an "I," morphing an "M" into a "W," losing the vision that can only be birthed through intentional play. Close eyes. Breathe. Slip back inside.

So much still to learn in this new language with its vocabulary of sight and touch. So much still to learn.

And yet, I have begun.

230 • DAWN BURNS

November 1, 2009
Layla Manjun and Steve Smith's Collaborative Sculptures

Title: "I Walk Into Your Wood to Find You"

> *I walk into your wood to find you.*
> *Roots trip my feet.*
> *Leaves clog my throat.*
> *You are not here and I am alone.*

© Smith-Manjun

Title: "I Walk Into Your Wood to Lose Me"

I walk into your wood to lose me.
Snakes fall from dead branches.
Twist inside my mind.
I am not here but I have my companions.

© Smith-Manjun

© z the goblin

Go to Hell

—From the Sunday, June 4, 2006, Associated Press news article titled "Hell, Mich., Heats Up for 6/6/06 Party"

They're planning a hot time in Hell on Tuesday.

The day bears the date of 6-6-06, or abbreviated as 666—a number that, according to the Bible's Book of Revelation, signifies the devil.

And there's not a snowball's chance in Hell that the day will go unnoticed in the unincorporated hamlet 60 miles west of Detroit.

Nobody is more fired up than John Colone, the town's self-styled mayor and owner of a souvenir shop.

"I've got '666' T-shirts and mugs. I'm only ordering 666 (of the items) so once they're gone, that's it," said Colone, also known as Odum Plenty. "Everyone who comes will get a letter of authenticity saying you've celebrated June 6, 2006, in Hell."

Most of Colone's wares will sell for $6.66, including deeds to one square inch of Hell.

Live entertainment and a costume contest are planned. The Gates of Hell should be installed at a children's play area in time for the festivities.

. . .

The 666 revelry is just the latest chapter in the town's storied history of publicity stunts, said Jason LeTeff, one of its 72 year-round residents—or, as the mayor calls them, Hellions or Hell-billies. But LeTeff wasn't particularly enthused.

"Now, here I am living in Hell, taking my kids to church and trying to teach them the right things and the town where we live is having a 6-6-6 party," he said.

* * *

The first time Sammy and I met Hell's self-appointed mayor Odum Plenty whose real name is John Colone, we were waiting for Screams Souvenirs from Hell and Helloween to open so I could buy Sammy a chocolate cone at the Creamatory, spelled C-R-E-A-M as in ice cream, not C-R-E-M like where people burn their dead. Sammy was wearing her red t-shirt printed with a suit of armor straight out of Iron Man, only instead of being the Iron Man suit, the armor had a bright yellow cross in the center of the chest with the words, "Armor of God" printed below in stencil font.

Sammy had worn that t-shirt every day for three weeks since she'd earned it by memorizing Ephesians 6:11 with the rest of her Vacation Bible School preschool class at God's Way Community Church over in Pinckney. I didn't mind Sammy saying the first part of Ephesians 6:11 which could almost have been an Iron Man thing, but the second part sounded more like something out of the Bible, which it was.

"Put on the full armor of God," Sammy had shouted with her arms raised as I'd pulled the t-shirt over her head that morning in my basement room in my parents' house, and though I could have almost been ok with her knowing that first part, when she growled "so that you can stand up against the devil's schemes," my whole body tensed like it was afraid of something my mind couldn't even remember. Sammy thought that last part was funny and soon she was shouting, "Devil's schemes! Devil's schemes!" as she jumped up and down, her thin girl's body clad in the cotton-polyester blend armor that came all the way down below her knees, giving her years of room to grow into God's full armor.

I didn't like that stupid t-shirt any more than I liked my memory of the God's Way t-shirt I'd worn as a kid, designed in yellow and green to look like the Subway logo, only the letters spelled out "GODSWAY" instead of "SUBWAY." It embarrassed me to think now about how many times I'd worn that shirt to Subway with my mom, how I had believed my wearing the shirt meant I was being a witness because Mrs. Burdock, my Sunday school teacher and the pastor's wife, had told us the world would see the light of Jesus burning extra bright in us whenever we wore our shirts out into the world.

Standing beside my mom at the Subway counter, I had hoped the teenager making my Cold Cut Combo would ask about my God's Way t-shirt as he arranged white triangles of American cheese on my white bread, then layered ovals of ham, salami, and bologna on top, all made of turkey which I now know but hadn't known when I was seven. If the worker had asked about my t-shirt, I could have said, "I'm going God's way, not man's way," and then added, "'There is a way that seems right to a man, but its end is the way of death.' Proverbs 14:12" to drive the point home which would have been the opening I needed, but because he didn't ask, I stayed silent, not knowing what else to say since soulwinning didn't come naturally to me the way it did my mom.

But that's about me, not Sammy, and what I thought of Sammy's t-shirt didn't matter any more than it had mattered that I hadn't wanted Sammy going to Vacation Bible School—VBS as the God's Way church people call it, like the acronym made it cool to spend a week of summer memorizing Bible verses which got glued onto crafts that Sammy brought home. When Mom put Sammy's VBS crafts on the refrigerator door, I really felt I had no choice and no say against what my parents thought was for Sammy's best.

After all, I'd been living in my parents' basement since that mid-February night four years ago when, terrified and feeling I had nobody else to turn to, I'd driven home from Spring Arbor University to tell my parents the unwelcome news that I was four months pregnant from a scheme I hadn't even seen coming from a man of God worse than any devil I could have imagined, a rape I hadn't even been given a chance to resist.

I had no choice.

Even thinking those words, my mind keeps whispering that something's wrong. Why wouldn't I have a choice and say about my own child? Why shouldn't I have a choice?

But I really felt I had no more say about Sammy going to VBS than I'd had about my own body that night four and a half years ago as a Spring Arbor sophomore. I lacked the knowledge and language to call what had happened to me "rape," which is what I now can say that it was, and can only say that it was because Professor Naomi used that word first when I confided in her after my television production class.

By the morning I stood outside Screams with Sammy, having made the choice to buy her ice cream at Hell's Creamatory with money my parents had entrusted to me when they left us alone for three days to attend the Prayer Prior to Sex retreat over in Climax with other married God's Way

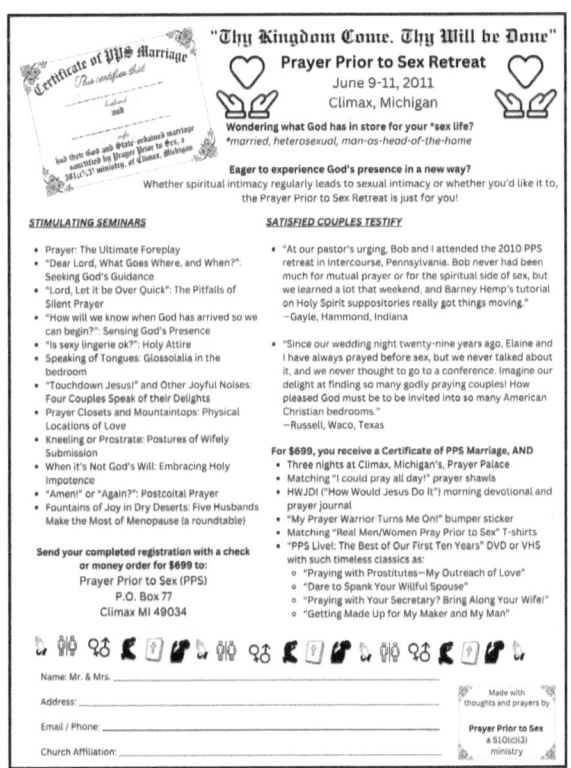

couples, I was beginning to recognize the icky feeling of having been taken care of my whole life, beginning to feel my own suppressed will spark and flare like I hadn't felt since I was Sammy's age.

I knew my strong will made me an outsider, both to my family and the family of God. But buying Sammy ice cream from Hell's Creamatory, when Dad, who could no longer even call me by my name and wasn't even home to condemn me if I bought that ice cream for my illegitimate daughter, was worth being burned in the fires of even a literal hell.

"You're an unwed mother now," Dad had said my first night home from Spring Arbor as I sat in the orange La-Z-Boy stroking Bubba's orange tiger fur from ears to tail, feeling the same way I'd felt as a child when I had been forced to listen to whatever Dad said I had done to once again disobey, disappoint, and dishonor him, my mother, and God. The fifth commandment had always been the hardest for me to keep, though I tried hard. Though I'd picked out Bubba as a sixth birthday gift when Pastor Burdock's wife brought the six-week-old kittens to VBS so she could both tell us about God caring for the smallest of creatures and so she could give all six kittens away, I couldn't remember a time Bubba hadn't been with me, like those years before I'd turned six hadn't counted for anything, like my sixth birthday was the day I'd been born instead of it being the beginning of the sixth year of my life.

Bubba had been the scrawniest in Mrs. Burdock's Chiquita banana box of kittens, the scrawniest and the only orange kitten when all his littermates had been black and white, and his mother had been too. But not Bubba. Not Bubba who was born orange and stayed orange which Mrs. Burdock said had to do with who the dad was, and I didn't care what she meant or didn't mean by this, just knew that Bubba was a spark of sunshine his monochrome brothers and sisters couldn't dim or understand. Bubba was curious, the kitten that ran over to me on and stood on his hind legs inside the box Mrs. Burdock had gotten from Busch's Fresh Food Market where she bought the Oreos and Kool-Aid for VBS because they gave God's Way a discount for all the good the church did in Pinckney.

When the orange kitten sneezed and fell over on his side, I picked him up and cradled him on his back in my arms, not caring that his eyes were matted shut because he looked perfect to me. I rubbed his belly with two fingers and his motor started up and he fell asleep just like that, purring in my arms. When I asked if I could keep the kitten, Dad said he would probably die, and Mom didn't disagree with Dad, but then she smiled at me at said the kitten would need extra caring, but that it would be good for me to learn how to mother something, and Dad couldn't argue with that.

So we took the kitten home and I named him Bubba like Bubba the Cave Duck in *Duck Tales* which I'd watched once when Mom took me with her to get an oil change at Pinckney Chrysler Dodge Jeep Ram, and *Duck Tales* was the only VHS tape they had, and there was no *Adventures in Odyssey* to be found. So I watched *Duck Tales* and afterwards we talked about how rebellious that Bubba Duck had been, which he was, playing rock music on a boom box in school and getting everybody—even his teacher—to dance. And because the kitten's fur was orange like Bubba Duck's hair had been, I knew Bubba was the name for him.

From the moment I held Bubba as a kitten, he had known when I needed him most, curling up on my lap and settling his calm body into my tense one. Bubba's motor was strong enough for me to feel his rumbling purr beneath my hands, but not so loud that my parents could hear him, and he always came to comfort me after my parents had spanked me with the wooden Spoon of Reproof.

"Look at me when I'm talking to you, Hanna Susanna," Dad used to say as I'd sit on that La-Z-Boy petting Bubba, my eyes studying the mulberry-stains on my fingers with their chewed-down nails which I pulled through Bubba's fur that parted like the Red Sea had parted for Moses as he led the Hebrew slaves out of Egypt and into a new life where no man—only God—could tell them what to do. I could almost feel how liberating and terrifying freedom must have felt with those walls of water standing up on either side as the Hebrews marched through, looking like that picture in *The Bible in Pictures for Little Eyes* Mom read from every night before I went to bed, each story a small paragraph with a colorful painting beside it that I could imagine myself inside.

"Look me in the eyes, Hanna Susanna," Dad said again, his voice sounding like the crash of waves that had drowned the Egyptians after the Hebrews had safely passed through, and I didn't want to be like the Egyptians, the Egyptians that disobeyed God. I was told they deserved death for what they'd done to God's people, must have deserved it the way I must have deserved this, the way Dad said I deserved this because I must listen, learn, obey. But I was just a kid who didn't understand why I had to go inside at exactly 7:35, why I couldn't stay outside on summer nights to watch the sky soften from blue to pink until it deepened into orange just before the sky darkened and the stars came out which was when my body wanted to sleep, but until then I wanted to stay outside and play.

Wanting to stay small and safe inside my own skin, I'd closed my eyes to see inside the darkness of my own heart, this darkness like the darkness I'd wanted to see in the sky as the stars were born, but Dad's voice insisted, "Your eyes, Hanna Susanna," so I made myself open and lift my eyes to his face which was shaved but not smooth, his face pocked with little craters like the craters on Earth's cold and distant moon, and though I looked close enough to Dad's eyes for him to think I was looking into them, my focus was on the deep squiggly pock at his right eye's outer corner that curved down to rest upon his cheek bone, a pock unlike all the others, as though put there by the sharp corner of a coffee table, which Dad had said it was, and that he'd gotten it from running in the house when his mom had told him not to, that he'd ended up with a scar because he'd been willful and disobedient.

It hurt my eyes to look into Dad's, so I kept my focus on his willful scar. That must have been close enough to what Dad demanded that he let me be, and in time I learned to lock my eyes on that scar before he could tell me to look in his eyes, and in this way he fashioned me into what he wanted, or most of me, because every single time a part of me ran away and hid deep inside myself, to keep my soul safe.

"You're an unwed mother now," Dad had repeated a second time, his voice as thin as his greying combover, as thin as his eyes which I could see out of the corner of my own even as I focused on the crescent scar that had remained a part of his face's geography all these years, and I focused on it as though it were my North Star.

"You're an unwed mother now."

And that was that. The moment Dad stopped calling me Hanna Susanna. The moment he stopped calling me "my daughter" and started calling me only "unwed mother" like I could no longer be his daughter and could now only be his shame. Even though I didn't know it at the time and couldn't tell for years, that was the moment my North Star fell into its galaxy's black hole and my name went with it.

Hanna Susanna. I had loved that name since I was a child looking out over the Hell Creek Dam from the back porch of our plain brown two-story house. Every spring I would grow flower seedlings in Styrofoam cups on the outsides of which I'd draw pictures of the flowers the seeds would one day bloom into—pink zinnias, orange marigolds, and purple petunias. When the tender green sprouts became rooted enough to grow on their own, my mother would help me plant them in the little mulched patch outside my bedroom window in the shade of the cottonwood tree that snowed down cotton every July.

I'd call the cotton snow magic and my mother would say, "No, Hanna Susanna, that's not magic. We don't believe in magic. We believe in miracles, and that's a miracle. One of God's many miracles." And then because my mother's voice was soft, and because I had learned to be afraid of magic which came from Satan, I'd call the soft puffs of falling cotton miracles, though when I caught the cotton in my hands, magic was what I felt.

Maybe Dad didn't realize how much I hated when he called me "unwed mother," or maybe he just didn't care and couldn't even hear me, wouldn't hear me, as though I'd changed from being a person to a problem, a sin that had been made manifest in my body as there was no denying now that I wasn't a virgin, and even I didn't know how I felt about that when I'd been raped. If rape was even the word for not having wanted to have sex but for having been made to have sex anyways, which even now I sometimes doubted.

What was it that had gotten me raped? Was it something in me that drew my professor to me? That made me the extension of Satan? A "Jezebel" as he called me afterwards? Was it my own willfulness? An unholy arrogance that I could control the situation?

"You've always been willful," Dad said, and Mom nodded. And that was that. Without even trying, without even knowing I was doing so, I must have led my professor astray by my own willfulness.

My whole life I had tried not to be a strong-willed child. When I was seven, I'd repeated First John 1:8-9 after Pastor Burdock when I'd prayed my first prayer of confession at the God's Way kneeling rail. Both Pastor Burdock's hands had been on me then, his right hand weighing down my right shoulder as he kneeled behind me, his left hand pushing my head down so low my chin pressed into my chest, making it hard to breathe let alone repeat the words that he said would save my soul.

I remember Pastor Burdock preaching, "As the word of God declares in First John chapter one, verse seven, 'If we claim to be without sin, we deceive ourselves and the truth is not in us.'" I had wanted so desperately to be full of truth that I'd worked up the courage to walk down the center aisle, my eyes on the red carpet beneath my feet, as the eyes of everybody at God's Way were upon me as they sang through the second verse of "Just As I Am," convicting me with each word.

Just as I am, and waiting not
To rid my soul of one dark blot;
To Thee whose blood can cleanse each spot,
O Lamb of God, I come, I come!

And then I was kneeling at the altar rail, Mrs. Butler still playing "Just As I Am" on the organ as Pastor Burdock prompted me with, "If we confess our sins," his hot breath smelling like his wife's deviled eggs left out too long in the sun at the church picnic.

If we confess our sins, I repeated, squeezing my eyes closed tight, believing the fate of my eternal soul depended on this, knowing that the sulfur smell of deviled eggs was nothing compared to the sulfurous Lake of Fire.

"He is faithful and just and will forgive us our sins," Pastor Burdock boomed, as though I were the only sinner in the sanctuary.

He is faithful and just and will forgive us our sins, I repeated, remembering how the night before at dinner I had refused to eat my broccoli, told my mom, "No. I don't like it," as I pushed my plate away and crossed my arms across my chest.

"And purify us from all unrighteousness," Pastor Burdock grunted, the full weight of him against my back as he wrapped his arms around me and with his sweaty bratwurst fingers pried open my closed fists, then slammed my palms together between his own, the way he said God wanted me to hold my hands when I prayed.

I wanted to throw up at the kneeling rail the way my mother had thrown up Mrs. Burdock's deviled eggs in the parking lot, but I wanted even more to be good, not bad. Not willful. I was able to name my particular sin even then because my mom always said I was strong-willed, full of pride and rebellion like Lucifer who had been cast out of heaven for having a will of his own, for thinking too highly of himself, for wanting to be worshipped like God, or maybe just for believing he was beautiful. I wanted to go up to Heaven to live with Jesus, not be thrown into the pit of Hell to burn with Satan.

Why was I always so bad when I tried so hard to be good?

"And purify us from all unrighteousness," Pastor Burdock said, his voice terrifying, soft.

And purify us from all unrighteousness, I repeated, my hands not moving from how Pastor Burdock had put them, my mouth still tasting the bar of Ivory soap Dad had shoved in my mouth the night before. Oh, how I wished then I had eaten the broccoli! Dad's voice soft, terrifying: "'Honor your father and your mother.' Exodus 20:12," and then, "You will not talk back to your mother."

Kneeling at the rail felt the same as kneeling over the bathtub, Ivory-so-pure-it-floats turning to drool that pooled in my mouth and dripped down my chin onto the porcelain-enameled tub. I needed to be taught obedience.

But that was age seven, and here I was now at twenty, knowing I hadn't sinned but I still felt so bad. It was like being a small child again, crying alone in my bed, my parents not coming to comfort me, like it was wrong to even cry when I had a nightmare.

So I learned.

Be quiet. Stay small. Stay as small as an unwatered Zinnia seed in a Styrofoam cup. Don't sprout.

It hadn't made a difference that I'd told my dad I hated being called "unwed mother," hadn't mattered that the phrase made me feel ashamed and unseen when he'd introduced me to others with it. I even told him I hadn't gotten pregnant on purpose, that I'd never wanted to have sex, let alone sex with Dr. Paul—Paul like the apostle who had written about putting on the whole armor of God—who taught Spring Arbor's History of Christian Belief class. Dr. Paul who had invited me into his office after his lecture on Genesis 38 and the etymology of onanism. Dr. Paul who didn't wear a condom when he raped me, who afterwards cried as he called me a Jezebel who had led him into sin. And my father continued Dr. Paul's judgment upon me, making me feel so ashamed. Just the words "unwed mother" brought me back to that horrible night.

What I keep remembering is apologizing to Dr. Paul for everything I could think of that could have been my fault. I'd worn a skirt too short for the Spring Arbor dress code. I'd sat on top of his classroom desk. I'd laughed at one of his many stupid jokes. I'd not stopped him from closing and locking his office door when everywhere at Spring Arbor the rule was that any meeting of a man with a woman—any woman, even a student—meant keeping the door open six inches.

I had done nothing to stop Dr. Paul when he pinned me, just laid there beneath him looking up at the drop ceiling stained with water marks that looked like Moses' stone tablets of the Ten Commandments only nothing was written on them for me to read.

Even if I had been strong-willed as a child, by the time I had gone to Spring Arbor I had learned not to be, and what I wanted or didn't want would not have mattered. Because I did not matter.

So I was a Jezebel unwed mother living in my parents' basement, but Sammy, my parents said, was a gift from God sent to be a living, breathing testimony to my mom's ministry—ironically called Fearfully and Wonderfully Made—where she mentored and loved teenage girls having babies out of wedlock. While I lived in the basement, Sammy lived in my old bedroom upstairs filled with the softest, pinkest things my dad's money could buy, and decorated with Cherished Twinklings prints my mom had chosen.

Mom's favorite, "A Woman's Only Joy," hung above Sammy's bed like a sacred icon, its baby-faced mother only looking like a mother because she was larger than her babies—a crying pink-diapered girl in her arms and a shrieking toddler in a nautical suit and captain's hat who gripped his mother's blue denim skirt with one hand, and with the other swung an orange kitten by the tail. I could not imagine the Cherished Twinklings mother not feeling exhausted, yet she smiled in a way too perfectly at peace to be real, that looked like I had never felt as Sammy's mother. But then it wasn't really me raising my child but my mother who had taken charge from the start. The Cherished Twinklings mother looked like my mom always had, both of them so good at smiling the eternal smile, both so good at performing their only joy.

I didn't know if "A Woman's Only Joy" was meant for my mom, only knew it wasn't meant for me, that the Cherished Twinklings picture didn't look like motherhood felt, this ache I'd had since Mom first packed up Sammy along with the pink lunch box that held bottles of my pumped breastmilk and walked out the front door, driving away to Fearfully and Wonderfully Made in her blue Ford Astro to hand over my daughter and a bottle of my breastmilk to a pregnant teenager practicing to be a mom.

Motherhood? I wasn't allowed motherhood, and I felt no joy. I felt so much anger I could not show.

As I watched Sammy run around my basement room in her armor of God t-shirt, I knew Vacation Bible School wasn't a hill I wanted to die on. I'd learned early to pick my battles, so Sammy went to VBS and learned about putting on the full armor of God so she could resist the devil's schemes, while I learned to keep my mouth shut, even telling myself that maybe Sammy would make some friends her own age. No harm, right? I mean, I'd grown up in God's Way Community Church, gone to Sunday school every week and VBS every summer, and I'd turned out alright, hadn't I? Well, "all right" aside from being a Jezebel unwed mother stuck living in my parents' basement whose child had hardly been made to seem like her own.

I hardly knew what to do with myself, how to be, as I stood in front of Screams Souvenirs with Sammy in her armor of God t-shirt. I had three whole days with Sammy while my parents were in Climax at their Prayer Prior to Sex retreat. Three days of being her mom uninterrupted. Three days to make choices for and with Sammy—what to eat and wear, when to wake up and go to bed, what to do together. Already things felt different, lighter. The night before, Sammy and I camped out in the basement in a blanket fort we'd built together, and when she woke up crying in the middle of the night, I lay down beside her and rubbed her back until we both fell back asleep.

And now here we were in a different Hell than where I'd always lived. Here we were in the Go to Hell tourist attraction where I'd always been forbidden from going even though I could see it from the back of my brown two-story house in the months the trees had no leaves. I grew up with a clear view of Hell's Chapel of Love with its bright red roof, and of the miniature golf course with all its crazy, colorful sculptures. My parents had always warned me against going down into Hell, just like they'd always warned me against listening to secular music, but then I'd gone away to Spring Arbor, away from home and away from God's Way, and I'd started to experience the world as just a bit bigger and less scary than I'd been told it was. And though I didn't ever fully tell my parents what I felt and thought, I still knew I thought and felt different things in different ways from them, and that those thoughts and feelings, like my anger, had only grown since the day Sammy had been born.

As Sammy and I stood in front of Screams, John walked up and introduced himself as Odum Plenty, the mayor of Hell, then crouched down on Sammy's level and asked, "How the hell are you?" in a voice that sounded like a smile. At the word "hell," Sammy scrunched up her face and puffed out her chest and said straight back at John, "My grandpa says you can't say that word or you'll go there."

John, still in a crouch, looked up at me, and though we'd only just met, I knew from his kind blue eyes that I didn't have to put up my guard, didn't have to feel embarrassed by what my dad said, didn't even have to believe what my dad believed because I was twenty-four now, and I was a mom—Sammy's mom—and my dad was an hour and a half away from here. I shrugged. "Sammy isn't wrong," I told John. "That is what her grandpa says."

"Oh, I know plenty what her grandpa Jason says," John said, standing now. "I grew up with your dad, and he didn't like my idea for Hell way back when we were in high school together and had to create business plans for a class, and he really didn't like that my plan to create Damnation University had made our teacher laugh. Now your dad's on town council," John said, "and every meeting brings up the idea to change the name of our small hamlet from Hell to Hiland Lake. He wants to get everybody to follow his rules, but the harder he tries, the more I laugh, and I laugh the most when I count out pennies to pay my town council fines." John laughed. "*Illegitimi non carborundum.* That's Dam U's motto and mine too."

Then John reached out his hand and said, "Nice to finally meet you, Hanna Susanna."

Hanna Susanna.

It felt so good to hear my name again, to be reminded that I had a name beyond "unwed mother" which I knew my dad called me everywhere, even on town council. Not John, though. Even though John and I had never met, he remembered my real name and used it. I reached my hand back out to John and said, "Nice to meet you too" and as we shook hands, every fear I'd ever had about going to Hell—whether the literal lake of fire or this fun tourist attraction on the other side of Hell Creek Dam—burned to ash and blew away forever.

Then the mayor of Hell crouched back down to Sammy wearing her armor of God t-shirt that definitely wasn't Iron Man, and he didn't skip a beat, just said, "Then how the heck are you?" Sammy laughed and I laughed, and from that moment I knew I was going to find a way to make Hell our home.

Before we left that first day, John gave me a red ticket printed with, "Hell. Admit One," and on both sides the numbers "666."

"Now Sammy," John said, "how would you like this?" And he pulled from a clothing rack in the children's section a bright red t-shirt printed with a young devil with horns and a pointy tail that said, "I've been to HECK, MI 'cause I can't say Hell."

Sammy looked at the t-shirt, then looked up at me, and when I nodded and smiled, she grinned and shouted, "Heck, yeah!" The first thing she wanted to do was put the t-shirt on, so I took her into the bathroom to change, and she came out saying, "Heck, Michigan! Heck, Michigan!" with as much enthusiasm as she'd been saying "Armor of God!" thirty minutes before.

While Sammy went off to look at the rack of postcards next to Hell's post office counter, John turned to me and said, "Now I don't think your dad will like that shirt, so if you want, I can keep the shirt here for her and she can change into it whenever you both want to come back, and I hope you will. You and Sammy are always welcome in Hell, Hanna Susanna. I can promise you that."

I thought about the offer—an offer that even two days ago I might have taken—but I liked the idea of Sammy wearing that t-shirt whenever she wanted, just like she'd been wearing the armor of God shirt from God's Way, so I told John,

"Thanks, but I think we'll take it with us," knowing that what I really wanted was for Sammy to be wearing it when my parents walked back in the house fresh from their retreat.

And then John said, "It would be so cool if she could wear the shirt to the 6-6-6 party" next month." So that is what Sammy did, and for myself I bought the t-shirt with the devil's face that says, "God is busy, can I help you" on the front in flaming red script, and on the back, "Once in a lifetime. 666. June 6, 2006. Hell, Michigan."

Hell is nothing to be scared of. Hell is simply where I live.

Hell is also where I work with John and Reverend Vonn, the "Official Minister of Hell" as she says John called her on her first day of work and the title just stuck. Vonn dresses in black, dyes her hair red, and officiates weddings at Hell's Chapel of Love, sometimes wearing horns and sometimes not. It's all pretty different from God's Way over in Pinckney. Reverend Vonn has never—not even once—made me feel scared the way Pastor Burdock once did, and I've stopped caring whether there's a literal lake of fire—that just doesn't concern me any longer. As for John, he's the kindest man I've ever met, and I don't know whether that's because he made it through Vietnam alive but not unscarred, or maybe because kind is just who John is.

Ask me who I am, and I'll tell you. My name is Hanna Susanna, and I live with my daughter Sammy in a little pop-up camper out past Hell's bathrooms on our own square inch of Hell (plus a little more) which we bought for $6.66 the day of the 6-6-6 party when almost 20,000 people came to Hell, including my mom and dad, though they stood on the opposite side of the road with Pastor and Mrs. Burdock and other God's Way members, holding signs that said, "Hell is Real" and "God Will Not be Mocked." Nobody on my side was mocking God, though, just having a little light-hearted fun at nobody's expense.

I work full-time at Screams Souvenirs, sometimes singeing postcards with a cigarette lighter at the post office counter and stamping them with a round red Hell postal stamp. Sammy, who's seven now, sometimes wears red devil horns and wants to dye her hair red like Reverend Vonn's. Sammy has a dozen t-shirts from Hell, her favorite and mine reading, "No worries, we're all accepted in Hell" beneath a row of rainbow flames. When kids come to Hell in the summer, Sammy gives them the full tour, even takes them down to walk the world's shortest boardwalk along Hell Creek and to point out the brown house on the other side of the dam where she once lived, and where I was once a child. I say "Welcome to Hell" and "Have a helluva good time" when guests enter, and sometimes for lunch I walk next door to Smitty's Hell Saloon where I swap stories with the bikers riding through.

For Sammy and me, Hell has become all the heaven we need. On mid-October days I'll sit behind the green shed, look out at the Chapel of Love, and feel the cool breeze as I watch for Sammy's school bus to drop her off behind the Scattering Yard. I'll wait for her to call out "Mommy!" and I'll shout back, "How the Hell are you, Sammy?" Then we'll both laugh as she comes running into my arms.

In October, Hell's bushes blaze red like Moses's burning bush only they aren't burning, nothing symbolic in a religious way, but more like their own magic.

© Nicole Miller

*incorporating Peter Beerits' mermaid sculpture
as photographed by Cathy Owen*

Epilogue

We are always pretending we are always real.

We are. Always. Pretending. We are. Always. Real.

We are always. Pretending we are. Always. Real.

We! Are always pretending? We! Are always real?

We? Are? Always? Pretending! We? Are? Always? Real!

We are. Always pretending we are. Always. Real.

We are always pretending. We are always real.

We are always.

—*Xavier Buttons, 1961–1982*

© Tammy Gordon and Mary Catherine Harper

Artists

While visiting Mary Catherine Harper in July 2025, we happened upon an idea: Why not invite artists to create original artwork for *A Green Glow on the Horizon*?

Mary Catherine had, after all, just created the book's original cover art by photoshopping the aurora borealis into a photo of Tammy Gordon's original tourist attraction blue boy quilt to give it a green glow. Then Ross Tangedal had set to work designing the cover in a style he had always wanted to try. We'd already experienced good creative synergy; why not keep it going?

When Ross said "yes" to including art, I emailed invitations and a different chapter to each of the artists, saying that if something sparked, I'd be delighted if they would join me in a "collaborative celebration of weird, beautiful creativity."

The response was overwhelmingly generous and generative, and by November 1, I had received all the art that now appears in the book in black and white, and on my website in full color.

My deepest gratitude goes to the artists who contributed their creative visions to making *A Green Glow on the Horizon* so rich, full, and multi-dimensional.

I am astounded and humbled by your art and honored to share this book with you.

Jan Bechtel (Vermilion, OH) grew up on the glacial till of north central Ohio, a few miles from the shores of Lake Erie. Her love for that land drew her to Dawn's story of Ruth and the Corn Palace.

Peter Beerits (Deer Isle, ME) is the sculpture artist behind the fantastical, historical, ever-evolving Nellieville at Nervous Nellie's Jams and Jellies. *https://www.nervousnellies.com/*

Lux Burns (Lansing, MI) loves acting, playing video games, and sipping tea while listening to bossa nova or watching *MirrorMask*. In the future, they hope to develop video games and own pet rats.

Kelcey Ervick (South Bend, IN) is a creative writing professor at Indiana University South Bend. She writes and draws stories of the creative life at her illustrated newsletter, *The Habit of Art*, and once volunteered as an Ask-Me Guide at Frank Lloyd Wright's Fallingwater. *https://kelceyervick.com/*

Heidi Reichenbach Finley (Petoskey, MI) is a recovering oil painter who is drawn to the stunning patterns and endless color combinations afforded by fused glass and Turkish marbling, both of which she teaches in her home studio. Her favorite place in the world is Cedar Point, Ohio! *https://www.marblingsupplies.com/*

Monica Friedman (Tucson, AZ) is author of *Bonnie Jo Campbell Comics Volumes 1-5* and *The Hermit*. She teaches creative writing to elementary students and edits a literary journal of children's work, *The Pencil Eaters*. Her favorite tourist attraction is Montezuma Well in Rimrock, Arizona. *https://qwertyvsdvorak.com/* and *https://www.redbubble.com/people/qwertyvsdvorak/shop*

Tammy Gordon (Cary, NC) teaches history and martial arts, and made her piece out of thrift store t-shirts, enjoying the possible stories these garments might tell. Once, outside San Carlos de Bariloche in Argentina, a smiling little white dog named Maria led her on the trail and then sat to meditate by the falls, her fur reflecting a beam of spring sunlight.

Mary Catherine Harper (Defiance, OH) was born and raised just east of the Rockies and northeast of the great American desert. Now she lives in the Great Black Swamp. Go figure! Alongside Dawn Burns, she has breathed life into Swamp-Fire since 2008. *https://marycatherineharper.org*

Bex Miller (Lansing, MI) is a poet whose "Writing in Clay" illustration was born in an instant from her mind's creative neighborhood. Her favorite attraction was Major Magic's All Star Pizza Revue (1982–2010) in Toledo, Ohio.

Nicole Miller (San Diego, CA) is a forever student of life who thrives professionally on solving marketing challenges with curiosity and collaboration. She is a lover of live music, travel, yoga, reading, and laughter who reminds herself—and you—to not take life too seriously.

Cathy Owen (Toledo, OH) seeks meaning, connection, and inspiration in the simple details of life through CaSu Photography. She thanks Dawn and her husband Mark for introducing her to eclectic tourist attractions by way of Deer Isle, Maine's, Nervous Nellies Jams and Jellies.

Julian Norwood (Coventry, CT) is an openly trans illustrator and writer living between a cult compound and university. He runs a small fish rescue, lives on a solar-powered micro farm, spends most days painting, and has been guest of honor at more than one niche nerd convention. *https://moose.ink*

ARTISTS

Sofia Pagen (Lansing, MI) was born and raised in Rio de Janeiro, Brazil, and moved to the United States in 2012, where her lifelong admiration for graphic novels, TV shows, and film evolved into a playful yet introspective art practice. She teaches art in Lansing and can be found at *sofiapagen @ tumblr / instagram*.

Mary Jane Pories (Grand Rapids, MI) is an award-winning visual artist, writer, Equity actor, and former mainstage cast member of The Second City. Her favorite attraction is Inn by the Mill in Saint Johnsville, NY, where she saw a manikin in the bathtub, the first robot ever invented, and plastic flowers ringing every window, molding, bed, and mirror. *www.maryjanepories.net*

Steve Smith (Angola, IN) is an old hippie and award-winning sculptor active internationally in humanitarian work. For thirteen years he served as a SwampFire teaching artist and retreat host. In his youth, Steve's favorite tourist attraction was Ohio Caverns; now it's Barcelona.

z the goblin (Winona Lake, IN) is a queer, painter, magician, and non-linear man raised and residing in the mostly abandoned efforts of generations of evangelical retreats in his tourist trap homeland. z feels deeply that these odd places are as wondrous and haunted as he. *https://www.zeebeasts.com/*

Erin "Z" Zerbe (Lakewood, WA) creates work that blurs the boundary between personal and mythical, transforming trauma into visual landscapes where beauty and unease coexist. When Z, a dual citizen of the U.S. and Ireland, visits family in Dublin, they love to go to Bray Waterfront in Wicklow County. *https://erinzerbe.com/*

Acknowledgments

> *"We are all characters in each others' stories."*
> —Bud Blackenberry

The summer of 1982, I saw my first jackalope.

My whole family—my mom, dad, big sister, and me—had been thirsty for Wall Drug's Free Ice Water when my dad pulled our family's green Plymouth Valiant off the road, and we all tumbled out. Earlier that day I had marveled at The World's Only Corn Palace in Mitchell, South Dakota, and now I stood staring at jackalopes on a wall at Wall Drug! At nearly nine years old, this was almost more wonder than I could handle.

For this moment—and for my undying love of travel and tourist attractions that underlie this book—I have my dad to thank. The wonder has never left.

As for *A Green Glow on the Horizon* being a proper book, I have many more acknowledgments to give, beginning with Albion College for the Faculty Development Grant (2001) that solidified my quirky ideas into a legit book project, and made it possible to drive across the United States visiting tourist attractions and writing stories. I am also immensely grateful for all the places I've visited and people I've met along the road, whether they made it into this book or not.

Thanks to the Society for the Study of Midwestern Literature (SSML) which awarded me a Paul Somers Prize for Creative Prose for "Raised in a Corn Palace," subsequently published in *MidAmerica* (2008), and to the Ohio Arts Council which awarded me an Excellence Award in Fiction (2014) on the basis of "Born Beneath Pedro's Sombrero."

Thanks also to Michigan State University's Department of Writing, Rhetoric, and Cultures (WRAC) for professional development funds supporting my travel to Michigan tourist attractions, including Hell, where I found my final story.

Thanks to my WRAC colleague Margaret Morris' Fall 2022 "Introduction to Grammar and Editing" class and her competent and enthusiastic student editing team led by SaMya Overall.

My gratitude extends to my local Lansing community. Thanks to the Arts Council of Greater Lansing for granting me Chris Clark Fellowship Program funds to promote *A Green Glow* at AWP 2026, and to Lansing's vibrant bookstore scene, including Scott Harris at Everybody Reads Books and Stuff, and Elise Jajuga and Christine Pfeffer at A Novel Concept. Let's keep working together!

To Dr. Ross Tangedal, publisher: when you said you would be "overjoyed" for Cornerstone Press to publish *A Green Glow on the Horizon*, I knew Cornerstone was the right home for my book. Thank you for caring passionately about both people and books. I'm honored to know you!

To managing editor Lilly Kulbeck: thanks for your work on *A Green Glow*. Your leadership helped shape this book into its final form while keeping me in the loop. I am thankful for you and each team member, including managing editor Brianna Loving, media director Samantha Bjork, sales director Sophie McPherson, sales managers Madison Schultz and Autumn Vine, and assistant editors Asher Schroeder, John Evans, and Oliver McKnight.

Finally, thanks to friends, family, and my generous and generative creative community!

ACKNOWLEDGMENTS

To Tammy Gordon: your tourist attraction blue boy quilt has been a constant reminder to keep going, keep writing, keep trusting the process. I so appreciate our conversations, your scholarship, and your unwavering friendship. Love you dearly.

To Bex Miller: you remind me that I can only do one thing at a time, travel with me to places you might not otherwise go, and love me always.

To my grown-ass kids Elliot and Lux: you don't mind that I'm weird and often join me in my fun. I'll (almost) always let you choose the music for our road trip adventures.

To Nicole Miller: your website and marketing expertise help keep me sane! You inspire me with your willingness to take risks and play!

To Cathy and Mark Owen: for keeping my books on your shelf. Mark, Percilla the Monkey Girl made it into this book because of you, and I couldn't be happier about that.

To SwampFire: you are the blazing soul of my creative community. I could name many names and not even come close to capturing who we are together.

To Steve Smith: for hosting SwampFire and teaching "word people" like me we can create beyond words.

To Bonnie Jo Campbell: for all your H House gatherings large and small. You build community and defend democracy with stories, grit, and love! I appreciate you (and Christopher!) and am grateful for friendship, camaraderie, and donkeys.

And finally, to Mary Catherine Harper. For twenty years, we have both lived with and worked on *A Green Glow on the Horizon: Tales from the National Association of Tourist Attraction Survivors*. When I shared that early draft of "The Thing Is" you didn't turn away but leaned in. Even then I could feel the electric crackle of the distant horizon's green glow, and now here we are at the edge of it, overcome with wonder! We did it!!

DAWN BURNS is the author of *Evangelina Everyday* (Cornerstone 2022) and founder and co-organizer of the SwampFire community of writers and artists. While thoroughly Midwestern, Dawn also loves to travel and is relentlessly curious about people and places. Dawn's creative nonfiction has appeared in *Lingering Inland: A Literary Tour of the Midwest*, and in *On an Inland Sea: Writing the Great Lakes*.

An assistant professor at Michigan State University, Dawn is committed to writing and community building as acts of personal and social change both in and beyond their classroom.

www.ingramcontent.com/pod-product-compliance
Lightning Source LLC
LaVergne TN
LVHW040042080526
838202LV00045B/3452